HUTCHINGS POINTED TO THE HOLOGRAPHIC MAP WITH A RED LASER.

"We call these areas the Forbidden Zones. We think that the Vapor probably lives somewhere on Level Seven. When he appears, *if* he appears, you'll know someone's invoked an Injunction and that we're close to being vaporized."

"I take it this Vapor person is your bogeyman," Klane said.

"*Our* bogeyman," Hutchings clarified. "Yours and mine. Trust me. You don't want to see him. He's a very sophisticated robot of some kind. When I arrived, he told me all the things we weren't supposed to do here. One of them was that we weren't to go looking for him in the Forbidden Zones. In fact, even attempting to enter the Zones is an Injunction itself. The second violation beyond that—any violation at all—brings out the Vapor, and he will pronounce his judgment."

"Then what?" Klane asked.

"We're dead," Hutchings replied.

CUTTING EDGE SCI-FI
NOVELS

FORTRESS ON THE SUN

*

Paul Cook

A ROC BOOK

ROC
Published by the Penguin Group
Penguin Books USA Inc., 375 Hudson Street,
New York, New York 10014, U.S.A.
Penguin Books Ltd, 27 Wrights Lane,
London W8 5TZ, England
Penguin Books Australia Ltd, Ringwood,
Victoria, Australia
Penguin Books Canada Ltd, 10 Alcorn Avenue,
Toronto, Ontario, Canada M4V 3B2
Penguin Books (N.Z.) Ltd, 182–190 Wairau Road,
Auckland 10, New Zealand

Penguin Books Ltd, Registered Offices:
Harmondsworth, Middlesex, England

First published by Roc, an imprint of Dutton Signet,
a division of Penguin Books USA Inc.

First Printing, July, 1997
10 9 8 7 6 5 4 3 2 1

 REGISTERED TRADEMARK—MARCA REGISTRADA

Printed in the United States of America

—For Patrick,
greatest prisoner of them all

Drenched in sunlight they are blind travelers.

—Norman Dubie
"New England, Springtime"

1

Emerging from a thicket of birch trees that flanked a narrow meadow, a man appeared in the quiet of the night. He was a large individual, yet he moved across the brittle grass with an athlete's grace. His was an intentional carefulness, not wanting his presence there to disturb the peacefulness they had worked so hard to achieve. In fact, he did not want his presence to disturb anything at all, ever again.

Ian McFarland Hutchings, Ph.D., renowned biotech chemist and history's greatest killer of men, made his way slowly across the meadow as he did every night at that hour. Hutchings was not prone to bouts of his community's mysterious new quick-sleep—or any kind of sleep for that matter—but making this final circuit of their little corner in Hell before turning in did seem to relax him somewhat.

During the daylight hours, Hutchings's mind concerned itself with the stewardship of the one hundred and three men and women of their community whose exile he shared. At night, however, his mind would fill with the banshee voices of a guilty conscience:

Murderer! those voices would whisper. *Annihilist!* *Suffer in Hell for the rest of your days!* Solace from those voices seemed to come only when he took his final tour through the meadow.

Illuminated by brilliant constellations overhead, Hutchings walked across the glade, mindful that his 250 pounds—forty of it contained in bracelets of solid gold at his ankles and wrists, his "shackles," as he referred to them—didn't further damage the hybrid grass of the meadow floor.

The meadow, however, could never offer him the genuine consolation he knew his conscience needed. Ultimately, the only acceptable expiation for his crimes would be his death, a demise that would more than likely come in the form of a few billion tons of super-heated hydrogen plasma imploding down around him. His life would be over in a trillionth of a second, well before his brain would even register the fact. One moment he would be alive, worrying about the welfare of his friends; the next, he—and those very same friends—would be atomic mist.

At the opposite end of the meadow, about forty yards away, lay Hutchings's pride and joy: a gazebo made of real, handcrafted wood. While the manufacture of the meadow had necessarily been a group effort, Hutchings himself had built the gazebo. It was based on one of the few childhood memories he had. His Uncle Buck owned a small farm on the outskirts of Lowell, Massachusetts. Adjacent to the farm were five acres of unmown pasturage surrounded by elderly birches. The meadow upon which Hutchings now stood had been modeled after it. Though a much smaller meadow—it was approximately fifty

yards wide and about eighty yards long—theirs was
just as real as his uncle's spread. The grass and the
trees most certainly were.

Hutchings was very proud of his creation.

Standing in the lower half of the meadow next to
the mirror surface of their fake pond, Hutchings happened to glance at his feet. There was no real reason
for it, really. Just instinct.

There in the fragile grass adjacent to the pond he
discovered several long gouges, dark moist earth
against the white of the sage. They were clearly divots, clumps of torn-up soil. He scanned the area
around him, squinting in the darkness, and noticed
several other ragged holes.

"Christ on a stick," he growled. The gouges were
hash marks, goal lines. That meant that several little
Boys, against orders, had been up there earlier playing football. To his further dismay, he found that a
large section of the meadow had been scrimmaged
upon. A *lot* of little Boys had been up there, it
seemed.

"Damn it! Com, open. Boys' dorm!" he snapped.

A faint chime went off beside his right ear as their
communications system opened a channel to the dormitory which housed their little Boys.

"Wake up, you little bastards! This is Hutchings and
I'm in the meadow. I want to know who was up here
this afternoon. Answer me or I'll tell the Spanker for
sure this time!"

A dozen little Boys roused from sleep started yam-
mering into the com at once, the cacophony of their
replies filling Hutchings's right ear. It was the threat
of the Spanker that got their attention. The Children

feared the Spanker as much as the adults feared the Vapor. And while the Spanker was a fiction, the Vapor most assuredly was not.

Hutchings did not wait for a confession. He had a good idea of who might have organized a football game. "Matthew White, wake up! You're responsible for this!"

"What? I didn't do anything!" piped a voice foggy from sleep.

"Don't give me that. You guys were up here this afternoon playing football. The place is wrecked now!"

"It's not wrecked, you big fat liar," the Boy protested.

"You ruined what took us months to cultivate!"

"Bobby made all the holes!" White contended.

"Bobby Nakamura is only five years old and he'd never disobey me. Besides, Lorraine said she *saw* you making a football in the Fiddler's den the other day. She told me."

"She did not, you liar!"

Hutchings shook his head in disgust. "Christ, I knew you'd do something like this. It was just a matter of time."

Several of the little Boys down in their dorm rooms started talking and hooting into their coms at once. *"Leave him alone, Ian!" "You're just a bully!" "You're a big fat bully!"* Several juicy raspberries followed from the little Boys' dorm.

"I'm going to tell you this one time," Hutchings said. "It took us a year to generate viable topsoil, and it's not for you to ruin. This place is off-limits from now on. Do you hear me?"

"Then where are we gonna play?" Matt White pro-

tested. *"The ball always bounces off the roof of the Rough-house and you can't tackle anybody there 'cause you slide and hit the wall."*

"The meadow was designed for general use. It's a *park*, not a football field."

"It's more like a cemetery, if you ask me."

"Watch it, Matt."

Matthew White, a twenty-eight-year-old shuttle pilot, had one of their worst cases in retrograde amnesia. His entire adult life had been erased from his mind, leaving him with the mental abilities—to say nothing of the concomitant maturity—of a seven-year-old boy. Hutchings should have known better than to leave any of the Children unsupervised, especially the little Boys.

Matt White then said, *"Hey, are you up there with your shackles on? I'll bet you are! I'll bet you're up there right now walking all over the place making holes with those big shackles on!"*

"Their weight is negligible," Hutchings retorted.

"I'll bet you're mashing all kinds of holes up there! I'll bet you a million bucks!"

Hutchings said, "Hey, I designed this place. I'm very careful where I go."

"You're such a liar, Ian! You're a liar and a bully! I hate you a million times! I hate you, I hate you!"

Hutchings heard the closing chime as the twenty-eight-year-old little Boy went off-line. The closing chimes of the other little Boys followed like tinny sprites vanishing into thin air.

He rubbed his eyes. The strain of the last three years was beginning to get to him. Lately, he seemed too quick to anger, too eager to lash out and vent his pent-up feelings.

Recalling his own mother's tirades, he knew that having a houseful of children was in truth Hell itself. Chaos ran amok, with Pandemonium right behind snapping at its heels. However . . . Hutchings had to remind himself that life with real children was only one kind of Hell. There was a much, *much* greater Hell still.

And he was living in it.

Hell was Sunstation Ra, a giant metals production factory floating on the surface of the sun where escape was impossible and death but an eyeblink away. The meadow upon which he stood had been built in what once was a spacious arboretum that occupied the two upper floors of the facility. Only recently had they got its ecosystem up and running, having taken nearly a year to cultivate the soil, breed the right kind of grass, then accelerate the growth of the dozens of bonsai trees which the former science crew of Ra had left behind when the System Assembly pulled them off.

Since its completion, Hutchings had been spending quite a lot of time in the meadow, particularly late at night. As present Administrator, his duties should have kept him so busy during the day that some form of rest at night was inevitable. But Hutchings rarely slept, thanks in part to certain biotech enhancements in his brain, as well as a haunting sense of moral obligation to make up for his criminal past.

No one else on the Hot Rock bore the weight of the crime he had committed, even if everyone there, including the severely memory-wiped Children, were also supposed to be the worst civilization had ever seen. In another life, they would have been executed. Yet, from the perspective of the System Assembly, the governing body that lorded over two planets, twelve inhabited moons, and two giant LaGrange colonies, it did make sense to locate them where they could do no harm, someplace, even, where they might be of some practical use. And that place was a battleship-sized fusion facility on the surface of the sun.

To Hutchings, it made sense in a very poetic—and quite ironic—way. Ra could not be operated efficiently by robots, yet it had been deemed far too dangerous for a crew of volunteers. So they were elected. Those Raians who were able, fused metal alloys in the Suncup—the gold in his shackles came from there—distilled from the 6,000-degree plasma that raged just beyond the Renner force-shield that protected them all. Other inmates tended to the station's basic maintenance; still others tended to those who could not tend to themselves: the Children and the bindlestiffs, inmates so devastated by the horror of their incarceration that they could not function at all. The 'stiffs spent their time wandering the free zones, sleeping in the halls when quick-sleep overtook them, eating whenever they could get near a food processor. But Children they were not.

To Hutchings, the memory-cleansing process was their most cruel and unusual punishment. And it made no sense to him that he, the greatest scourge mankind had ever seen, could remember up to his postdoctoral days in college—but *not* his specific crimes—while some inmates were reduced to the mental states of three-year-olds. If the punishment fit the crime, then he should have been regressed to an embryo, if not executed outright. Instead, he was a twenty-eight-year-old postdoctoral student stuck in a middle-aged man's body.

Hutchings tamped down the divots as best he could. In the morning he would put a few eager Fiddlers, once-engineers barely at the level of college, to repair the damage. The Fiddlers were always looking for something to fiddle with.

Hutchings turned his attention to the gazebo. The wooden edifice actually served a dual purpose. Its stage concealed the Shunt platform upon which they had arrived three years ago. It was a moment Hutchings remembered well—for he had been the first to set foot on that fantastic island on the sun. He was the first to be told who they were and why they were there; he was the first to be told what they could do to redeem themselves: send the System Assembly newly fused metals and the SA would mark their effort. As such, for some, parole off the Hot Rock was possible.

But not for the butcher of a billion people.

Hutchings searched the stars of their planetarium sky. Once a week their Suncup engineers sent up ingots of precious metals forged in the Suncup's fusion chamber. An unmanned ore scow, protected by a Renner shield of its very own, would dip into the sun's twenty-million-degree corona, lock onto Ra's Renner-protected matter-transmission corridor, and take back Ra's plasma-fused booty in one big tele-ported gulp.

So they did their good deeds, some of them. They maintained the sunstation, some of them. They maintained each other, some of them. And Hutchings did what he could, though none of his efforts counted for anything in the eyes of the System Assembly.

Hutchings ran a hand through his bristly white hair. He guessed that he was about forty-five years old, but he felt as if he were a thousand. He shouldn't have barked at Matt. After all, the Boy was only seven years old, just a kid.

Hutchings looked up one final time into their glittering starscape, feeling the winds of October drift across their ersatz meadow. He sighed.

Then stumbled backwards.

A bright star had suddenly appeared overhead, a star that wasn't there a few moments ago . . . a star that didn't belong in any constellation of their artificial night sky.

"Yes!" Hutchings shouted. *"Yes!"*

Their main computer had been programmed to project onto the planetarium dome any ship that aligned itself with the monopole transmission corridor above the sunstation. But by the size and shape of the "star" overhead, Hutchings knew that this ship was different. Glowing a brilliant green, it meant that the ship was *Bold Charon*, the System Assembly's personnel transfer shuttle.

It was not an ore scow: People were coming down!

Hutchings stared at the gazebo's stage. The green "star" rolled across Ursa Major's generous ladle as it aligned itself within the monopole corridor a million miles above the sunstation, the only place, and a dangerous one at that, where any kind of teleportation could be done.

They had waited three years for this moment.

Hutchings ran toward the gazebo where a gossamer haze had begun to manifest on the stage. There, he counted the human forms now appearing. One, two . . . three, four . . . five, six.

Six new inmates!

The star representing *Bold Charon* overhead then vanished as the ship dashed away from the dangerous solar atmosphere, its purpose fulfilled.

"Meadow!" Hutchings shouted. "Lights up, twelve noon!"

The planetarium night vanished with astonishing suddenness as a brilliant blue sky speckled with clouds took its place.

On the stage six startled human beings stared with amazement at the world about them—the meadow, the forest of stately white birches, and the huge man with the massive golden wrist- and ankle-bracelets standing next to the mirror of a fake pond.

"Welcome to Hell," Ian Hutchings said breathlessly. "Welcome!"

2

Six more astonished individuals could not have been sent from above. Hutchings could see that they had not believed that the System Assembly's nasty little secret in the sky—a rumored prison facility on the sun—actually existed. Each had obviously assumed they were being teleported to their deaths, much the way Hutchings and his friends had believed at the time of their Shunt three years earlier.

"This is interesting," said a very tall man who wore a name patch that read: N. KLANE. He stood close to seven feet tall and his platinum-blonde hair nearly brushed the rafters of the ceiling. "Certainly not what we were expecting."

"Don't get your hopes up. It's still Hell," Hutchings said. He pointed beyond the gazebo. "Go one mile that way, or—" He indicated the opposite direction. "One mile *that* way and you'd find out quick enough."

"You mean this goes on for miles?" the tall Mr. Klane asked.

"No. This is just an arboretum," Hutchings reported. "From here it extends about two hundred and fifty feet to the inner bulkheads. Beyond that are a million layers of Renner shielding and *then* it's the surface of the sun."

Klane stepped down the short flight of steps to the meadow. "Quite an illusion," he remarked. "And a forest as well. Very impressive."

Of the others, one man had collapsed backward against several transfer crates which had also ridden the Shunt with the new prisoners. The stencilled name on his duffle read: E. PLAINFIELD.

The third man, D. OAKS, had quick, brown eyes, dark, unruly hair and practically no forehead. He was short, almost the size of a child. He blinked a few times as if to clear his head from the effects of the Shunt. He then slipped under the railing, jumping to the meadow. "Wow!" he said. "Look at this place!"

Of the women, one had jet-black hair with flecks of silver gray at her temples; she might have been in her late thirties. The other was a redhead with a face harsh and tough that indicated a difficult life had been hers. The name patch of the former read: A. ADAMSON; the name patch of the latter read: C. PICKER-ALL. The third woman, a blonde, seemed the most distraught of the three as she appeared to be weeping. Her duffle bag read: R. BARRIE.

The childlike Oaks came around to Hutchings. "Are we really on the surface of the sun? I mean, it's out there, isn't it?"

Hutchings nodded. "Actually, the sun doesn't have a normal surface. It's mostly hydrogen plasma clouds that get denser the farther down you go. We're about

fifty thousand miles above the first striations of pal-
pable surface in the photosphere where it's cooler
than the corona by a factor of ten."

"Wow," Oaks repeated. He turned to the tall Mr.
Klane. "So we made it, Klane. We're alive!"

Klane didn't appear to be all that impressed.

"Enjoy it while you can," Hutchings said. "We
could implode at any time. The Renner shield is extremely powerful, but nothing lasts forever. Second
law of thermodynamics and all that."

"Will we know it if the end comes?" Klane asked.

"Not really," Hutchings said.

Klane snorted in fatalistic disgust.

At that point, the com-chime sounded in Hutchings's right ear. A resonant voice followed it. *"You're
not in your quarters. So where are you?"*

The women crowded at the gazebo rail. The black-
haired Adamson asked, "Who is that? Who's talking
to you?"

"One moment, Hugh. Pause," Hutchings said. To
the group on the gazebo, he said: "I'm speaking with
Hugh Bladestone, our physician. I need to see what
he wants. Com, continue. I'm up in the meadow,
Hugh, making the rounds. What's happening at
your end?"

"I'm with Kate," the doctor said. *"She's had another
one of her nightmares. She came out of it screaming this
time."*

"That sounds bad."

*"It's the worst one yet. I had to give her a mild sedative.
Aren't you two bedding each other these days?"*

"On occasion. I was a little restless tonight."

"You know it's the best medicine for her. I think she

should be sleeping with you for the next several nights so you can keep an eye on her. I don't want to lose her."

"Neither do I," Hutchings said. "Is there anything else?"

"Larry called from the Brains. He says the Man logged a handshake signal to the gazebo. That the Shunt platform's been activated. Has it?"

"I was about to call you," Hutchings responded. "It has. We've got some new people."

"That's fantastic! That's absolutely fantastic! How many did we get?"

"Six."

"Just six?"

"Six for now. You'd better come up. And bring a few parrys with you, while you're at it."

"I'm on my way! Com, out."

The tall Klane hovered over Hutchings, which was no mean feat, given Hutchings's own height of six feet three. "You have a doctor down here?"

"Yes. Fortunately for us. He's a good man."

"Is he a prisoner like we are?" asked Oaks.

"Do you mean is he a *criminal* like we are?" Hutchings said. He nodded grimly. "That's what the Screws tell us."

"So who's the boss down here?" Klane asked. "You?"

Hutchings again nodded. "I'm our Administrator. For the period of this term, anyway."

Klane seemed to be making note of Hutchings's compelling size. "Of course," he said. "You would be."

"How did you do that?" Oaks asked, scurrying

up to Hutchings. "How did you talk that way to that man?"

"It's our shipwide com-system, something we dreamed up. You'll be fully briefed on it when you're ready to receive your implants."

Oaks gazed at the forest. "Hey, are those *real* trees?"

Hutchings nodded. "Yes. They're from bonsai plants left by the original crew. They also left behind seeds for several different kinds of plants as well as the grass you're standing on."

"What about bugs? You got any bugs and spiders?" Oaks inquired. "Hate spiders."

"Not unless they're hitching a ride on you," Hutchings said. "All our fauna is microscopic and limited to the soil here in the meadow. Everything else we grow or manufacture—"

"Pardon me," Klane announced, gazing past Hutchings. "But what is happening right there?"

Klane was pointing to what was designed to appear like the flat surface of a small pond in the meadow. It was actually the polished metal door of their main lift. Now it was retracting beneath the shaggy grass of its banks.

Rising up into the meadow appeared a black man dressed in the bright white of a physician's tunic. He was roughly sixty years old and had close-cropped white hair that dipped in a slight widow's peak on a high, intelligent forehead. He carried a small black bag.

The women on the stage huddled close together.

"Easy," Hutchings said. "This is our doctor, Hugh Bladestone. He won't hurt you."

"How do you do, people?" the doctor said with a smile. "Welcome to our little community."

"Be careful of that bag," Klane said threateningly.

"There's nothing in here but parrys," the doctor said.

" 'Parrys'? What's a 'parry'?" Klane demanded.

The doctor placed the bag at his feet. From it, he removed several bracelets, each with an oblong face scrawled with computer circuitry. He then gave one to Klane, then Oaks, who were nearest. He then passed one each up to the women on the stage. "These are for you," he said. "If you want them."

"What are they?" Oaks asked. "What do they do?"

"They generate a personal protection shield," Hutchings said. "We call them parrys. You might want to wear them until you feel safe here."

None of the new people knew what to make of the strange bracelets.

"Go ahead," the doctor urged. "Put them on. You initialize them with your thumbprint. As long as you wear your parry, no one can physically assault you."

Oaks clamped his on immediately and activated it. Klane clamped his on as well but with much less enthusiasm.

Oaks looked up at Hutchings. "Why do you call them parrys? What do they do?"

"They'll ward off anyone who attacks you or any object thrown your way. A knife, a bullet, a fist. Just about anything."

"This is *neat*," said Oaks, admiring his bracelet.

"Now do you feel safe, little man?" Klane asked Oaks mockingly.

"So how do they work?" Oaks asked Hutchings.

"Take a swing at Mr. Klane and see what happens."

"I wouldn't do that—" Klane started.

Oaks went ahead anyway. He reared back to take a swing at Klane, but Klane thrust out a hand, intending to push Oaks's small head away from him.

Klane's hand, however, encountered a spider of black energy that blossomed suddenly around Oaks, shielding him. Klane pulled his hand back and Hutchings knew that it was tingling with dissipating energies. Oaks's shield lifted and Klane gripped his hand. He looked disgusted but no less worse for wear.

"Wow," Oaks breathed.

"Our engineers designed them," Hutchings said. "They're based on Algernon Renner's equations for his force-field technology, the same thing that protects us here on the sun."

"Why don't *you* have one?" Klane asked.

"Probably because I don't need one."

Oaks's eyes widened with sudden recognition. "Hey, are you that Eradicator guy?"

"The term is 'Annihilist.' But I'd rather you call me by my name. Ian Hutchings. That's all I go by down here."

"Major Ian MacFarland Hutchings?" the tall man asked.

"That's me."

The three women on the stage slipped their parry bracelets on and activated them.

"They told us you might be dead," the dark-haired Adamson said in a rather husky voice.

"Nope. Still here."

Meanwhile, the doctor had stepped onto the gazebo to examine E. Plainfield, the man who lay curled up next to the transfer crates. The doctor gently rolled Plainfield over and looked into the man's eyes which blinked uncomprehendingly.

"I go Baba's home?" Plainfield asked softly.

"I'm afraid you're going to be with us for a while," the physician said. "Are you in any kind of pain?"

"Want my bankie," Plainfield said. He stuck his thumb into his mouth and began to suck. As he did, his forefinger caressed his slightly curved nose.

"Oh, brother," Klane said, rolling his eyes.

The redheaded woman, Pickerall, glared contemptuously at the tall man. "Leave him alone, Klane. This isn't easy for any of us. They said this might happen."

"Ian," the doctor signaled. "You might want to look at this."

"What's wrong with him?" Hutchings asked.

"It looks like he's been powerfully regressed," Bladestone said. "Perhaps as far back as infancy."

"What do you mean 'infancy'?" Adamson asked darkly. "He's sixty years old, if he's a day."

Bladestone stood up, knees cracking from the effort. "How old are you, Miss—" He looked at her name patch—"Adamson?"

The dark-haired woman suddenly had to think about it. "I don't remember." She seemed surprised. She turned to the other two women. "I don't remember."

"What's the last thing you do remember?" the doctor asked. "I mean of your life before they sent you here."

Adamson's brow knitted. "I remember a canal

race. Yes, that's it! They were going to flood one of the southern plains and all the Mars middle schools were allowed to float pod-teams down the main channel. I was . . . I was a cheerleader! That's what I was! I was a cheerleader for the Mad Mesa pod! We were going to race the Jiu San Industrials pod and . . . and—"

She stopped. She suddenly realized that an enormous hunk of her life had been scalloped from her mind.

"I think you're probably sixteen, maybe seventeen years old—mentally," the doctor told her. "Given how old you look now, I'd say they removed twenty years from your memory. But it looks like this man has lost more than that."

Only then did the new people seem to fathom what had been done to their minds.

"We'd better get all of you down to the infirmary," the doctor said. "Com, open, Diane."

"*I'm here,*" a woman's voice broke inches from the doctor's right ear.

"Wake Kristen and bring a gurney up to the meadow. We've just had a Shunt."

"*A Shunt? A people Shunt? Really? How many did we get?*" Diane Beckwith asked excitedly.

"Six," Bladestone told her. "Three men and three women."

"*Just six? I mean, weren't we supposed to get twenty or twenty-five new people?*"

"Well, it's just these for now. Go ahead, wake Kristen."

Klane reached a long arm through the gazebo railing and retrieved his duffle bag. "I take it you thought more would be coming."

"They told us to expect Shunts of twenty-five new prisoners every three years," Hutchings said. "Three years our time."

"Looks like they changed their minds," Klane said.

"So you're all that're coming?" Hutchings asked.

Adamson followed Klane onto the meadow. "It's just us," she said. "There's no one else."

Oaks grabbed his duffle and slung it over his shoulder. "Hey, we heard that you guys eat your dead down here. Is that true?"

"It hasn't come to that yet," Hutchings said.

"What *do* you people do down here?" Klane asked.

"You'll see."

3

The past was beginning to catch up with Katherine Ariella DeWitt. During the day she might elude her guilt by keeping busy. But at night, in her dreams, such evasions were not possible. The past thundered toward her, just over the far range of hills: stampeding horses, horses in the thousands—all of them just out of sight and heading her way in the dream.

But why horses? And why now after all these years?

Whatever the reason, they were coming for her and there wasn't anything she could do about it, except perhaps kill herself. That would definitely end the terror of their approach.

Kate was thirty-eight or thirty-nine years old, but like much else in her life, she wasn't certain about it. The Wall of her amnesia blocked memories of her life after her twenty-sixth birthday.

Growing up, she had never once thought of the fury of the sun or that she would end up in a prison tethered to its surface. Now she thought of the sun always; that, and the statistical inevitability that some day the Renner shield would collapse. Oh, sure, their Fiddlers had made a redundancy back-up field around the sunstation just beyond the hull. But entropy always humbled the best efforts of Man. Just ask King Ozymandias. But unlike Shelley's narcissistic king, she would have no statue half-covered by desert sand to speak of her existence. When the end came, she would ride the solar winds in a billion blown atoms. Her epitaph would be written in the luminescent scrawl of the aurora borealis.

Lately, however, Kate had grown tired of thinking such thoughts. She had grown tired of thinking any thoughts whatsoever.

Her emotional deterioration, however, had not gone unnoticed by either Ian, her bedmate, or by Hugh Bladestone, their doctor. On Hugh's advice she had taken up temporary residence near the infirmary so she could be monitored. This meant time away from Ian, even if Ian rarely spent a full night with her. He had his own Eumenides. The unsettling ghosts of a billion human beings would keep anybody awake. Kate had trouble enough with the 191 people she was accused of slaughtering.

Now they were coming back to haunt her in her dreams—stampeding horses, just out of sight, beyond a nearby ridge. And lately, the animals seemed to be getting closer.

This was a shame because she loved horses. She had grown up with them in Wyoming. Her father had given her a bay gelding for her twelfth birthday named Nietzsche. Nietzsche was an intelligent animal, full of spunk. She showed Nietzsche at 4-H fairs, barrel-raced him at rodeos. She thought of him as just another member of the family, a person disguised as a horse.

Her dream-horses, however, were nothing at all like Nietzsche.

It is a crazy dream, always the same. In it she finds herself running out across a snow-dappled pasture toward the force-fences behind their ranch. The sky is pink, the clouds are yellow. She hears the calls of the frightened horses. She does not see them yet, but she knows they are just beyond a ridge which has just appeared. Their heads—she can see them!—barely crest the hill, rising and falling as their hooves rumble across the cheatgrass and sod.

Though the horses are saddled, no one rides them. The saddles are almost alive with beauty. They are made of embossed silver and pearl, riveted with rubies and gold—spectacular!

But what's happened to the *riders* of the horses? Where are they? The cries of the animals make her feel as if some pure evil is following close behind them, after anything it can sink its teeth into.

Kate's dream has always stopped there. For whatever reason, though, that night her dream went just a bit further. She had managed to climb the crest of the hill. She wanted to reach the horses before they disappeared again. She wanted to ride off in one of those beautiful saddles, never to be seen.

Hugh Bladestone, however, had stopped her—again. The monitor above Kate's bed had picked up her frantic REM and had notified the doctor. He came armed with a mild dosage of diazepam which should have allowed her to sleep, bypassing her dreams altogether.

But now she was too exhausted to sleep.

Everyone on Ra had strange dreams, a side effect of their amnesia. Remarkably, the memory-specific mind-scouring process did not affect the skills and abilities they needed to operate the sunstation. Those abilities they kept, though they did not know how the mind-wipe process allowed such a thing to happen.

Kate did know that she had grown up in Juliene, Wyoming, but left to attend the University of Texas at Austin where she majored in nuclear-fusion technology. Later, she lived in Galveston and interned at one of the wildcat fusion companies that plumbed the waters of the Gulf for its hydrogen. In that time she had flown to Luna on several occasions. *Had she committed her awful crime there? If so, why?*

Kate did know that she had had at least one child. Her lower abdomen bore a white caesarean-section scar. She also had the tell-tale wrinkles of suckling around the nipples of her breasts. But had the child been a boy or a girl? And who had been her husband? Did she even *have* a husband?

The Wall of her amnesia held all of that information like a dam holding back the waters of a flood. In her case, however, that dam was not likely to burst any time soon.

Kate got up from her bed not too long after Hugh had left her and donned her bathrobe. In the small bathroom she applied cold water to her face and stared at herself in the mirror. Her eyes looked—and felt—like rusted ball bearings. Were there any others on the Hot Rock ready to cash it in?

Kate stepped out into the deserted corridor and walked the short distance to the infirmary. The corridor wasn't quite deserted, however. At the far end of the curved hallway a small cylindrical tent lay off to one side. A pair of feet stuck out and snores could be heard coming from within. *Yes, there were others. The bindlestiffs.* They were the victims of the mysterious quick-sleep, a kind of vicious narcolepsy which had only months ago beset them. The worst affected became bindlestiffs and they had to carry flops around with them, tents that unfolded automatically whenever quick-sleep struck.

Perhaps it was time for her to start carrying a flop.

The lights were low inside the infirmary lobby. It seemed as quiet as a mausoleum. Several computer monitors were on and that meant that Hugh was still up. But he was nowhere about.

A nearby wall held their pharmaceutical cupboard. Kate walked up to the monitoring plate and tried several commands to get it to open. The cupboard, however, remained locked. Hugh always locked it when he retired for the night. He was not a careless man. He knew the dark places to which a human soul could plummet. And suicide was no stranger to Ra.

Kate leaned against the wall and slid to the floor. "Well, then," she said to no one in particular, "I guess a rope will have to do. A rope and a stepladder. Maybe a chair."

That wouldn't work either. Nor would a razor across the back of her wrist. Since Marlissa Madrigal and Kerry Harland had killed themselves, the Meadow Council got the Fiddlers to develop "eyes" for the station, to watch everyone. A pair of those eyes approached Kate just then. It came in the form of a bright yellow toy dump truck. It had apparently heard her muttering to herself and sensed the note of despondency in her voice. The Tonkas were unusually intelligent and ever alert.

"Go away," she said to the yellow toy.

The dump truck did not move. Whether Lorraine Sperry or one of her deputies was watching her through the toy's eyes, she did not know. It could have been acting autonomously. That certainly was within the parameters of its AI circuits.

"Ian," she whispered in her dejection. "Where are you?"

"I'm in the pond lift coming down to the infirmary," Ian's voice suddenly barked in her right ear. *"Why? Where are you?"*

She jerked her head up. "What?"

"I said I'm in the main lift. Where are you?"

Damn! The Tonka, following one of its busybody programs, had automatically engaged Kate's com-link when it had sensed that something was amiss.

Outside the infirmary she heard a commotion in the corridor. Hugh Bladestone then burst into the lobby, followed by his two assistants, Kristen Barron and Diane Beckwith. Kristen and Diane, in turn, commandeered a floating gurney upon which lay an elderly man—a man who was sucking his thumb.

Behind them appeared several more individuals, none of whom Kate had ever seen before. The new people each wore Shunt mufti.

Ian reached a hand down to assist her to her feet. "There you are," he said. "We could use your help."

He made no mention of the fact that she was sitting at the pharmacy cupboard where Death lay waiting.

Kate asked, "Who are—?"

A very tall man, the tallest Kate had ever seen, stepped into the room. His thin smile was without any humor whatsoever. "I believe we are 'new meat'," he said.

The haze that contained the memory of the riderless horses vanished from Kate's mind. The situation before her was entirely unprecedented. And unexpected. A miracle all its own.

She would save her death for another day.

4

Hutchings tried to conceal his surprise at finding Kate sitting on the floor next to the pharmacy cupboard. He didn't need his adrenalized left-brain biotech boosters to help him figure out what Kate might have been seeking.

Kate was usually a miniature dynamo, full of life and enthusiasm. Though just five feet two, she commanded the respect of the other Suncup engineers, and the Children loved her dearly. She certainly had salvaged him from many a depressive episode. Lately, however, Kate's reserves of morale appeared to be running low. Finding her this way wasn't a good sign.

"This is Katherine DeWitt," Hutchings told the new people. "Kate's our chief Suncup engineer. She'll help you get settled."

Kate was on her feet and straightening out her bathrobe. She tucked back a strand of brown hair. "This is rather sudden. I'm glad to meet you," she said somewhat embarrassed.

"Com, open, Ramirez," Hutchings said. "Pablo. Wake up."

"Jesus-what's-his-name! What time is it?" piped a mouselike voice beside Hutchings's ear.

"Oh three-hundred," Hutchings said. "Rise and shine."

"Call me tomorrow."

"It is tomorrow. Wake up. We've had a Shunt and we've got six new people in the infirmary."

"Huh?"

"Get down here and bring your Gleaner. We only walked across the meadow and took the pond lift down."

"Say what?"

"Quiet. I don't want your bedmate to hear."

"You don't have to worry about that. Claren's sleeping with Constantine now. I'll be there in three minutes. Out."

"Who was that?" the dark-haired Adamson asked.

"Pablo Ramirez, our chief Fiddler. He's perfectly harmless."

"You mentioned something called a 'Gleaner'," Klane said. "That didn't sound perfectly harmless."

Hugh Bladestone had just emerged from the adjacent room where Plainfield had been taken. "There's nothing for any of you to worry about. You'll see in a minute."

Klane smirked, but said nothing to that.

The infirmary had several side rooms that could be expanded or partitioned off to suit the doctor's needs. Diane Beckwith, a woman with very short light-brown hair and a no-nonsense attitude, had placed Plainfield on a waiting bed in one of those wards. Kristen Barron, a tall, leggy woman of Scandinavian descent, engaged the modest monitoring computer above the headboard to keep a medical eye on the old man.

"Nice place you've got here," Klane said. "Do you have occasion to use it much?"

The doctor seemed only slightly miffed at the insinuation. "We aren't barbarians, Mr. Klane. We try to take care of each other. We're a fairly close-knit community down here."

"What if we don't wish to be part of your 'close-knit' community down here?" Klane asked.

Hutchings stood before Klane. "Look, once Hugh determines that you made the Shunt in one piece, you can go your separate ways. We'll show you where you can eat, where you can sleep and where you can shit. What you do beyond that is up to you."

The doctor's two angels of mercy reconfigured the ward into two separate sections, one for the men, one for the women.

"Kate," the doctor said, "you can help the women get settled in the next room."

Kate pulled the collar of her bathrobe tighter around her throat. "Follow me," she said.

The blonde woman, R. Barrie, hugged her duffle. "What are you going to do to us?" she asked.

"We're not going to do anything to you," Kate said. "No one's ridden the monopole corridor down to the sunstation in three years. We need to see if you're reasonably intact."

Barrie seemed to accept this, but Adamson's eyes flashed. "The first person who touches me gets his arms pulled out."

Adamson, Hutchings noticed, had large, capable

hands. He wondered what sort of damage those hands had done in-system.

"Look," Hutchings said. "This'll just take a few minutes."

The doctor, who had a more practiced bedside manner, intervened. He said, "Ms. Adamson, we're just following protocol. We don't want to incur a Vapor Injunction. This is for everyone's benefit, not just yours."

Oaks looked up. "A Vapor Injunction? What's that?"

The doctor said, "Our computer is programmed to destroy us if any of the major station rules are violated. Two Vapor Injunctions and the computer will shut down the Renner shield and we'll be vaporized. Mr. Hutchings will provide you with a list of the violations that the System Assembly Penal Committee left us with. You'll want to memorize them."

Klane frowned. "You mean that if we don't go in there—" He nodded at the men's ward—"that we'll be incinerated?"

"It's possible."

"That's the most ridiculous thing I've ever heard," Klane said.

"Nonetheless," Hutchings said, "we go by the rules here. The doctor has to examine you and you're not leaving until he does."

Klane then shrugged. "Why not? We've got nothing to hide."

"You never know!" announced a short, yet clearly athletic man of bronze skin and jet-black hair standing in the doorway behind them. He walked in wearing a bright yellow jumpsuit and an olive-green tank connected to a hose strapped to his back. The snout of the hose looked as if it once belonged to a vacuum cleaner.

"Don't point that thing at anybody just yet, Pablo," Hutchings said to their chief Fiddler. "We're still a bit jumpy."

"Jumpy's not the word," Klane said. "Point that thing at me at any time and I'll break you in half."

Pablo Ramirez blanched at the tall man's words.

"This is Mr. Klane, Pablo," Hutchings said. "He thinks we're out to get him."

"Is he kidding?" Pablo asked.

"Apparently not," Hutchings responded. To the new people, he said, "This is Pablo Ramirez, our chief engineer. That thing on his back is called a Gleaner."

Oaks scurried up to Ramirez and, in a childlike voice, asked: "What's it do? How does it work? Can I try it? Let me see!"

"I'll show you," Ramirez said. He stepped back, aiming the Gleaner's black nozzle at the small man's boots. The device then began humming softly.

"I don't feel anything," Oaks said, staring at his feet. "Is it working? How come I don't feel it?"

"It's a matter-absorber. But you shouldn't feel anything," Ramirez said. "My guys back-engineered it from Shunt schemata we found in an unprotected computer file."

"You did?" Oaks asked with apparent incredulity.

Ramirez nodded. "The Gleaner absorbs all kinds of microscopic biodebris. Bacteria, virus fragments. Even loose, biotech components or nanobots you might be carrying."

"I see you've accomplished quite a lot down here," Klane said.

Hutchings scrutinized Klane. It was too early to know what to make of him other than he was a very bitter and cynical man.

Ramirez, however, had yet to be put off by Klane's condescending manner. Instead, he swept the nozzle across the floor of the infirmary. Pablo then said, "Anything we glean, we turn around and compound it in the Sally." He pointed to a cubbyhole set into the wall nearby. "The Sally can make mulch as well as food. Tons of it, in fact."

"The Sally?" Oaks said.

"That's short for 'Salvation Army'," Hutchings said. "We get our meals free from the Sally."

"Why not call it a 'food processor'?" Klane said. "Which is what it is."

"Because 'Sally' ties us to our past," Hutchings told him. "It ties us to the worst period in American history, the Great Depression where all Americans were bonded by a crisis."

"That was over a hundred and eighty years ago. Ancient history," Klane said.

"That doesn't matter. It's for *our* memory. You can call it a food processor, if you want," Hutchings said.

Ramirez walked into the men's ward and stood before Mr. Plainfield. Kristen Barron was smoothing the new man's brow with a motherly hand. Plainfield seemed to be asleep.

"What's wrong with him?" Pablo asked.

"We don't know yet," Kristen said.

"Can I Glean him?" he asked Hutchings.

Kristen looked at Hutchings who nodded his approval. Ramirez then proceeded to scan the old man where he lay.

"Find anything interesting?" Hutchings asked when the Fiddler switched the Gleaner off.

Ramirez consulted a data card to which the Gleaner had transmitted its preliminary assessment. "Umm . . . just planetary dust. Could be lunar or cometary. And some of the usual organic debris. Bits of skin, hair, and stuff like that."

Pablo glanced past Hutchings to where Kate and the doctor had gone with the new women. "How many women did we get?"

"Three," Hutchings said and Ramirez grinned.

Klane saw the grin. He looked down at the diminutive engineer. "Do not go near them," he said threateningly. "If you want to see another day."

Ramirez looked at Hutchings.

"It's not what you think," Hutchings said. "He's just interested in their hair."

"What?"

"Hair is like a big net," Ramirez said. "There's no telling what sorts of things they've picked up."

"That's all that interests you?" Klane asked.

Ramirez turned to Hutchings. "What's with him?"

"I'll let you know when I find out," said Hutchings. "Go on and Glean the women, but keep your distance. We don't want to set off Mr. Klane here."

Ramirez left the room.

"What's that man in for?" Klane asked Hutchings.

"Thirty-three counts of first-degree murder and conspiracy to undermine the System Assembly."

"Him?"

"That's what the Roster said. We think Pablo

might have done something to an assembly of Quorum Elders. There are usually thirty-three elders in a plenary session. But that's only a guess. Speaking of which, did they give you a Roster?"

Klane fished a hand into a tunic pocket. He pulled out a domino-shaped iridium-titanium tile which he gave to Hutchings. "The Screws gave it to me just before they threw me into the Shunt."

Hutchings took the tile and pocketed it for safekeeping. "We'll download it when the whole station is assembled at oh nine-hundred. Right now, we have enough on our plate."

"You have such an interesting way of putting things," Klane remarked.

"That's me."

Hugh Bladestone returned to the men's ward. "Please, Mr. Klane." He beckoned to one of the beds. "This will take just a few minutes of your time."

"All I've got is time."

"Then let's make the best use of it. This way please."

Klane reluctantly followed the doctor. Hutchings noticed how every move the man made was informed by deep and seething resentment, perhaps even a murderous one.

Klane, he decided, would bear watching.

5

Across an immeasurable sea of darkness, the plaintive voice of a woman calls out to Dr. Bladestone: *"Hugh! Hugh, darling, please!"* He does not know what to do. His thoughts are sluggish. He can barely move. He seems to be dreaming. *Yes, that's it. I'm dreaming.* A bout of mysterious quick-sleep has sucked him down from the bright surface of the waking world. *The bright surface of the sun. . . .*

The voice changes to that of another woman: *"Dr. Bladestone, please report to Emergency Dock Alpha as soon as possible. Dr. Bladestone, please report to Emergency Dock Alpha!"*

Inexplicably, he's back at Chicago Mercy. There, in the real world, he had interned immediately after graduating from medical school, working eighteen-hour days as an ER physician. Mercy was one of the best hospitals on the planet, but now it was being pushed beyond its limits. Everything around it is turning to a landscape of silver and ice.

In the dream, Bladestone is staring out of a third-floor lounge window where he has been contemplat-

ing the fury of the snowstorm. Snowflakes the size
of silver dollars are falling. Experts are calling this
another "little Ice Age," similar to the one in the
fourteenth century that turned Greenland white and
Europe into a frozen wilderness that set the stage for
the Black Plague. Above him, ambulances descend to
the landing pads of Chicago Mercy, their antigravity
plates glowing neon-blue. Once down, their bays
open and gurneys are whisked through the emergency entrance by harried landing-pad attendants.
The snow is deep and getting deeper. Entire sections
of Chicago have no power. People are freezing to
death in their homes, their cars, their offices. News-
casters are now calling the dead of Chicago "Ice
Men."

And some of these Ice men are women.

Hutchings clamped a firm hand on the doctor's
shoulder where Hugh had been sleeping at his desk.
Clearly the doctor had collapsed out of sheer
exhaustion.

"Are you still with us?" Hutchings asked.

The doctor jerked. "I think so. Yes."

"Don't tell me you're coming down with quick-
sleep," Hutchings said. "That's all we need right
now."

Bladestone looked around blearily. "I'm just beat,
that's all. What time is it?"

"Oh-eight-fifty. Not quite the crack of dawn."

"God, what a night," Bladestone muttered, rubbing his eyes.

Hutchings himself had gotten thirty minutes of compressed sleep, the usual for him since his mind rarely,

if ever, shut down. He had been experimenting on himself lately in an attempt to repair his memory damage by employing a navy of metamphetamine facilitators and endorphin packets produced by protozoa-sized nanofactories he had recently devised. Those factories built machines whose task it was to rebuild the neural tissue of his amnesia-damaged brain—if such a process were possible. To do that, his brain cells needed stimulation, hence the need for the amphetamine boosters. Hence, his constant insomnia.

What little sleep he did get that night he got with Kate in her temporary room down the hall from the infirmary. He made sure that she slept between himself and the wall so she wouldn't wander off this time and find some other, more efficient means to kill herself.

Hutchings and the doctor found the new people, minus Mr. Plainfield, having breakfast in the infirmary lounge. Lorraine Sperry, their African-British security chief, stood watch, sipping her usual morning cup of Earl Grey.

"Good," the doctor said. "Everyone's up."

The three new women seemed to have resigned themselves to their fate, but each exhibited that resignation differently. Barrie seemed the most hopeless. Pickerall, if anything, was nervous and alert. Adamson merely smoldered. She seemed to snarl, if wordlessly, at Hutchings when he entered the room.

As for Klane and Oaks, the one ate his breakfast with the elegance of a heron dipping its long neck down into a swamp to spear food; the other gobbled his eggs and bacon and pancakes as if they were his last meal.

"I see we've learned to work the Sally," Hutchings said.

"I told them not to waste food," Lorraine added. "Our first rule. What they can't eat I'll take upstairs to the little Boys."

"Is this one of your 'Vapor Injunctions'?" Klane asked.

"Not quite," Hutchings said. "We just don't like to waste food. It's a little voice in our heads."

"We feel it in our bones," the doctor said.

"With your access to pure hydrogen," Klane observed, "you could fill this room with food, from now until forever and still never run out. Sounds like a superstition to me."

"Nevertheless," Hutchings said solemnly. "We don't waste food here. We either eat it or recycle it. After a while, you'll feel it down to your bones, as the doctor just said."

Behind them a new man walked in from the main infirmary lobby. He wore a teal-blue jumpsuit and he carried six thin-leafed booklets.

"Elliot," Hutchings said.

"I've got your guidebooks, as promised," Elliot Shoemaker said. He stood five feet eight inches and had graying black hair packed in small curls on his head. His hazel-green eyes shone with intelligence. "Is our sixth man still down?" he asked the doctor.

"He is," Bladestone responded.

Shoemaker looked around. "So where's Kate? We should have the entire Meadow Council present for this."

"She's with the little Girls," Hutchings said.

"We're trying to keep all of the Children out of the loop for the time being. She'll view all this later."

"What about the little Boys?"

"I think they're in the Roughhouse," Hutchings said. "Maybe they can stay occupied until the assembly is over."

At the opposite end of the lounge was a blank wall. Hutchings walked over to it and said, "Computer, on." The wall came alive with a display menu that advertised a number of functions. He then said, "Open access from here to all common rooms and all other on-line monitors."

Hutchings turned to the new people. "As Administrator, I am required to play the Roster and introduce you to various sunstation functions. You will otherwise not be interrogated at any time beyond this meeting. Any information you want to give us yourselves is entirely up to you. Otherwise, no one will bother you from here on out."

"We have your word on that?" Klane asked.

"I personally guarantee it," Hutchings stated. "I'll enforce it, in fact."

Klane made a characteristic smirk.

Hutchings went on. "Despite what the SA might have told you, you haven't lost any of your human rights by being sent here. Any behavior on our part which you consider to be harassment report directly to Lorraine here or you can let me know. We don't take any shit down here, especially from ourselves."

Lorraine Sperry nodded as she leaned against the back wall, her concussor pistol, their only real weapon, holstered and ready at her hip.

Hutchings engaged the Roster. "Open directory,"

Hutchings said. "Access Readme file, with full visuals."

On the blank wall of the lounge, the visage of a hooded Ward Judge appeared, a veritable tzar of fear. The Hood, cloak and mask were a dark green and on the man's chest was an obscure symbol, perhaps that of a bell or a beehive. *The newest in fascist evening wear*, Hutchings thought acidly.

"On this day, April 18, 2095, Common Era, we, the Elders of the System Assembly Quorum, sentence the following humans to Ra," the Ward Judge announced.

Elliot Shoemaker whispered, "Hey, it's 2095! That means a whole decade's gone by on the outside! It's just three years to us—"

"Shh!" Lorraine Sperry hissed.

The screen then divided in two. Beside the Judge appeared the booking photograph of a horrified old man who looked as if he were standing before a firing squad. The Judge said, *"Edward Plainfield for crimes of subversion, sabotage, and felony insurrection. Lifetime sentence. No possibility of parole."*

Next appeared the 2-D image of Oaks. "That's me!" cried Oaks.

"Dylan Oaks," the Judge intoned, *"for theft and illegal transport of weapons-grade materials; unauthorized detonation of a nuclear device; four-thousand-eight-hundred-and-six counts of felony murder. Lifetime sentence. No possibility of parole."*

"I did that?" Oaks asked wondrously.

"Be quiet, little man," hissed Klane.

The image of a defiant Klane appeared next. The Judge said: *"Newsome Rhajo Klane, for conspiracy against the System Assembly; illegal orbital alteration of a planetary body; destruction of Martian habitat; forty-thousand-one-hundred-and-sixty-three counts of felony murder. Lifetime sentence. No possibility of parole."*

Nobody said anything to that, not even Klane.

The image of Klane was replaced by that of the dark-haired and belligerent Adamson. The Judge said, *"Arliss Caroline Adamson for crimes against the System Assembly; prostitution; blackmail. Fifteen years. Possibility of parole in six."*

Adamson seemed unfazed by the Judge's pronouncement.

Pickerall's image appeared next. Her red hair had been cut brutally short in the booking photograph. *"Clarissa Marilyn Pickerall for crimes against the System Assembly; unlawful manufacture of controlled substances; conspiracy to distribute controlled substances; pandering; prostitution; attempted murder. Sentence: twelve years. Possibility of parole in six."*

Barrie appeared next. *"Rhonda Alison Barrie for the crime of treason. Sentence: ten years. Possibility of parole in three."*

The image of Rhonda Barrie blanked out. The woman sat aghast, not quite believing what she had just heard.

The Judge resumed. *"Sunstation rules and basic functions should now be discussed. These should include those procedures which allow a prisoner to earn credit toward parole. Resume on your command."*

Hutchings prompted the computer to manifest a 2-D cutaway of the sunstation next to the frozen image of the Ward Judge. The sunstation itself resembled a squat mushroom with a strange bell-like structure hanging at a considerable distance beneath the narrow "stem" of the mushroom. Everyone could see that the "cap" of the mushroom—the living and working areas of Ra—had eleven levels, the top two of which comprised the meadow.

Hutchings took out a laser pointer and needled a red beam at the diagram. "This is Ra," he said. "The main living facilities are in the 'cap' and the ship's vital functions—the main engines, the Renner-shield generators and the main computer housing which we call 'the Man', are locked away, down here in the 'stem'. This structure dangling below the stem is the Anchor, which is probably some sort of tug or shuttle. Its principal function is to hold us in place. We assume that the Renner shield pinches off somewhere below the Anchor, but the monopole alignment signal is grounded all the way to the Van Flandern Discontinuity at the center of the sun. It's what keeps us locked in place so that alloy shipments and prisoner exchanges can come and go via the top part of the monopole corridor, here."

Hutchings then drew a red laser-line of light to the midpoint of the sunstation where the cap rested upon the stem pedestal. "Much of Level Seven and all of the 'stem' are unaccessible to us. We call these areas the Forbidden Zones. The Vapor probably lives somewhere on Level Seven. When he appears, *if* he appears, you'll know someone's invoked an Injunction and that we're close to being fried."

"I take it this Vapor person is your bogeyman," Newsome Klane said.

"*Our* bogeyman," Hutchings clarified. "Yours and mine. Trust me. You don't want to see him."

"What is he?" Rhonda Barrie asked at the other end of the table. "I mean, is he human?"

Hutchings shook his head. "It's a very sophisticated robot, a kind I'd never seen before. When I arrived, he told me all the things we weren't supposed to do here. One of them was that we weren't to go looking for him in the Forbidden Zones. In fact, even attempting to enter the Zones is an Injunction itself. The second violation beyond that—any violation at all—brings out the Vapor, and he will pronounce his judgment."

"Then what?" Klane asked.

"Poof," Hutchings said.

Elliot Shoemaker handed out the booklets he had brought to the meeting. "You'll find listed in the first chapter the twenty main activities that evoke a Vapor Injunction. Memorize them and make damn sure you don't commit any of them."

The new prisoners leafed through their booklets.

Hutchings added, "Vapor Injunctions also include attempts at sabotage—the environmental systems, the Sally, the secondary fusion generator which runs the free zones. The Suncup and the main internal gravity systems are included in these as well. And, of course, you are forbidden to kill anybody."

"The book says that?" Klane asked, looking up.

"No," Hutchings said. "That's *my* injunction."

Oaks held up his left wrist with its glittering parry. "I thought that's what these things were for."

"They are. We're just covering our bases," Hutchings said.

Clarissa Pickerall pointed to the 2-D cutaway of

Ra. "What's that area at the top of the 'stem', right there in the middle of the station?"

A lozenge-shaped cavity, glowing a bright yellow, hung in the center region of the sunstation. Hutchings said, "That's the Suncup facility where we earn points toward parole. At least those of us who are allowed to earn points toward parole."

"Your Suncup is not in the Forbidden Zone?" Klane asked.

Hutchings shook his head. "No. We have complete access to it, inside and out. If we didn't, we wouldn't be able to maintain the Suncup properly."

"As it is," Shoemaker added, "we've already had one major accident in the 'cup. We were fortunate that we didn't incur a Vapor Injunction."

"What happened?" Arliss Adamson asked.

"We had an escape attempt a year ago," Hutchings said. "One of our technicians tried to use the Suncup matter-transmitter to escape the station during a standard alloy Shunt."

"I take it he failed," Klane said.

"*She* failed," Hutchings said grimly.

"She?" This came from Rhonda Barrie.

Hutchings nodded. "The 'cup is hardwired to send only single elements or simple alloys, depending on what the System Assembly requests that month. It won't send anything as chemically complex as a person."

"Someone tried to use the Suncup to escape?" Rhonda Barrie asked.

Hutchings nodded. This was really Kate's bailiwick, but he answered in her stead. "One of our best engineers, Marlissa Madrigal. At the time we were preparing to send up several tons of pure iron which had been recently fused from solar plasma. Marlissa accessed the chamber without anybody knowing about it."

"What happened?" Barrie asked. "Did she go up?"

"Yes. Part of her, anyway."

"Which part?" Klane asked.

"The iron part. The rest of her stayed behind because that's all we were Shunting at the time. It was rather grisly."

The new prisoners glanced at each other. The reality of their incarceration seemed to be sinking in.

Hutchings went on. "Because there are so many Vapor Injunctions, we would appreciate it that when you try to escape you run your plans past the Getaway Team and see what they have to say."

"Getaway Team?" Klane asked. "What the hell is that?"

"It's a committee run by two of our inmates, William Woodfield and Alan Balter," Hutchings said. "They've compiled a book that lists our escape attempts and a few we haven't tried yet."

"I take it you think we're going to escape," Klane said.

"You will, if you're like the rest of us," Hutchings said. "We just want to make sure that you don't do anything stupid."

"Anything that might make us go pop?"

"Exactly."

Klane folded his mantislike hands. "Well, nobody tells me what I can or cannot do and I certainly don't need anybody's permission to escape from this place."

Hutchings leaned over the table. "Let me be clear

about this, Klane. Screw up and you stand a good chance of killing us all. It's *my* job to see that you don't do that."

Klane's ice-eyes locked onto Hutchings.

Hutchings stood and faced the monitor wall. "Resume program," he commanded.

The Judge continued. *"The following individuals have been granted parole and will be removed in a standard parole Shunt in forty-eight hours. Anyone other than these nine humans attempting to board the parole Shunt will be destroyed upon arrival. Parole has been granted to Staff Sergeant Armando P. Chavarin, Corporal Steven Welch, Corporal James Harrington, Corporal Wanda Pease, Corporal Suzanne Alcott, Private Thomas Geyer, Dr. Janice Koetzle, Captain Lyle MacKenzie, and Lieutenant Katherine Ariella DeWitt. End communication."*

Silence fell about them. Hutchings blinked. He was utterly flabbergasted and so were his friends in the room. To the five new prisoners, though, the parole announcement meant nothing at all.

Hutchings looked at Hugh Bladestone, stunned. "My God. Did you hear that? They want Kate."

The doctor countered: "Kate? Ian, they want *Lyle.* What are we going to do about Lyle?"

Hutchings had no immediate answer to that. This was a development he hadn't expected. Parole. For Kate *and* Lyle.

And what *were* they going to do about Lyle?

6

While Ian had been preparing for the morning assembly, Kate had gone to the dorms where the little Girls slept. Two vast beds usually allowed three physically adult Girls to sleep together like real four- and five-year-olds at a slumber party. Occasionally, they'd push their beds together and they'd run back and forth in their jammies and make a mess of things.

When Ian sneaked away at 07:30 to prepare for the assembly, Kate, still groggy from the tranquilizers Hugh had given her, went to sleep with the little Girls. They were glad to have her. It didn't take long before they were all back in slumberland fast asleep curled amid their bankies and dollies with everyone but Kate sucking their thumbs in blissful oblivion. Kate would view the assembly tape later. For now, she wanted merely to be in the company of the innocent—the members of her adopted family.

Kate remembered her brother, Kingston. It was her first cattle drive just south of Sheridan, Wyoming. She was fourteen. Several head of cattle had wan-

dered up a narrow canyon the night before and
hadn't come back out. Nietzsche maundered along
with a gentle rocking motion as Kate and her brother,
on his horse Django, tracked the heifers up a cold-
creek canyon of succulent spurge. Blue jewels of
water burst around the hooves of their horses as Kate
and Kingston followed the crescent moons of cattle
hooves like fossil trilobites on the muddy shore.

As the morning wore on they found the animals,
one by one. However, the last animal, when they
found it, had fallen onto its side. The beast had
gorged itself on the burdock and spurge and its
stomach, full of fermenting debris, had bloated
hugely. The creature couldn't move and moaned
mournfully.

From a saddlebag Kingston removed a tubular
contraption. He then jumped from his horse and
crashed across the creek to where the wretched animal lay. Over his shoulder, Kingston said, "I'd get
upwind, if I were you, kid. You won't like it."

Kate didn't move. She was fascinated. She hadn't
the slightest idea what the thin silver tube was for.
If anything, it resembled a long hypodermic needle
with a valve at one end.

Her brother sank one knee in the creek, chaps and
all, and gingerly began probing the animal's belly
with a gloved hand. The poor beast lowed at the
pressure of Kingston's hand.

When Kingston found the spot that he was searching for, he thrust the tubular device directly into the
beast's stomach. The animal let out a terrible cry.
Kingston quickly opened the petcock at the rear end
of the tube and fetid air suddenly came whistling

out. Kingston then pushed his shoulder into the creature's gut, hastening the egress of the sulphurous mulch.

The gas from the animal's stomach gathered itself in the still air above the creek. Its scintillating silver particles then fell about Kingston like a vengeful genie released from its bottled prison.

"Don't breathe it, Katie!" Kingston shouted to her. *"Don't breathe the traces! Don't let them in!"*

Kate jerked awake coughing and gasping for air. A silver glitter seemed to have coated her throat. She fell back onto her pillow. It had been a dream! But this dream had a new wrinkle. The traces. Kingston never used that expression before. What did it mean?

"I want French toasts and *lots* of syrup," said a small voice beside her. *"Big* toasts. Real big toasts and *lots* of syrup."

Sitting on the floor beside the bed was a pretty blonde woman of about thirty-five. She held a blanket to her cheek and sucked her thumb. She had removed her thumb to make her pronouncement. Once the announcement was made, the thumb went back in.

From the opposite side of the bed another little Girl's voice broke in. "You had French toasts yesterday. You don't get any toasts today. *I* get French toasts."

Kate fought her way from the dream's seductive clutch. "Bebe, Junie—quit arguing."

Bebe Wasson, on the floor with her bankie, scowled at the little Girl lying on the other side of Kate on the immense bed. Junie Russell, clutching her stuffed tiger, stuck her tongue out at Bebe. The Girls were five and six, respectively. Bebe Wasson, their youngest Girl, had platinum blonde hair done up in pigtails. Junie, a rather buxom woman of thirty-eight, had rich brown hair which had only recently begun turning gray. Of the fourteen female Children on the station, only Junie looked her age.

"I get toasts," insisted Bebe.

"You don't either."

"Girls," Kate said.

"Then I get to sing my birdy-nose song," Bebe announced.

"No birdy-nose song!" Junie shouted, jumping up on the bed.

"Birdy-nose, birdy-nose . . . knock, knock, knock!" sang Bebe.

"Stop it!" shouted Junie. She clamped her hands over her ears. "I don't like the birdy-nose song! No birdy-nose song!"

"—knock, knock, KNOCK!" Bebe said louder.

Kate sat up. Another Girl walked into the large bedroom. Following her on the floor was a red toy firetruck, a sturdy observant Tonka. Lisa Anderson was a slightly built woman of about forty with short brown hair and elfin features. She had an impish gleam in her eyes.

"You get to go *home*," Lisa said to Kate. "You're *proled*."

"I get to go home, too!" Bebe said.

"You don't, either," said Junie. "You're staying here 'cause you've been bad."

Kate blinked. "What are you talking about?"

Little Lisa Anderson, still in her jammies, walked

over to one of their many toy boxes and came up with a small container of crayons and a coloring book. "You're proled. Somebody said."

"Who told you that?"

She shrugged. Drawing pictures was more important now.

"Com, open, Ian," Kate said.

"Right here," he returned. *"What's going on at your end?"*

"I've just been told I've been 'proled'. Does that have anything to do with being *paroled?*"

"Probably. You and eight others have been paroled. It's on the Roster that came down with the new people."

"When . . . when do we go?" Her heart was now beating so rapidly, she hardly knew what to think.

"Subtracting a few hours, about two days."

"Who are the others?" she asked.

Ian rattled off the names.

"Lyle got paroled? But, Ian, he's—"

"I know, I know. We're still trying to figure out what we're going to do. Are you still with the Girls?"

"Yes."

"We'll discuss this later. Have the Girls gotten break-fast yet?"

"No," Kate said. "That was next on our list."

"Yay!" said Junie, jumping up. Her adult mass made the bed rollick like a Hatteras sea swell.

"Take your time. We'll get together as soon as you feed the kids. Buzz me when you're clear. Com, close."

"You're! Going! Home!" Junie Russell chanted as she jumped about the rumpled landscape of the bed.

"And I'm having French toasts!" said Bebe Wasson, rising to her feet and heading for the clothes closet to select the day's apparel.

Lisa Anderson, meanwhile, was drawing pictures of two fat little Girls, one blonde, the other brunette, singing to herself. She hadn't a clue as to what was going on.

Neither had Kate.

Level Four of the sunstation was given over to inmate quarters. The floor, however, was only one-third occupied; as such, several inmates often took possession of a nearby room or two. Ian was one of these. Ian's second room was actually a private laboratory he'd constructed which Kate rarely visited. When she wasn't at the Suncup, her duties often centered around the Children.

On the same floor was common room number six where everyone met to share their meals. When Kate and her Girls arrived at the common room dressed for the day, they found several Children in the midst of their own brunch. Actually, they were in the midst of a food fight, buoyed by the excitement of having new people arrive.

"Help!" huge Bobby Nakamura shouted from behind an overturned table. "He's attacking me! Help!"

"Hey! Hey!" Kate said. "Who started this?"

The place was a colossal mess.

Matthew White, lanky and towheaded, stood with a fistful of gooey oatmeal which he was about to fling at Bobby Nakamura. "Bobby started it!" Matt said accusingly.

"I did not!" Bobby shouted back.

"Well, it's over now. Straighten this place up," Kate demanded.

The little Girls marched in and stuck their tongues out at the stupid little Boys. They walked over to the Sally like perfect little protopersons and began dialing their favorite morning foods.

"But it's Bobby's fault!" Matt whined.

"You know we don't like to waste food, Matt. Wait until Ian hears that you guys were having a food fight."

"But this isn't *food*," Matt said.

Kate pondered a bowl of oatmeal on a table that had not been capsized during the skirmish. It looked perfectly normal to her.

"It's yucky," Matt pronounced.

Quite a lot of the oatmeal had been flung about. Bobby Nakamura, being the largest target in the room, was covered with it. So, too, were the other little Boys, most notably Terry Hummer, Danny Stryk, and Brucie Weigl—adults with a mental age of six, seven, and eight, respectively. At ages eight, nine, and ten were Minnie Marcroft and Lissa Van Fleet and Cory Hales. Even though the Boys had started the fight, the three little Girls had obviously also participated. They were spattered with their own badges of oatmeal.

"It was new, so I tasted it," said Minnie Marcroft, a perky, fortyish woman with a healthy head of wavy brown hair.

"*I* tried it first," announced Melissa Van Fleet, a stunning, soft-featured blonde who, because of her comeliness, was always the target of pranks by the little Boys.

Danny Stryk, a timid little Boy, came over to Kate. "Do we have to eat it? Matt made Sally give us *gobs* of it."

Kate considered the bowl of gruel in Danny Stryk's hands. Oatmeal was usually one of their favorite breakfast foods.

"It tastes *awful!*" said Brucie Weigl. "I don't like it."

Kate took up a spoon and sampled the oatmeal. It *was* awful. More than that, it had a faint metallic residue that didn't seem natural at all.

"Christ," she whispered. No wonder they'd had a food fight.

Kate put the bowl in the waste cubby where it quickly dissolved and its molecular compounds were returned to the Sally's element stock.

Danny Stryk pouted. "Will the Spanker come out and spank us?"

"I don't know," Kate said. "He might."

"Eddie Brickman said that the Spanker would get us if we did anything bad," insisted Brucie Weigl. "Will he?"

"I'll bet he won't come out if we can clean this place up," Kate suggested.

The little Boys found this agreeable and started picking up after themselves.

At the Sally, Kate punched up her usual batch of eggs over easy, toast with marmalade, grapefruit juice, and coffee, then returned to the little Girls at their end of the table when the Sally delivered its fare. The Girls, as she knew they would, had loaded up on syrupy goodies.

Everyone but Kate proceeded to gobble their goodies while the little Boys did their cleaning. The peace lasted only five minutes.

Bebe and Lisa, who were sitting next to one another opposite Kate, looked up from their French toast. The other Children froze where they sat. Matt, on his way to the recycler, held a bowl of unused oatmeal. A fresh spoon angled in it.

The very tall and very scary Newsome Klane had entered the room, wearing a nylon white jumpsuit with silver trim that ran down the arms and legs. The Boys and Girls hadn't seen any of the new people before this moment.

"Ah, the monsters at breakfast," he said with a tilted smile.

"It's the Spanker," Bobby Nakamura said loudly.

"It's okay, Children," Kate said quickly. "This is Mr. Klane. He's one of the new people. He came to us last night."

But the Children were wide-eyed with terror as Klane walked into their midst. He paused before a stunned Matt White and looked down at the little Boy.

"Ah," Klane said, taking the bowl of unabused oatmeal from Matt's hands. "You have anticipated my very desire. A hearty bowl of oatmeal."

Matt's eyes were as wide as a pair of breakfast eggs.

"Let us not waste good food, now shall we?" Klane said. He took a large spoonful of the oatmeal, levered it into his wide mouth and swallowed with hardly a pause to chew.

"Mmm," Klane said. "Mighty good."

The Children saw the man's smile, dropped everything, and ran screaming from the room.

7

So how *do* you kill a billion human beings? How do you kill that many people without the impact causing the absolute collapse of civilization?

The enormity of his crime was never far from Hutchings's thoughts. The arrival earlier that day of the new prisoners only served to remind him of the horror of his deed and the extremes to which the System Assembly went to insure that he would never again pose a threat to humankind.

As he lumbered slowly around the gravity-amplified track in the deserted Roughhouse, he thought about his earlier life, the life he led before the Wall. He remembered his graduate studies at the Media Lab at MIT in nanorobotics and biotechnology. He even recalled his dissertation: *Thermoelastic and Phonon Viscosity Loss in Nonisothermal Processes.*

As he plodded around the Roughhouse track at three Earth gravities he tried to conceive how a biotech application might have led to his crime. Even in grade school he knew that biotechnology had revolutionized medicine. Biotech machines could function as waldo-like attachments to white blood cells or act as a set of propellers to plasma-borne enzymes. Also used were chemical-warhead delivery systems with protein sensors for use in cancer therapies. There were even "pox boxes," large polymer molecules that surrounded malignant cells and collapsed about them, rendering them ineffectual.

What were the applications for murder from such a technology? Perhaps he had wiped out all the plankton in the sea. Perhaps he had killed off a species of vital insect. Bees, perhaps. Or perhaps he had caused the bonding elements of pollen molecules to unravel. The death of pollen alone would cause a *lot* of damage.

And what about the deed's aftermath? Bodies of the dead would have clogged rivers. Islands of them would be floating in every ocean of the world. The stench alone would be unprecedented. Putrescent clouds of it would choke whole continents.

Yet neither he nor his friends could remember anything approaching the magnitude of such a deed. What information he had of his crime came with the Roster the Vapor had given him upon his arrival. However, when Hutchings asked the robot why the System Assembly simply didn't execute him for what he had done, the Vapor said the Quorum valued every human life. Capital punishment was no longer an option for the enlightened State.

Hutchings managed four laps around the rubberized track in his shackles, which was about usual for him. He leaned over, drenched in sweat, gulping huge lungfulls of air. During the Middle Ages they would have called this self-immolation or flagellation, a self-imposed punishment to expiate his sins.

One billion counts of felony murder.

Perhaps a heavier set of shackles would do. Eighty pounds instead of forty. Kate could easily make him a new set of alloyed shackles in the Suncup. . . .

Yet, *how* he had killed so many people mattered less to him than *why*. What sort of karmic curse from a former life would lead him to kill so many people in this life? Taken in its reverse: What specific punishment did someone living in, say, Sunnyvale, California, or São Paulo, Brazil, require that they be put to death by *him*? His father, a descendent of New England Puritans, had become a devout Vajrayana Buddhist (to spite those Puritans); his mother, Presbyterian, became a Sufi. In fact, when he was eighteen, he and his mother had made a religious pilgrimage to India, to the tomb of Meher Baba. It had been one of the seminal events of his life. The avatar's shrine had been like a spiritual generator, powering so much of what was to come in his life after that. That he could *remember*.

Despite his physical size, he wasn't a particularly violent man. He had been in the usual adolescent scrapes when he was a kid. He played football in high school, rugby in college. But he had no recollection of ever having clobbered anyone out of sheer meanness at any time in his life. As the current Administrator of the sunstation he often had to deal with recalcitrant little Boys or bratty little Girls, as well as the occasional bindlestiff who wouldn't stay put (or who wouldn't even eat). It was only in the Roughhouse where he, Eddie Brickman, and Lyle

MacKenzie would often beat the shit out of each other in games of Zero Ball. But that's what the Roughhouse was for—sport.

Had he killed a billion human beings out of some sort of *sporting* impulse? Had it simply been a mere whim?

Bent over on his hands and knees, gulping air, he said, "Com, open, Elliot."

"I'm right here," Shoemaker returned.

"Where are you, exactly?"

"Up in the Fiddlers' lair. Lorraine and I are showing the new women through the sunstation. We've done the meadow and the Underworld. We're working our way down. What's on your mind?"

"I need a favor," Hutchings said.

"Shoot."

"Do you think you and Lorraine could bring the women down to the Roughhouse? I'd like to speak with them, if I could."

"Let me consult our guests. Pause," Shoemaker said.

Seconds later, Shoemaker was back on-line. *"If there's nobody else down there, they said it would be all right. We were going to tour it anyway."*

"Well, it's just me."

"We'll be down in a few minutes. Out."

Hutchings sat back, feeling the brutal crush of three gravities upon him. The Roughhouse had originally been set aside to be a dormitory for female inmates. But the floor above was able to hold all the people on Ra and then some. So the Fiddlers knocked out the walls and installed gravity plates in the floor and ceiling and turned it into a multipurpose gymnasium. The Roughhouse could accommodate a basketball court and two tennis courts. A running track, an eighth of a mile long, circled the whole affair. At either end of the oval track were observation decks and bleachers behind a wall of shatterproof glass.

Elliot and Lorraine soon appeared in the primary observation deck where the gravity was always Earth-normal. Hutchings reclined on the empty track in his sweats, about ten yards from them trying to look as nonthreatening as possible. The new women came in behind Lorraine and Elliot in their white jump suits. They seemed alert but suspicious.

"Here we are," Shoemaker said. "The Roughhouse. You might be spending some of your rec time here. That booth up there"—he pointed to an elevated chamber just above and to the right of the entrance to the room—"controls the gravity environment. And *this* is the running track—"

They turned their attention to the track beyond the protective glass wall. "And Mr. Hutchings, as we can see," said Arliss Adamson in a dour voice.

"Ian would like a word with you," Shoemaker stated.

Lorraine Sperry leaned against a far wall, watching like a referee.

"Hey. I thought you said we wouldn't be interrogated by you or anybody else," Adamson began.

"I'd like to ask you a few semipersonal questions. It's not an interrogation at all."

"Do we have to answer your questions?" Adamson asked.

"No. Of course not."

Rhonda Barrie stepped forward. "What do you

want to know?'' she volunteered. ''I'll tell you anything I can.''

Adamson stared hostilely at her.

''Okay. I was wondering if any of you have any
idea of the crime I was supposed to have committed.
Oaks knew that I was called something like the Annihilist. I thought one of you might know more.''

''You don't *know* what you did?'' Adamson asked.
She managed a bitter laugh, not quite believing that
Hutchings had asked the question in the first place.

''Not really,'' Hutchings admitted. ''The Vapor said
I had a billion counts of felony murder charged
against me. He didn't say what I did. I just wanted
to know if it had happened on the Earth or out
among the System Assembly settlements.''

Barrie said, ''I remember something about New
York.''

''Don't cooperate with him,'' Adamson hissed.
''You'll only make it worse for the rest of us!''

Adamson, Hutchings realized, was starting to get
on his nerves.

''Make it worse?'' he asked. ''Make what worse?''

''It's a wonder you haven't killed us already,'' Adamson said. ''All this is just a setup.''

''What *are* you talking about?''

''What the hell do you think?'' Adamson said.
''You're trying to make us think that we're safe here.
But we know what's going on. You'll get us sooner
or later.''

Hutchings was taken by the woman's energetic
strain of apparently unbridled paranoia.

Lorraine Sperry said, ''Nobody's going to 'get' anybody down here, not while I'm around.''

"Oh, right," Adamson mocked. "Like you and that popgun of yours can do a lot of damage."

Lorraine frowned and said, "You've got your parrys. Your private rooms have coded locks on the doors and your coms will put you in touch instantly with anyone on the sunstation. And you know about the Tonkas. I or one of my deputies can be at your side in less than forty seconds from the moment you call. Nobody's going to 'get' you."

"Ha," Adamson said. She obviously didn't believe a word of it.

"And this isn't a popgun," Sperry told her. "It's modeled after the Mills concussors. It'll blow anybody apart with a direct hit."

Hutchings looked at Rhonda Barrie. "Did you see or hear anything from the crew of the Shunt vessel before you were sent down here?"

The short-haired blonde shook her head. "I . . . have this vague recollection of asking one of the guards at the Shunt chamber where I was going. He said I was going to Hell."

"Did he say any more than that?" Hutchings asked.

Barrie seemed to struggle through the fog of her transfer shock. The Wall, they knew, did not become entirely solid for about forty-eight hours. "Well, there was one thing one of the guards said—"

Barrie thought about this for a moment, but ended up shaking her head with frustration. "I'm sorry," she said. "It had to do with you. I know it did. I'm sorry. I *know* it's there!"

Adamson turned to Sperry. "So are we done here? Is that it? Can we go now?"

Lorraine consulted Hutchings. "Ian?"

"Well, I suppose—" Hutchings slowly started climbing to his feet as he spoke.

He then jumped at them. Or so it seemed.

His body shot across the few yards between them and the glass partition of the observation deck in a powerful expression of his muscled legs.

"*Whoa!*" Hutchings shouted, crashing against the indestructible glass wall.

The three women screamed and jumped backwards. The leap had even startled Lorraine, who flinched and instinctively drew out her concussor pistol.

Hutchings careened back away from the glass wall, his nose bloodied and globules of crimson floating around like red snow.

Someone had changed the gravity settings. It had gone from plus-3 Gs to a flat zero in an instant.

Then into the observation deck thundered half a dozen little Boys. One of them—Bobby Nakamura or Matt White—had commanded the Roughhouse to reduce the gravity without checking to see if the place was currently occupied. Laughing and shouting, they dove into the gravityless arena, swimming through space. Hutchings, by then, was tumbling away cupping his nose.

The three women, though, had fled the room in absolute terror. Ian didn't blame them. It looked as if he were springing at them, perhaps having lulled them into thinking that he was harmless. A spider with three yummy flies just waiting to be caught.

Lorraine went after the three panicked women.

"Now what?" Elliot called after Hutchings through the door of the observation room.

"Beats the hell out of me," Hutchings said, floating upside down. "I guess I won't be talking to any of them anytime soon."

"Maybe it was the zero gravity," Elliot told him. "I mean, did you see the way they spooked?"

"I think my nose might be broken," Hutchings said, moving his nose from one side to another. "Damn."

The little Boys were hovering in a clot several yards away, busy choosing sides for a game of Zero Ball.

"Elliot, find out what sort of damage I inflicted," Hutchings requested of his vice-Administrator. "Try to convince them I'm not an ogre."

"Sure."

Shoemaker left the room. He didn't want to see what Hutchings was about to do to the little Boys who, this time, deserved everything Hutchings had to throw at them.

8

Hugh Bladestone's dream came back to him almost the instant he closed his eyes. . . .

He is again at Chicago Mercy and the situation seems to have worsened. All across Chicago people are freezing to death. The machines of industry everywhere are failing. Snowflakes the size of saucer plates whirl on the wind. They seem almost alive, driven by their need to strike down humanity. And in the dreams, this seems to be the greater menace.

Bladestone stands exposed to the night on the hospital's E deck. The multiplex of Chicago Mercy rises behind him, a city unto itself. Bordered on the east by ice-locked Lake Shore Drive and on the south by what used to be Lincoln Park, Chicago Mercy stands as a bastion against the forces of Mother Nature. But how long can this last? It seems as if the very cold of outer space has fallen upon the Earth itself.

EXPERTS CONFIRM IT'S AN ICE AGE, that morning's *Chicago Tribune* on-line service read. FAIRBANKS UNDER MILE OF SNOW another headline proclaimed. Still another: ASTRONOMERS BLAME TRACES ACROSS THE SUN.

Chicago Mercy's fusion generator is working around the clock now. City planners, meanwhile, are doing what they can to link up nearby buildings. The famous Steinhoff Foods processing facility, three-quarters of a mile to the west, is now joined to Chicago Mercy via underground tunnels. Glass-enclosed walkways and tram systems link it to the half-mile-high Dylie residential complex to the southwest. Soon, Chicago Mercy will be a lost oasis in the snow, home to about ten thousand people.

An emergency vehicle appears overhead. Its anti-gravity plates glow a furious blue as it lands. There is so much that Hugh has forgotten. As it is, he barely remembers medical school. He can barely call up the sems he had taken which were supposed to bolster his abilities as a physician. But the biotech installed memory packets—miniature "semesters" the same as one might take in college—were known to dissolve if the knowledge wasn't used soon after the implant.

The cold has lined his ears with rime and the breath in his lungs seemed to fill a large frozen cavern in his body. *The traces*, he thinks. *This is the fault of the traces.*

The rear door of the ambulance pops open and several EMS personnel jump out like commandos hitting the beach. They guide a floating gurney between them bearing some very important person. It has to be. The resources of an ambulance service and half a dozen EMS personnel would otherwise not be squandered in this way. It is not efficient. It wastes calories, burns vital heat.

But the snow seems to be winning. Eventually the cold will slow down the progression of the entire universe.

Perhaps, he thinks, *this is where entropy starts . . . and humans begin to lose. . . .*

By the morning of the second day after the arrival of the new people, the excitement seemed to have died down. Though the gawkers and busybodies among the crew—most of them at least—had gotten their fill of the new people, the incident in the Roughhouse indicated to Hutchings that the three new women were still skittish. He asked if Lorraine Sperry's Tonka corps could keep a special eye out. She then placed the diligent toys at various locations throughout the free zones to watch for unusual behavior, particularly among the little Boys. They were the most likely to get themselves into trouble and Hutchings didn't want any more surprises—*especially* if one of those surprises might bring the Vapor out of hiding.

When Hutchings wasn't thinking about the welfare of the new people, he was thinking about Kate. Matters weren't made any better when they received an unprecedented communication from *Bold Charon* later that morning.

Larry Voorhees, a slender, sandy-haired late Adolescent who looked as pale as the soil of his native Oklahoma, had just logged onto his usual shift in the Brains when the Man suddenly announced that a message had arrived. A delivery vehicle had appeared, fired off the message, then shot back out, barely waiting to get an acknowledgment from Ra that the message had been received. By the time he had summoned Hutchings, *Bold Charon* was already millions of miles away, where there was no possibility of a dialogue exchange between them.

The Brains was actually a secondary command facility. The primary command facility was somewhere down in the Forbidden Zones, but they didn't know precisely where. Matt White, whom they suspected might have been a pilot in his former life, was the only one of them who harbored a desire to take control of the sunstation and fly away. Matt had made several attempts to find the flight center of Ra, but the Forbidden Zone's mysterious repelling forces always kept him away. Perhaps to make up for this, the Boy had made a mock-up of a pilot's chair and controls all from memory in his room and spent many an hour there taking Ra into the cold reaches of interplanetary space, as far from the sun as his imagination could take him.

At the time he received Voorhees's summons, Hutchings had been checking into the condition of a bindlestiff sleeping in the hallway outside the Brains. He was thus able to reach the secondary command center with no loss of time.

"Did you see the doctor out there?" Voorhees asked. "I left him the message I sent you."

"I didn't run into him."

Three yellow Tonkas were at Voorhees's feet in various states of repair. As a balm to the boredom of sitting at the Big Board, Voorhees occasionally repaired the toys for Lorraine.

"You look a little ragged," Voorhees then said. "I hear you don't sleep anymore. Is that true?"

"I get some sleep. Every now and then."

"What has happened to your nose?"

"I've just returned from Rome."

"What?"

"Forget it."

Voorhees shrugged. "So, did you see my new 'stiff out in the hall?"

"Yes, I did. It's Susan Britton," Hutchings said. "I didn't know she'd been experiencing bouts of quick-sleep."

"I think it just crept up on her," Voorhees said. "Like it's probably going to do to the rest of us sooner or later."

"Are you getting it?"

"Not that I can tell so far," Voorhees said.

"Well," Hutchings began, "I'm sending up a report on it when the parolees ride their Shunt tomorrow. I don't think the System Assembly knows anything about quick-sleep. Hugh doesn't remember it from his college sems and there's nothing in his med computer. And I don't have it in any of my sems either."

"I had an ancestor once, a great aunt who was narcoleptic," Voorhees said. "She'd fall asleep anywhere, anytime. Then again, she also weighed three-hundred pounds and smoked like a fiend. In fact, she moved to Louisville when every state but Kentucky banned tobacco in 2018. She fell asleep and her house burned down around her. What a way to go. Ah, here's the doctor now!"

Hugh Bladestone walked in, cradling a steaming cup of coffee and looked as if he needed its physical contact to warm his soul. Hutchings thought he recognized the residue of quick-sleep in his friend's eyes.

And what would they do if their physician became a bindlestiff? Could they get by without his expertise?

Hutchings knew the answer to that. He himself had gotten very ill once a year ago and almost died from it. He couldn't imagine what their lives would be like with Hugh down and out.

"We got some sort of message?" the doctor asked.

"Sort of. They sent us a duty roster for the new people," Voorhees told him. "Take a look."

A message scrawled across the Big Board's main screen. It read: NEW DUTY ROSTER: ARLISS ADAMSON—INFIRMARY—CLASSIFICATION: FIRST ASSISTANT. RHONDA BARRIE—STATION MONITORING—CLASSIFICATION: SECOND ASSISTANT. NEWSOME KLANE—STATION MONITORING—CLASSIFICATION: FIRST ASSISTANT. DYLAN OAKS—SUNCUP—CLASSIFICATION: SECOND ASSISTANT. CLARISSA PICKERALL—ENVIRONMENTALS—CLASSIFICATION: SECOND ASSISTANT. THIS IS NONNEGOTIABLE. NONADHERENCE WILL BE CONSIDERED A VAPOR INJUNCTION. TRAINING AND LOG-IN TO BEGIN TWENTY-FOUR HOURS AFTER PAROLE SHUNT.

Voorhees leaned back and said, "So I'm thinking: they risked a shuttle vessel to send us this? They could've waited until tomorrow, until we made the parole Shunt. What's twenty-four hours to those people?"

Hutchings was thinking the same thing.

"I'm supposed to put Arliss Adamson in Diane's place as first assistant?" the doctor said. "Does Ms. Adamson have any medical training? What do we know about her background?"

"You'll have to ask her yourself," Hutchings said. "I don't think she'll be talking to me any time soon."

"She might have had some college-level sems implanted when she was still in high school. Lower divisional requirements, basic anatomy, that sort of thing," Voorhees said. "Chemistry sems are the easiest to plant and to access once they're in."

Bladestone brooded over his coffee. "Diane went to Johns Hopkins, which she remembers quite well. She's got five hundred seminar hours that she knows of, all of which appear to still be intact."

"What about Plainfield?" Hutchings asked. "They forgot about him. Is there any more to the message?"

"Nope," Voorhees said. "This is it."

Hutchings didn't need a flotilla of mentation-enhancing nanobots in his brain to help him figure out this one. "Looks like they've written him off."

"That means they knew the condition he was in when they sent him to us," the doctor said. "Bastards. He needs qualified people to look after him. He doesn't belong here."

"Nobody belongs here," Hutchings said.

"What do you think about Dylan Oaks as a Suncup?" Voorhees asked. "From what I hear, he's the last person I'd assign to the Suncup."

"Same here," Hutchings said.

The three men were silent for a moment. The glowing letters of the message on the Big Board's main screen seemed carved in stone: DO IT OUR WAY OR DIE.

If Eddie Brickman was there, Hutchings thought, he'd probably drop his pants and moon the Big Board. . . .

At that point, a chime went off in Hutchings's right ear and Lorraine Sperry's voice appeared. *"Ian, are you up?"*

"I've been up a while. What's going on?"

"A Tonka watching a bindlestiff in corridor S6 just registered a trespass into the Forbidden Zone. I'm getting a visual feed from it. I think you should see this. Are you near a screen?"

"I'm down in the Brains," he responded quickly. "Patch it to Larry's board here."

On one of the secondary screens an image appeared. It was the view from the tiny eyes of a yellow Tonka road grader. The "trespasser" walked out ahead of it like a giant on the Earth, so tall did he seem.

"Oh, no," the doctor breathed.

It was Plainfield and he appeared to be sleep-walking. Hair askew, thumb in mouth, he padded down the empty hallway, "bankie" at his cheek.

However, he was sleepwalking in a *very* dangerous place, just a few yards from the invisible boundary to the Forbidden Zone.

Hutchings turned to Hugh. "Wake Diane and Kristen. Get them down there with a gurney. One with straps. I'll get Plainfield."

"Right," Bladestone said.

To Voorhees, Hutchings added, "If you see the Vapor, stall him."

"Stall him?" Voorhees yelled out as the two ran from the room. "How the hell do you stall the Vapor?"

Voorhees sat back in his chair, alone with the message on the wall before him. "Jesus," he whispered. "And I just came on shift. . . ."

9

Despite his size and the weight of his shackles, Hutchings was rather quick on his feet, the product of months of bone-crushing exercise in the Roughhouse. He raced from the Brains, sprinting down the corridor toward the lifts.

However, instead of taking the main lift which was far too slow, Hutchings opted for his own lift: a former ventilation shaft that he and a few of the Fiddlers had built strictly for his use. He called it the "spook hole" for the frightening character of its gravity-powered ride and for what lay at the bottom of the shaft. The lift was *very* fast and at the bottom of the shaft lay the Forbidden Zones. A simple grate he'd welded in place was all that stood between him and fatal madness. It was a devil's lair, a spook hole.

"Open up!" he said to a panel set in the wall. A blank section of wall suddenly snapped open, having registered the signature of his voice.

Once inside Hutchings said, "Suncup!" The door clamped shut and down he went.

He plummeted in the shaft like a message in a

pneumatic tube and was summarily spat out into the corridor near the Suncup facility. All this happened in the space of a single heartbeat. He raced for corridor S6. That's where Plainfield seemed to be heading.

He rounded the corner and saw the vigilant Tonka that had made the discovery and reaching the intersection, Hutchings quickly found the old man.

But he had already wandered past the boundary of the Forbidden Zone.

"Plainfield!" Hutchings said. "Stop where you are!"

Astonishingly, the old man had penetrated the Forbidden Zone by at least ten yards. Another ten feet or so and he would reach the only door they knew that led directly into the Zone.

"Plainfield, step back," Hutchings said, trying not to sound overly alarmed.

Even here, Hutchings could already feel the mysterious aura of the Zone affecting his mind. Their Warders had made the zone impenetrable by virtue of a force-field that broadcast the essence of absolute fear. How this was possible, none of them knew. But the Zone did not repel them so much as it frightened them off.

Yet Plainfield had wandered further into the Zone than any of them had ever attempted, farther even than Eddie Brickman had gone. Unlike Eddie, however, Plainfield was miraculously still on his feet.

"Hey, little guy," he coddled. "Why don't we come back this way, okay? How does that sound? Come on back this way and we'll go have some breakfast. How does that sound? We can have waffles and pancakes. Doesn't that sound yummy?"

But Plainfield's infant mind was elsewhere.

"Com, open, Ramirez," Hutchings said in a sharp whisper. "Pablo, get your ass down here."

"Huh?" Ramirez mumbled as he came on-line.

"Wake up and bring a rubber-tipped grapple down to S6 with about thirty yards of nylon cord. And a compressor gun!"

"What?"

"Now. As fast as you can."

"All right, all right. Jesus, what a grouch."

Hutchings inched forward, fighting his rising fear with each step he took. Amazingly, Plainfield didn't look at all terrified. He seemed befuddled more than anything. It was either that or he was so brain-blasted from the Zone that there was nothing left in his skull *to* be filled with fear.

Plainfield then plopped down, as if suddenly sleepy, and rolled over onto the floor. Facing away from Hutchings, Plainfield began humming a lullaby. He continued to suck his thumb.

Hutchings couldn't get any closer for all that he tried. His heart pounded and every nightmare, phobia, or anxiety he had ever experienced raced through his fevered mind. His bowels began to loosen. *There's nothing to be afraid of . . .* he kept telling himself. *It's all in your head . . . nothing's going to happen.*

That, however, wasn't true. Hutchings after all *had* seen the Vapor. Anything could happen.

Hutchings heard the pounding approach of several feet behind him in the corridor. Pablo Ramirez came scurrying around the corner in his yellow jumpsuit. He was accompanied by his most reliable Fiddlers, the two Bobs—Bob Peters and Bob Cady. Each of the Bobs happened to have had parents who had brain-boosted their education far beyond the normal sems given to the average child. Though now approximately seventeen years old and about as mature, the two Bobs were nonetheless useful engineers.

Ramirez held his men back when he assessed the situation.

Hutchings inched back himself. "This is where the Zone starts, at least for me. Right here." He pointed along an imaginary line across the floor.

Ramirez saw where Plainfield had established himself comfortably in the middle of the hallway. "How did he get that far in? He couldn't have jumped. How'd he do it?"

"We'll have to figure that out later, if there *is* a later. Right now we've got to get him out."

"Have you tried talking to him?"

Hutchings nodded. "But he just sat down and rolled over. The way you see him now."

"He'll be brain-fried, for sure," Ramirez said. "I don't think the System Assembly will like that if they find out."

"The System Assembly? What about the Spanker?" Bob Peters asked. Peters was an intensely blond-haired man with pale, narrow eyebrows of a near-albino hue.

"There's no Spanker, stupid," said Bob Cady. "It's the *Vapor*." Cady was a solid, fireplug-shaped man who they thought had played Australian Rules football in college. His nose had been smashed flat at least half a dozen times.

Hutchings turned to the Bobs. One held a long

nylon rope, the other a peculiar-looking gun with a compressor attachment.

"The rope," he said to Bob Cady, who handed him the coiled silver-white rope. "The gun. Let's have it," he said to Bob Peters, who passed the gun along.

"Hold this." Hutchings gave Ramirez the free end of the rope. Ramirez wrapped it around his forearm and, with Cady and Peters behind him, prepared to act as anchors.

"We're set," Ramirez said.

Hutchings took aim with the grapple-gun, then pulled the trigger. The gun coughed and a three-pronged metal claw tipped with special rubber pads shot out.

The grapple went wide and clattered to the floor. Plainfield had no reaction whatever to the metal apparatus which landed beside his head.

"Rats!" said Cady.

Hutchings quickly reeled the grapple back and reset the pressurized gun for another shot.

This time, the claw popped out with more accuracy and impacted on Plainfield's right calf, instantly closing over it.

"Hooray!" said Peters.

Hutchings began carefully pulling at the cord.

"I don't think it'll hold," Cady said.

"It'll hold."

"No, it won't."

Cady was right. It didn't hold. So thin were Plainfield's shanks that the grapple simply slid off and came away.

"Told you," Cady said.

"Then we'll try again," Hutchings glowered. He reset the pressure gun for another shot.

"Let's use a *metal* grapple," Peters suggested. "I can get a metal hook and we can drag him out!"

"What do you think we're dealing with here?" Ramirez asked. "A fish? He'll bleed all over the place."

Peters pointed to the old man. "But the doc can patch him up after we get him."

"You got shit for brains, or what?" Cady said slapping Peters on his forehead.

"I'll betcha it'll work!" insisted Peters.

"Forget it," Hutchings said. "He's not a piece of meat."

All this time, Hutchings had been keeping an eye on the door just a few yards opposite Plainfield. It was the door the Vapor had disappeared behind three years ago after he had taken Hutchings on his private tour. It could just possibly open up and the Vapor could step out and nail them all, then and there.

Hutchings took aim and pulled the trigger. But the shot once again went wide of the mark. It landed with a noisy *clank*!

Ramirez decided to shout at the old man. "Hey, Plainfield! Snap out of it! Grab the goddamn clamp!"

His voice echoed in the hallway. But no response came from Plainfield.

"We have to do something," Hutchings admitted. "I don't know how much longer we can risk having him in there. Maybe a hook isn't a bad idea."

"Are you nuts?" Ramirez said. "You want us to *spear* him and drag him out?"

"Maybe," Hutchings conceded. Or was it the Zone talking? "We might be able to hook him without injuring him."

"You really are ruthless, aren't you?" Ramirez commented.

"We *have* to get him out," Hutchings snapped.

Ramirez turned to his two assistants. "Go upstairs, get a hook, a *big* hook, and a pole that's long enough to reach Plainfield. We'll need duct tape and that forever-glue."

"Really?" Peters asked. "You're gonna try and hook him?"

"Yes!" Ramirez said. "Go!"

The two Bobs took off.

Hugh Bladestone and Diane Beckwith passed them as they ran toward the main lift, having just emerged into the hallway. A hover gurney floated behind them, steered by Kristen Barron.

The doctor said, "I'm sorry, Ian. Plainfield walked off when we weren't looking. We should have thought of something like this."

"It's my fault. I should have tied him down," Kristen said contritely.

Hutchings waved away their apologies. "We didn't know what he was capable of doing. It's not your fault he wandered off."

Hutchings stood at the fringe of the Forbidden Zone and shouted in his loudest possible voice: "Plainfield! Get up off your ass and get back here! *Now!*"

Diane Beckwith whapped Hutchings on the arm. "That's no way to talk to him! He's just a baby."

Plainfield continued to suck his thumb, ignoring them.

Hutchings faced Ramirez. "What if we attached a pair of waldo arms on a remote Tonka, send it in and grab him."

Ramirez said, "That might work. But it would take us a couple of hours to build it. Maybe less if we—"

"Perhaps I can be of service," a voice behind them suddenly announced.

From an intersecting hallway, Newsome Klane appeared. Hands deep in the pockets of his silver-white jump suit, he looked like a man out for his morning constitutional.

"What appears to be the problem?" Klane asked.

"The old guy's wandered into the Forbidden Zone," Pablo Ramirez said. "If we don't get him out soon, we'll probably get slapped with our first Vapor Injunction."

"There is also the possibility that Mr. Plainfield will go insane with impacted fear," the doctor added. "Too much exposure to the Zone can easily kill a person."

"Then why don't you go in and get him?"

"Because we *can't*, Klane," Hutchings said. "That's the whole idea. The Zone keeps us out."

"He can't survive in there too long," Diane Beckwith said. "The Zone does something to the brain that we don't understand. We've got to get him out before he suffers permanent brain damage."

"I will do it."

"Not so fast, Klane," Hutchings started.

But the tall man walked past him without a second

thought. He stopped, however, just a few yards inside the Zone, well short of where Plainfield lay.

Klane returned to the gathering. He seemed more pale than usual. "I thought you were kidding." Beads of sweat dappled his forehead and he looked genuinely affected.

"Told you," Ramirez said.

Klane considered their problem for a moment, then said, "Give me your rope."

Ramirez looked to Hutchings.

"Go ahead," Hutchings responded. "Let him have your rope."

Ramirez handed over the rope.

Dr. Bladestone grabbed Klane's arm. "You just felt a small bit of the Zone. It gets worse the deeper you go. A *lot* worse."

Klane bent over like an exotic bird and tied one end of the rope securely around his ankle.

"What are you going to do?" Hutchings asked.

"I'll see if I can grab him. If I can't get him out on my own, you can pull me out." He handed the rest of the rope to Hutchings.

Without further discussion on the matter, Klane took a running leap into the Forbidden Zone.

Klane's forward arc carried him just far enough to reach Plainfield's feet. The tall man's right hand clamped firmly on an exposed ankle. Plainfield, in turn, made no response whatsoever to the fact that someone had just grabbed his leg.

"You may pull me out now," Klane said.

Hutchings pulled powerfully on the rope attached to Klane's leg. Klane held onto Plainfield's ankle and within a few seconds they were removed from the peril of the Forbidden Zone.

Klane stood up uneasily. His bravado and practiced arrogance did not belie the fact that he had been shaken by the experience.

"The System Assembly seems endlessly inventive in its cruelties," Klane said. "That *is* a brilliant weapon." He began massaging his temples with the tips of his long fingers.

Dr. Bladestone looked at Klane. "You've just done the impossible. Do you know that?"

"I will most certainly think twice about it the next time I have to do it."

"Let's hope it doesn't come to that," Hutchings told him.

Plainfield was then loaded onto the gurney, his eyelids twitching. It wouldn't have surprised Hutchings if Plainfield's brain had been entirely scrambled by the incident.

Even so, the occasion did call for a reassessment of Klane's character. *And* his physiology. The tall man had gone where no one else had gone . . . and come out reasonably intact.

That was better than Eddie Brickman.

10

While the rest of the sunstation was absorbed with the arrival of the new prisoners, Kate had withdrawn into her own private world to watch the hours tick by until her departure. She tried to avoid Ian as much as possible. With a day to go, neither one wanted to face the fact that they were about to lose each other and that the loss would be emotionally devastating.

She otherwise did not deviate from her usual routine, which was to keep watch over the little Girls, particularly during their sleep periods. Bebe Wasson and Junie Russell had been so spooked by Newsome Klane that they couldn't take naps by themselves and sought consolation with Kate, sometimes in Kate's own bed in her regular quarters.

Unlike the bed in Kate's temporary quarters in the infirmary, the bed in her regular room was quite large, configured to conform to Ian's massive presence. The bed could therefore easily accommodate three physically adult women.

However, Kate wasn't thinking of Ian at the moment. Bebe Wasson had had another nightmare. She woke up crying and her "bankie" was soiled with the sweat of her fever-dream. The blanket Bebe so loved was a patchwork quilt Kate had made for her composed of cloth taken from a wide range of materials left behind by Ra's former crew. It was a mélange of discarded shirts, tunics, coveralls, and other kinds of odd abandonments.

The quilt to Kate seemed filled with all sorts of irretrievable histories. It made her wonder if she would be able to "patch" her own history back together once she was in-system. Because they suspected that the Renner shielding created a time-dilation effect, which slowed them down relative to the outside universe, she wondered if there would be anything recognizable for her to go home to. If the most recent communication could be trusted, ten time-dilated years had passed on the Outside. Were her parents still alive? Was Kingston? Was her husband—assuming she had one—still alive? What about the child she'd had? Was he, or she, all grown-up now?

Such thoughts kept Kate from sleeping after their lunch: whether she wanted it or not, in less than twenty-four hours, she was going to get a few answers to some of those questions. But right now, she had the little Girls to tend to.

Junie and Bebe, usually quick to fall asleep, were both sleeping uneasily. Perhaps it was the excitement of the new people . . . or that scary Mr. Klane. But it was during their afternoon nap that Bebe had her nightmare.

"Don't you bump me! Don't BUMP me? Mommy! Mommy! Ow!" Bebe cried out in her sleep.

"Bebe, sweetheart," Kate said, shaking her softly.

Suddenly the Girl lurched sideways as if trying to flee the thing that pursued her in the dream. Holding onto the quilt, the little Girl began making frantic gestures at her right hip as if something had nipped her.

"Bebe!" Kate said.

Junie Russell, on the opposite side of the bed, was now awake, watching with big brown eyes.

Kate sat up. "Sweetie, you were dreaming. It was just a bad dream."

"They came after me," Bebe cried, opening her eyes. "They wanted to *touch* me and bite me! Ow!"

Listening to Bebe's small, desperate sobs, Kate had a startling recollection: *She was living near the University of Texas-Houston Bergenholm Fusion Reactor complex. A summer storm impended. Brash forks of lightning made a devil's playground in the sky; winds rattled the bedroom window. Her son was crying out for her . . . beyond the window were the tresses of a killer tornado which the Weathermasters hadn't been able to destroy. . . .*

Kate gasped. She'd had a son. She knew it with absolute conviction. Then the memory vanished, yanked back behind the Wall.

Bebe sniffled, her nose running now.

"What was your dream, sweetheart?" Kate asked Bebe softly.

"Cactuses," Bebe said. "Big cactuses with arms." Bebe held out her arms. "They wanted to touch me!"

They had long suspected that Bebe—born Elizabeth Wasson—had come from the Desert Southwest,

Phoenix or Tucson, where saguaro cactuses happened to look remarkably like human beings with their arms thrust to the sky. The dreaming mind of a Child might give them legs as well as arms and an evil intent.

"They *got* me and I couldent *run* anymore!" Bebe said, sniffling. "I was *stuck*! My does went down!"

"Does?"

"Toes," Junie said. "She means 'toes'." Junie wiggled her own toes beneath the blanket covering her.

Kate got a tissue from the nightstand and helped Bebe blow her nose. "That's better, isn't it?" Bebe nodded.

"I was a bam*boo* tree," Junie announced, not to be ignored. "The wind blew and I sang all day long. I had holes in me and I made music. I was silver and *real* shiny."

Kate hadn't heard this before.

"They wanted me to be a *cactuses*," Bebe countered. "My *toes* got longer. Don't like cactuses."

Junie sat up and looked to Kate. "Are you going home? Bobby 'n' Matt says you're going home!"

"Maybe," Kate said. "Maybe not."

"Not," said Bebe, sucking her thumb.

"I don't know yet," Kate told them both.

This surprised her. She didn't know about the other parolees, but she now realized that her true family was here. When she and Ian met three years ago in the ramshackle arboretum after her Shunt, he acted like a solicitous big brother in helping them all get settled. Everyone there owed their lives to Ian, who, along with the dashing Lyle MacKenzie and that crazy Eddie Brickman, had managed to keep everything from descending into chaos.

"Will you let me run the Suncup?" Junie then asked.

Kate said, "You're too young, sweetie. I think it'll be Sheila's turn. She's next in line."

Junie pouted. "No fair. *I* want to be a Suncup."

"Sweetie, it takes Grown-ups to run the fusion chamber. We've got a little piece of the sun in there and we have to be extra-special careful all the time."

Junie's pout deepened. "Only Suncups get to go home."

"That's not true," Kate returned. "The parolees come from all duty-stations on the ship. You might be able to go home someday."

"Will you 'member us?" Bebe then asked. The diminutive blonde seemed calmer now that she was fully awake.

"Of course I will," Kate said.

But Kate wasn't too sure about that. Nobody knew if the Elders would allow them to remember their time on Ra. After all, if they could selectively purge them of their memories during the time they were criminals, the System Assembly could just as easily purge them of their time on the sunstation. That notion had a frightening plausibility: lingering memories of Ra might inspire a parolee to commit an act of revenge on behalf of their brethren. It was just possible that Kate could lose memories of *both* of her families, the one she left behind on the Earth and the one she had been adopted into on Sunstation Ra.

Kate eased out of bed and stood on the floor in

her bare feet. The cold crept up through the soles of her feet.

Maybe life as a silver tree singing in the wind wouldn't be so bad. Especially if it lasted forever and she didn't have to fret any more about what she was possibly missing in-system.

Then she thought: what if one day she went riding across the Wyoming plains and happened to glance up into the sun? What would the golden visage of the sun remind her of? Would it evoke the people she had come to love, the *family* she left behind her in Hell ninety-three million miles away?

No matter where she would be on the Earth, without her family, *this* family, it would be Hell above and Hell below. No freedom at all. It would merely be a continuation of her punishment.

She looked at the bright and innocent eyes of the two little Girls. They had their own spark of sunshine which she did not want any shadow to cross.

"Would you miss me?" Kate asked.

Both Girls nodded vigorously.

"Okay," she said to them. "Then I won't go."

"*Yay!*" the Girls shouted.

Kate suddenly felt terribly courageous and she managed a bright smile of her own.

Meanwhile, the little Girls began jumping up and down on the bed. It was the happiest they had been since . . . since the night before when they had sparkly chocolate cake for dessert, part of the updated software that scary Mr. Klane brought down with him, a present of the System Assembly engineers who thought new food software might be useful.

Kate suddenly felt very happy . . . but she also knew that she couldn't tell Ian of her decision until the very last minute. Telling him beforehand might cause trouble. Ian had enough to worry about at the moment.

Meanwhile, Kate felt suffused with a profound feeling of warmth. Family made the difference. Life was meaningless without it.

11

"Hello?" a voice called out from behind Hutchings. "Are you busy in there?"

Hutchings had been sitting at his workbench, working on an aerosol spray delivery system for his most recent tinkering, a flotilla of biobots designed to combat their amnesia. He was having better success with the spray system than in the capsule form he had originally devised. The capsules had caused him to become violently ill once, and that had raised the suspicions of their doctor. *He knew he had to be careful this time regardless of what he came up with . . .*

Hutchings turned around. Rhonda Barrie stood at the entrance to the lab, having come in through his bedroom. The lab occupied the room adjacent to Hutchings's main quarters and he usually kept the door to his apartment unlocked.

"I thought we'd talk," she said. "If you think it's safe."

Hutchings couldn't have been more surprised had a house fallen on him. Barrie stood in the door with her arms crossed. Besides noticing the contour of her breasts, he also noticed that she was not wearing her parry bracelet.

"Do *you* think it's safe?" he asked. "That's the question."

Barrie stepped forward. "Actually, there's one of those little yellow trucks in the hallway. It knows I'm here."

"Then you're safe," he said, pointing to the cluttered room. "Grab a seat, if you can find one."

The blonde woman glanced around the strange laboratory. "What is this place? Your mad-scientist work room?"

Hutchings's main apartment—large bedroom, small kitchen, small bath—was always neat and tidy. Mostly because Kate made him keep it that way. His workroom, however, was a spectacular mess.

"Hobby room, I'd call it. We've got so much living space that some of us have built workrooms next to our quarters. You people can do the same, if you want, since you're all the System Assembly sent this time."

"How many inmates can the station hold?"

"Comfortably? About two hundred and fifty. Twice that, if the Screws get mean about it."

Barrie nodded. She seemed momentarily lost in thought. She had something on her mind, but Hutchings knew he had to be circumspect with all of the new people, especially since the incident in the Roughhouse.

"You're not wearing your parry, I see," he said.

She shrugged. "I feel safe. So far. But I've noticed that hardly anyone wears theirs. Why is that?"

"There's really no need. And I've got these—" He

held up his right arm with its tight-fitting ten-pound shackle. "If I wore my bracelet, it would just get in the way."

"You always wear those things?"

"Mostly."

"Even in the shower?" she asked with a smile.

"Gold doesn't rust."

"Don't they get in the way?"

"That's the idea."

Barrie turned her attention to a hovering holograph of Ra which Hutchings had been studying at his main desk. The floor where the Suncup was located—particularly corridor S6 on the opposite side of the sunstation—had been highlighted. Barrie pointed to it. "Your holograms of the station are remarkably detailed. I would have thought the Screws would have purged the computer of any schemata they might have left lying around."

"Actually," Hutchings said, "we wrote this program based on our own explorations of the sunstation, inside and out. It's only the Forbidden Zones and the Anchor facility that are still mysteries to us. We tried to reach the Anchor once, but that didn't turn out well. What you see here is mostly guesswork."

"Did I hear you right?" she asked. "You said you got *outside* the sunstation?"

"It's in the Getaway Book," he said. "Did Elliot give you one yet?"

"Last night. But I haven't looked at it yet. Why?"

"It's important that you do, even if you don't think you're going to try to escape."

"You think I might?"

"Somewhere down the road. We know that Oaks is going to try and the odds are good that Klane will as well. My guess is that Adamson will also try—eventually."

"How do you know this?"

"Oaks has already canvassed the free zones of the sunstation and has been asking a lot of questions from some of the members of the crew. He's also gotten into the station computer and pulled up several station tutorials."

Barrie's eyes narrowed slightly with suspicion. "You've been spying on us?"

"We call it 'monitoring'," he said. "We can't have a repeat of yesterday's adventure down on S6. We were fortunate that we didn't wake the Vapor. That would have been bad."

"So you *are* spying on us."

Hutchings sighed slightly. "Look, we're all in this together. We don't want to go *poof!* because somebody wandered where they weren't supposed to. We have to follow some rules down here."

Barrie pondered the holograph of Ra. "You said you've been outside the sunstation. That doesn't seem possible."

Hutchings pointed to the floating 3-D image. "There are several million layers of shielding generated by the Renner engines. The striations are constantly shifting in strength, depending on the surface conditions outside. The layers rotate inward until they reach the hull where we've got it down to about room temperature. This puts less stress on the actual metal of the hull."

"And you've been outside, on the hull?"

He nodded.

"How?"

He shrugged modestly. "Since the layers of the Renner shield closest to the hull are at room temperature, we got the idea that if we could pump breathable air outside the hull we might be able to get outside the ship. Eddie Brickman found an exterior lock which he could open, so we tried it. About six of us went outside."

Barrie seemed stunned. "What's it like? Outside, I mean."

"It's the blackest night you'd ever want to see. The Renner layers absorb the entire electromagnetic wave spectrum," Hutchings said. "It certainly leaves no light to die by."

"Someone died? Who?"

"Eddie Brickman."

"How?"

"He disappeared over the rim of the ship," Hutchings said. "We'd made our own mountain-climbing equipment, but the environment suits we wore were a bit too cumbersome. Eddie slipped and fell off the edge. He probably fell past the Anchor and dropped into the lower cone of the Renner shield where it squeezes down to the width of the monopole corridor. He was probably dead long before being sucked into the Van Flandern Discontinuity at the heart of the sun. None of us took his loss very well."

"What in the world were you trying to do out there?"

"Mostly, we wanted to see what we could see. We're like a room full of monkeys. We're always working on something." He indicated the beakers, the processors, the extensive homemade equipment of his laboratory. "And you had to know Eddie. He could talk you into sawing your leg off."

"How many others have died?"

"Inside? A few. Kerry Harland, Marlissa Madrigal, who was a Suncup engineer, and Lyle MacKenzie. Only Marlissa's death was an escape attempt. At least that's what we think she was trying to do."

Barrie paused for a moment. "I guess it must have been hard to recycle your friends, once they died. Except for Mr. Brickman, I mean. I don't know if I could do something like that."

"We didn't recycle them."

"You didn't?" she asked, surprised.

"We never considered it. Why?"

"What did you do with them?"

Hutchings said, "There wasn't much left of Kerry or Marlissa, but when Lyle died, we decided to give him a proper burial."

"You *buried* him?"

Hutchings nodded. "In the meadow. That's what it's for."

"How did Lyle MacKenzie die? Did he blow himself up, too?"

"We don't know how Lyle died. He fell into a coma one day and several hours later he expired."

"He died? Just like that?"

"It might have been delayed transition shock. We don't know. He died six months after we came here. We kept his body in a stasis chamber until we developed the meadow, then we buried him. It seemed the most humane thing to do."

After a moment, Barrie said, "I would have reprocessed them. That's SOP to all habitat communities in the Solar System. Their constituent elements would be . . . priceless.''

"They are priceless. But as human beings, not as elements," Hutchings remarked. "Those people were our friends, not elements from the periodic table."

Barrie brooded. "This place is nothing like I thought it would be. Those strange toys, the grown-up Children, even those homeless people sleeping in their tents—"

"The tents we call 'flops'."

Barrie glanced down for an awkward moment rubbing her hands together. "This is a very strange place," she finally said.

"Welcome to Ra. What else would you like to know?"

Barrie looked at him directly. "I think I have an idea what you might have done. Back on the Earth, I mean."

"What? What was it?"

'I'm not exactly sure, but when I was lying on my bed after the mind-wipe session, I overheard two technicians. One of them said he was glad he wasn't stationed on the Earth anymore."

"Did he say why?"

Barrie nodded. "I got the impression that some sort of mind-deadening organism—an artificial organism— had gotten loose. One of the techs talked about his family in New York. He made it sound as if it had started there."

"It started in Manhattan?"

"No. Palmyra. Isn't that in New York?"

"It's in upstate New York. What else did you hear?"

"I was groggy through a lot of it. I got the idea from the other tech that the disease spread rapidly around the world. Only the far space colonies were immune."

"But you don't remember anything on your own?"

Grimly, Barrie said, "No. I've tried to, but I can't."

Hutchings sat back, baffled. He rubbed his chin and pondered some of the nanobot kilns lining the far wall. "Have you spoken with any of the others? Can they corroborate what you overheard?"

She shook her head. "I don't think so. If they can, they're not talking to me about it. But something very big happened."

Hutchings thought about this. He said, "I remember when they built that storage dome on the far side of the moon to cache the last specimens of Earth's major diseases. It was built in the Tellenes Redoubt— the *'Fortaleza de Soledad'*."

"The Pox Palace," she said. "I remember. We read about it in grade school."

"I've often wondered if I had broken into it," he said. "Maybe I figured out a way past the Redoubt's antimatter shields and stole one of their precious bugs."

"Maybe," Barrie said. "But I don't know how that would be possible."

Hutchings shrugged. "Hell. Maybe Eddie Brickman helped me. Eddie could have pulled off a raid on the Tellenes Redoubt all on his own. And Pablo and his boys can get into anything. With Lyle and Kate—Elliot and Lorraine, especially Lorraine—we'd have been an unbeatable team. For all I know maybe the bunch of us together *did* do something terrible."

"And they didn't say anything to you during your own Shunt . . . when was it—three years ago?" Barrie asked softly.

"All I recall is appearing on the Shunt platform and staring down at the Vapor with him staring up at me."

"The Vapor," Barrie said. "I'd hate to wake up to something like that. Not after the mind-wipe. I'd probably—"

At that point a chime sounded in Hutchings's ear and the com system came on-line. He raised his hand, stopping Barrie in midsentence. "I'm here," he said in response to the hail.

Hugh Bladestone's voice in Hutchings's right ear was audible enough for Barrie to catch. *"We've got a problem, Ian,"* the doctor said gravely. *"It might be a serious one this time."*

"What happened?"

"You remember how Lyle went?"

Hutchings looked at Barrie. "We were just talking about Lyle. What's going on?"

"Plainfield is starting to show the same symptoms Lyle had at the end."

"Are you sure?"

"Reasonably. Plainfield's fallen into a low theta-wave coma and his temperature is up one degree. I can't account for it. His blood's full of toxin killers and I'm showing traces of omnipox residues. So he's inoculated against the usual diseases. It's as if his body's shut down so that it can deal with something on the inside."

"Can you wake him?"

"Kristen and I have tried. It was time for his feeding and he didn't come out of it. He's even stopped sucking his thumb. It looks like a total systemic shutdown."

"That does sound like Lyle," Hutchings said. "I'm on my way."

Hutchings turned to Barrie, rising from his seat. "You might be interested in this."

"Won't they mind if I tag along?"

"You're one of us now."

"All right, then," she said. "Lead the way."

12

Hutchings and Barrie took the main lift down two levels to the infirmary. When they arrived, they encountered a small army of Fiddlers standing in the narrow hallway outside the infirmary. They stood, Gleaners ready, dressed in their ominous protective yellow suits with dark-visored hoods, clearly with the expectation of something to Glean. A bad sign, Hutchings thought.

"What are you guys, vultures?" Hutchings snarled. The Fiddlers parted to let the two of them pass.

"We heard the old guy's got a disease," one of the Fiddlers said. It was Bob Cady, his voice muffled by his protective hood.

"Pablo said we could have it," said Bob Peters, brandishing his Gleaner's nozzle in Hutchings's face.

Hutchings pushed the nozzle aside. "Plainfield doesn't have any sort of disease. Beat it."

"That's not what we heard," Peters argued.

"Clear the deck, you guys," Hutchings growled. "This place is off-limits until I say otherwise. Scram."

"What about her?" Cady said, pointing to Rhonda Barrie.

"She's an adult. She can come and go as she pleases."

"We're adults, too!" said a Fiddler.

"Not adult enough," Hutchings said.

"How come we never get to have any fun?" Peters asked. "You never let us do anything!"

"Go away or I'll break your legs," Hutchings said.

The Fiddlers walked off in their bulky suits, sulking every step of the way.

"Sorry about that," Hutchings said to Barrie. "They're barely out of high school and hard to control sometimes."

In the infirmary, Hutchings found the doctor and his two assistants standing before the glass door that led to the room where they had sequestered Plainfield. After the fiasco on S6, they thought it advisable to put him where he wouldn't be able to wander off so easily.

The doctor stood aside so that Hutchings could see. Plainfield appeared to sleep, but he did so rather uneasily. The old man twitched now and then, as if caught in a desperate fight to regain consciousness. But he was still dead to the world.

The doctor eased open the door and they entered the ward. "I want to show you something," the doctor said.

Bladestone bent over and pried open Plainfield's eyelids with the pressure of his thumbs. The pupils of the old man's eyes appeared to dilate, then shrink. At the same time they jerked around spasmodically. Plainfield's sleeping mind was scanning the violent night of his coma. What he saw there apparently terrified him.

Bladestone stood. Hutchings noticed that the doctor's eyes weren't looking so well, either. They were bloodshot, dark with rings of worry.

"This is what happened to Lyle," Hutchings observed.

Bladestone nodded somberly. "I don't recall anything in my seminar implants describing this. His temperature is up and his lymphocyte level is elevated, but his blood doesn't indicate any kind of toxicity. There's nothing there to fight."

Rhonda Barrie looked at the doctor. "This happened to Lyle MacKenzie?"

"Yes," the doctor said. "It did."

"What could it be?" Barrie then asked.

Bladestone rubbed his jaw. "Until now I've always thought it was a prior condition. But Lyle had a strong heart, strong physique. He was as healthy as a horse. He just stopped . . . functioning."

"I just told her about Lyle," said Hutchings. "And Eddie."

"Yes, well," Bladestone said, continuing. "Lyle's body simply shut down. His autonomic regulatory systems switched off and he died—just like that." He snapped his fingers for emphasis.

"But he lapsed into a coma before he went," Hutchings said. "That appears to be very important."

"How long was he in the coma?" Barrie asked.

"About half a day," Hutchings told her. "We thought it was just quick-sleep at first. We found out it wasn't."

"Quick-sleep? Like what those people in the tents have?"

"The bindlestiffs, yes."

"What's the difference between the two?" Barrie asked. "I mean, between what Mr. MacKenzie got and the quick-sleep?"

"The difference is," the doctor said, "that its onset is gradual and eventually you wake up from hours of quick-sleep. No one stays down forever."

Diane Beckwith, who had been standing close by, added, "But even quick-sleep . . . we don't even know what *that* is. But those who get it, like the doctor says, wake up now and again."

"What this looks like to me is a form of anaphylactic shock," Bladestone then said.

"But one without a cause vector," Kristen Barron said.

"Without a what?" Barrie asked.

"Without a known causative agent. A bug. A virus. A chemical. That sort of toxic intrusion into the system."

The doctor turned to Hutchings. "Ian, we're going to have to do full physical examinations on the new people. And probably on those of us first exposed to them."

"A physical?" Barrie said. "Why? You think we brought something down?"

"Maybe," Hutchings said. "If they wanted to kill us off, this would be a good way of doing it."

"They would never do anything like that," Barrie insisted. "Half the Quorum Elders are physicians."

"Sure they could," Hutchings said. "People change their minds all the time. Besides, a navy of small polymer nanomachines would go undetected by any sort of chemical analysis. They could latch onto non-vascular cell walls so they wouldn't show up in blood work, then after a period of time, they could float wherever they needed to go. It's easily done."

"That's unthinkable," Barrie said. "It's inhumane."

"This whole *place* is inhumane," Hutchings said flatly.

"The System Assembly wouldn't do that," Barrie insisted. "It's beyond their moral code."

"The victors have the luxury of writing whatever moral codes they want," Hutchings said.

The doctor rubbed his eyes. "Be that as it may, we probably should've done a thorough autopsy on Lyle when we had the chance. It's my fault that I didn't press for one."

"There was no reason to do an autopsy," Hutchings said. "We all thought we'd die one way or another. You did what you thought was best under the circumstances."

"That's no excuse."

"It wasn't meant to be," Hutchings said. 'Com, open, Ramirez, private."

Beside Hutchings's ear Pablo's voice appeared. *"I'm here. What's up?"*

"Where are you?"

"I'm in common room three, playing with the Sally. Why?"

"We need you in the infirmary. Bring your best Gleaner. And don't tell any of your engineers. I chased the Bobs out already."

"What about the Deyerberg women? I trust them."

"At the moment, I just want you in on this."

"I'm halfway there. Out."

"Do you think this is really serious?" Rhonda Barrie asked.

"It's too much of a coincidence for it not to be," Hutchings said.

Hutchings turned to the doctor. "You know, if there's a pathogenetic cause to Plainfield's condition we could have a control problem on our hands. There's no telling what the others will do if they think they've been abandoned by the Assembly."

"But you don't know that's what's happened," Barrie insisted.

"The parole Shunt is coming up," Diane Beckwith interjected. "Some might try to get off the station when that happens. Remember the Dark Ages? We're lucky no one got killed back during those days."

Moments later, Pablo Ramirez appeared with his Gleaner. He hadn't had time to change his tunic, and his arms were soiled up to his elbows with some sort of brackish goop.

"I thought you were in common room three?" Hutchings asked.

"I was."

"You look like you've been in hydroponics."

"We pulled up some really bizarre food files in the tiles Mr. Klane brought down with him," Ramirez said. "Some of them had these funky titles and we wanted to see what they were."

Diane Beckwith crinkled her nose. "It smells like pig slop."

"It could very well be," Ramirez said. "Whatever it is, it's not food."

"What's it doing in the Sally's software?" Hutchings asked.

"That's what we're trying to figure out," Ramirez said.

Diane asked, "How much of it did you call up?"

"A whole tub full. I was working on it when Ian called."

"You needed a whole tubful?" the doctor asked. "That's a terrible waste of food."

"Doc, this isn't food," Ramirez said. "But we'll make use of it someplace. It's nitrogen-rich, so it'll go either into the hydroponic tanks or we'll use it as fertilizer for the meadow. So what do we have here?"

Hutchings pointed to Plainfield. "I want you to scour Mr. Plainfield for the smallest possible microscopic artificials you can sense, especially anything broken down into pieces, even if they're just a few molecules long. Can the Gleaner be that precise?"

Ramirez nodded. "Do you want me to remove it if I find something?"

"No," Bladestone said. "We'll do this in stages. If it's a Trojan Horse or a timed device of some kind, we'll have to be very careful. We just need to double-check to see if there's something we've overlooked."

Ramirez engaged the device and drew the flat nozzle plate slowly across Plainfield's recumbent form, moving from the man's feet to his head then back again. He then considered the Gleaner's readout card. "I'm picking up residuals from various plassteel bone replacements, probably in his hips, knees, and ankles. Looks like he's got four dura-aluminum ribs, some metal shoring in his upper vertebrae. Considering how old the guy is, I'd say it's normal for all the body hardware he's got. All the free-floaters look like they're from the implants."

The doctor brooded. Hutchings could almost feel the man's frustration, as well as the unsettling terror at being confronted with a nemesis he didn't recognize, especially one which he might not have the tools with which to fight.

Just then a com chime sounded out beside Rhonda Barrie's ear. It surprised them all. Everyone turned to her.

A voice croaked weakly in the space beside Barrie's right ear. *"Rhonda. I'm . . . sick. I'm . . . really sick. I can't—*

"That's Clarissa Pickerall," Hutchings said.

"I'm not going to make it," Pickerall said. *"Seizure . . . please . . . help—"*

The voice cut off when the com link failed.

Hugh Bladestone looked at Hutchings. "Did she say 'seizure'?"

"I think so," Hutchings said.

The doctor considered the form of Edward Plainfield on his med-bed in the isolation ward. "If I didn't know any better, I'd say that Mr. Plainfield is suffering from the aftereffects of some sort of seizure."

"Do you think it could be spreading?" Kristen Barron asked.

"We don't know that yet," the doctor said. "We don't even know what it is."

"Then I think we should do everything we can to find out," Hutchings said.

He turned and left the infirmary as fast as his gold-weighted legs could carry him.

13

After Kate dispersed the Girls to their usual stations of play in the Playroom—where they would be watched by the diligent Tonka corps—she decided to do a little investigating of her own. Her decision earlier not to accept the System Assembly's gift of parole would have its repercussions. The Elders did not take disobedience very well; Ian probably wouldn't either. She had to know if she was doing the right thing.

In a deserted common room, she probed the Man's files, using a dozen different subject searches, trying to track down the rules of parole. However, the Man had only basic law texts, as well as the standard histories of mankind's more notorious penal institutions—Alcatraz, Lubyanka, Portmeirion, and the like. Nothing regarding Ra, or its uniqueness as a prison, could be found in the station computer.

This came as no surprise. The Getaway Team had searched the Man's files for months looking for anything that might be of use in their situation and they were looking still. The Getaways couldn't even find a reference to Amnesty Interplanetary's Ethical Protocols of 2066 C.E. that might help them understand how the System Assembly could legally—let alone ethically—put them in a place of so much danger.

Kate, however, was less concerned with the System Assembly than she was with Ian. Ian would not hesitate to boot her off the sunstation if he thought it was in everyone's best interests to do so. He'd *especially* do so if he thought it was in *her* best interests.

Kate gave up the search after about an hour and decided next to pay a visit to the meadow. It was unlikely that Ian would be there, since he rarely went there during the two day-shifts. She didn't want to face him just yet.

However, Kate's reason for going to the meadow had quite a lot to do with the upcoming parole Shunt: She wanted to see if their artificial meadow would remind her of the Earth—the Earth of real meadows and old-growth forests—which she would undoubtedly never see after tomorrow.

Kate did not take the main lift to the meadow, but climbed up one of the maintenance tunnels instead. If the meadow was otherwise occupied, she would descend into the Underworld and come at another hour.

It was still night in the meadow. She emerged near a faux game trail and saw that the last person to visit the meadow had neglected to reactivate the day/night rotational program. The deep darkness of the woods, however, suited her.

Kate stepped onto the meadow as the slightest of breezes played in the trees. Part of her wanted to languish there forever, send out roots into the marl of the soil and luxuriate in the wind. At least you wouldn't have to suffer the travails of being human. You would just have to hold out your arms and take in the sunlight during the day and the moonlight at night.

Kate sat down at the meadow's edge. In the eastern sky, just beyond the gazebo, the illuminated tail of Boörstam's comet was beginning to make its appearance. Most cultures on the Earth considered comets as harbingers of misfortune, the majii of bad times to come. Sighting the comet just now she wondered if *this* might be an omen. But then, she had seen it hundreds of times before and nothing bad had ever happened. In fact, she had helped Larry Voorhees write the comet's program for the planetarium's computer. To them, it was just light in the sky.

She heard a commotion in the woods off to her right. Someone was coming. However, she didn't move from her position. She was now too comfortable, and if it *was* Ian, she'd—

It wasn't Ian, however. Ian would have immediately returned the planetarium to its proper day/night cycle, evoking the brightness of day. He was a stickler for regularity.

Two yellow-suited Fiddlers slugged their way through the brush, having also entered the meadow through a maintenance tunnel. However, any stealth they might have gained by sneaking up one of the hidden shafts, they had lost by their clumsiness.

Kate recognized them immediately. They were the Smith brothers, Thomas and Don-Don. Though they were in their mid- to late forties, they had the personalities of a fourteen-year-old and an eleven-year-old, respectively. Their tinkering habits in the Fiddler's den, however, indicated that they might have once been adept engineers in their former lives.

They hadn't noticed that Kate was sitting so close at hand.

"Over here!" Tom, the older, whispered.

The two adolescents wore Gleaners strapped to their backs. Tom pointed the nozzle of his Gleaner directly ahead of him. "Let's unload it right here!"

"No. This is my spot," Don-Don gestured with his Gleaner. "I like this spot best—"

Kate couldn't imagine what the two were doing there. But within seconds a large mound of an indistinguishable substance appeared where they aimed their Gleaners. Everything about their movements suggested a jape of some kind—and one that was probably at Ian's expense.

Kate got up and approached them. "Boys. What are you doing?"

The Smiths jumped up at the sound of Kate's voice. They also tried to hide their Gleaners behind their backs.

"We weren't doing anything!" Tom said, hood knocked askew.

"Honest," responded his brother.

Kate turned her attention to the black spot in the meadow. "What *is* this stuff? Fertilizer?"

"The Sally had it," Tom said. "It was new."

"I think it's poop," the younger Smith claimed.

Kate recalled the food fight some of the little Boys had gotten into earlier with their strange oatmeal. But the substance before her now wasn't oatmeal. At least it didn't *smell* like oatmeal.

"Don't tell Ian," Don-Don pleaded. "He'll beat us up."

"I don't think he'll do that," she said calmingly.

Kate understood their worry. They did not like to waste food, but only Grown-ups could use the recycler. So the Smiths, not being entirely stupid—and actually being quite clever—sought to conceal it in the meadow where it could possibly be taken for the regular mulch and compost designed for the soil.

But what was a file for manure doing in the Sally's menu directory? Kate wondered.

Kate scanned the dark meadow. It was almost like Earth. *Almost.* Except for the two mind-wiped grown men squabbling like little boys and the extraordinarily advanced matter-assimilation technology strapped to their backs. *And* the unexplained substance scattered on the grass . . .

How could she leave any of this behind?

"Lookit!" Don-Don suddenly pointed. "Someone's coming!"

The mirror surface of the meadow's singular pond began sliding back into its recess heralding the emergence of someone rising into the meadow via the lift hidden beneath.

"It's Ian!" Don-Don said in a panic. *"Run!"*

They dove into the trees to hide; Kate merely stepped back into the brush to watch. Intuition told her that this wasn't Ian.

"Is it Ian?" Tom asked in a trembling whisper.

"I don't think so," Kate said.

The lift locked into place and in the darkness Kate

could see that it definitely wasn't Ian. It was Clarissa Pickerall.

This piqued Kate's curiosity even more. She kneeled down and watched as the new woman staggered onto the grass. She seemed dazed, lost. Kate couldn't possibly imagine what she was doing there.

Pickerall turned toward the gazebo and began walking toward it uneasily.

"She wants to go home," Don-Don said from the trees behind Kate.

"Fat chance," Tom whispered.

"Boys," Kate admonished in a low voice.

A few yards from the gazebo, Pickerall paused and gazed at the constellations as they wheeled slowly across the ersatz firmament. She looked to the east, then let out a small cry. She stumbled backwards in shock.

To Kate, it appeared as if Pickerall had just seen Boörstam's comet and it frightened her. The woman then fell down and began backpedaling desperately in the grass as if to distance herself from the hoary apparition in the sky.

The woman choked and started speaking into her com, summoning help.

Kate stepped from the trees and walked quickly over to the woman leaving the Smith brothers alone in the brush.

"Clarissa?" Kate said, kneeling. "It's Kate DeWitt. What's the matter? Is something wrong?"

The woman appeared to be undergoing an epileptic seizure. Her breath came in labored gasps and she trembled from head to toe. The look in the woman's blue eyes was one of panic, trapped in a land of fear from which she couldn't escape.

"I can't . . . make it . . ." the woman whispered. "Seizure. . . ."

"Com, open, Ian!" Kate said. "Ian, where are you? *Ian!*"

As if on cue, an enormous figure shot out of the trees, several feet from where the adolescent Fiddlers crouched. Ian appeared as if propelled from a cannon.

Somehow, some way, Ian had known what was happening.

"Meadow lights, on!" Ian said loudly, rushing over to the two women.

Bright morning light appeared as Ian knelt beside them. Pickerall, meanwhile, twitched furiously, her pale lips pressed tightly together, forming a white spittle.

"She said she was having a seizure," Kate reported.

Ian gently peeled back the stricken woman's eyelids. Pickerall's eyes scanned some terribly distant sky, helpless. She was neither conscious nor unconscious, but some place in between.

"The same thing's just happened to Plainfield down in the infirmary," Ian told her.

"Is she having an epileptic seizure?" Kate asked.

He gently lifted the woman and carried her toward the pond. "Hugh doesn't know. But he thinks it might be what happened to Lyle."

"That can't be."

"It's what Hugh thinks."

"All of a sudden? Like this?"

"*That's* the problem," Ian said. "Let's go."

Kate looked back at the two Fiddlers, waving them down. The Boys vanished. She rushed to join Ian on the pond, leaving the Smiths alone in the trees.

14

With Kate following behind him, Hutchings raced into the infirmary cradling Clarissa Pickerall.

The infirmary staff had by then prepared a bed in the isolation ward. It lay next to the one upon which Edward Plainfield fought the goblins of his own delirium. On Dr. Bladestone's recommendation, Diane Beckwith and Kristen Barron had also begun preparing beds for the other new people. This, Hutchings observed, was probably wise, but it did not bode well for what it implied.

"Where was she?" the doctor asked as Hutchings swung into the special isolation ward.

"The meadow. A Tonka was tracking her, since she isn't wearing her parry."

"Was she able to tell you anything?" the doctor asked.

"No. She was like this when I arrived." Hutchings backed off so the doctor could examine the stricken woman.

"I was there just before she collapsed," Kate said.

"She said she couldn't 'make it'. She was trying to reach the gazebo. Maybe that's what she was referring to."

Rhonda Barrie had been standing to one side, out of everyone's way. She wore an expression of profound concern. Hutchings turned to her. "Do you know what she was talking about?"

Barrie was as baffled as the rest of them. "I haven't the slightest idea. I barely know the woman."

"You think this is a seizure?" Hutchings asked.

"It's possible," the doctor responded. "But epilepsy can be controlled with gene therapy and medication."

"Was there anything on the Roster about her medical history?" Kate asked.

"No," Hutchings said. "Nor was there anything on any of the software data tiles that Klane brought down with him."

"She might not have known she was epileptic," Diane Beckwith offered. "The Wall could be hiding it."

"What about Plainfield?" Kristen Barron countered. "What abut Lyle? Could they *all* be epileptic?"

The doctor did a cursory examination of Clarissa Pickerall. When he finished, he said, "The symptoms appear to be the same. Her blood pressure is up and so is her body temperature."

"But is it epilepsy?" Kate asked.

The doctor frowned. "I don't know."

"Lyle wasn't epileptic," Diane Beckwith said. "He was as physically capable as anyone. We never saw him this sick."

"Until the end," Bladestone muttered.

The doctor then said, "We need to get the others down here right away. We've got to find out what this is."

"I *know* I don't have anything like this," Rhonda Barrie told them all.

"We don't know that for sure," the doctor said.

"There is one other possibility," Kate said.

"What possibility is that?" the doctor asked.

"The Children are pulling up tainted files in the Sally's new software. That could be due to faulty reassembly in the Shunt. Is it possible that the Shunt might not have reassimilated the transferees properly?"

Improperly reassembled organic molecules were the bane of matter-transmission technology. Guinea pigs, cats, dogs, and monkeys by the hundreds perished in the first trials before human volunteers were used. Even then, glitches still managed to occur, with highly tragic consequences.

Kate went on, "The monopole transmission corridor is only a few angstroms wide inside the Renner shield."

"*We* got down here in one piece," Hutchings said.

"But Lyle eventually died and two people went crazy later on."

"Might I suggest something?" Barrie offered.

"Please do," the doctor responded.

"Would a deep-scan of their brains show any kind of neurological damage?" she asked. "At the very least you could eliminate epilepsy as a possibility because epileptic lesions will show up on a simple MRI."

"That might not be a bad idea," Hutchings admitted. To the doctor he asked, "We never did that to

Lyle. Do we have the equipment to do a deep brain scan?"

Bladestone's brows knitted in concern. "We've got a simple axial tomographic scanner, but anything beyond that we're going to have to engineer. Remember, they only outfitted us with an infirmary, not a hospital research center."

"Yes, but then what are we going to do after that?" Kristen Barron asked. "How would we cure them?"

"First things first," the doctor said. "I like the idea of knowing what's inside their brains before we attempt anything like brain surgery. We'll worry about what to do next when we get there."

"You think it'll come to brain surgery?" Hutchings asked.

"I sure hope not," Bladestone said.

"All right, then," Hutchings announced. "We need to find out as much as we can before tomorrow's Shunt. We might have to send proof to the System Assembly. Photographs, readouts, data tiles—everything relevant. Otherwise, the Screws aren't going to believe us."

It turned out that three Fiddlers, two Suncup engineers and one of the Getaways had sems specifically related to medical technology and they were able to modify the simple MRI in the infirmary. Hugh Bladestone wanted the machine to serve as an MRI with X-ray readouts and axial tomographic graphs that could be printed out. They needed hard proof and hard copies for the System Assembly.

Hutchings lent his skills to the effort, even though he wanted desperately to be with Kate. Kate, however, had gone to check on the little Girls. A bad little Boy had told them that the Spanker was after them and Kate had to assure the Girls that he wasn't. Hutchings, for his part, was thankful that they were both occupied. He couldn't face the reality that he was going to lose her, and soon.

When they were ready, Hutchings helped the doctor's assistants lay Clarissa Pickerall on the omniscanner's pallet, easing her head into the scanner's cylindrical ring.

Bladestone engaged the scanner, watching the console with its many video display screens. On one monitor a series of EEG readings appeared.

Kristen Barron pointed to the multiple sine waves. "She's showing a high theta-wave pattern with spikes into beta. It's as if she's trying to wake up, but can't."

Bladestone gently moved the pallet through the ring, pausing at a point just below Pickerall's skull. On the main monitoring screen the woman's brain appeared in three dimensions and full color—the hologram being a Fiddler modification.

"What the hell is *that*?" Ramirez asked, stepping close.

Inside Pickerall's skull, entwined deep inside her brain, there appeared to be delicate filigrees throughout her limbic system.

Everyone gathered around the main console screen.

The filaments rose upward around the basal ganglia, cradling the cerebellum with an almost surreal beauty. Hutchings thought the anomalous structure looked like a flower of extremely delicate gold or silver leaflike convolutions. It had silver-blue petals, tendrils of crimson silver and a stem of a copper-gold color. Yet it wasn't a flower. It was hardly anything at all. The computer registered only the barest traceries of linked molecules.

"It looks like a tattoo," Ramirez commented.

"That's a hell of a place to put a tattoo," Kristen Barron countered.

"That's no tattoo," Bladestone said. "It's a definite structure of some kind."

Hutchings flushed with sudden revelation. "Hugh, you think that's the thing responsible for our amnesia?"

The doctor shook his head. "Memory is holistically distributed throughout all areas of the brain. This thing seems to be centered around the posterior spinocerebellar ganglia. We'd have to look deeper to see if it's infiltrated the cerebellum."

Kristen Barron said, "Even so, this whatever-it-is is still intrusive enough to affect neuromuscular function. At the very least, this could be the cause of Pickerall's seizure."

Bladestone eased the omniscanner ring farther down Clarissa Pickerall's delicate neck, stopping just at the woman's shoulders. The micron-thick structure in her brain appeared to fade into molecular invisibility, just below her neck somewhere, neatly ensconced in the nerve channels of her spinal cord.

Bladestone studied his screen. "There's some lateral accumulation on the ulnar and radial nerves with some clear definition along the intercostal nerve tract. It runs parallel to the upper-respiratory nerve network, but doesn't seem to interfere with it."

"Is it benign?" Kristen asked.

"Damned if I know," the doctor admitted. "I've never seen anything like this before."

"Let's take a look at Mr. Plainfield," Hutchings then suggested. "I have a bad feeling about this."

It took them several minutes to put Pickerall back on her own bed and hoist Plainfield onto the scanning pallet. What they saw didn't surprise them. Plainfield had the same sort of structure at the base of his brain. The colors were somewhat different and there appeared to be more copper than silver. The structure also extended farther down the old man's spine, by several inches.

Ramirez keyed the computer to analyze the structure. "Whatever it is, it contains small elements of lithium and titanium. It also shows traces of niobium. And it appears to be sheathed in some sort of polymer, a kind of protective coating."

"That's definitely no tattoo," Diane Beckwith said.

Bladestone stood back from the omniscanner console. He seemed deeply disturbed. "We're going to have to biopsy this," he said grimly. "I don't know what it is and I don't like it."

"A biopsy is not necessary," came a voice from the doorway behind them.

Every head in the infirmary turned to see who had spoken.

Newsome Klane stepped into the special room, having only now chosen to answer the summons of his presence in the infirmary.

"You know anything about this, Klane?" Hutchings asked, indicating the hologram of Edward Plainfield's brain.

"Not nearly as much as you do," Klane said.

"As I do? What do *I* have to do with this?"

Klane seemed surprised at the question. "You mean you don't know?"

"No, I don't know. Why should I?"

Klane remarked, "Because you invented them."

"*What?*"

"What's more, we all have them in our brains." Klane poked the side of his head with a bony finger. "In here. Thanks to you."

Silence fell about them as everyone turned to Hutchings, who, for once, was mute with complete astonishment.

15

"Okay," Hutchings said to Klane. "Explain that."

Newsome Klane gazed with apparent remoteness at the two stricken individuals before them. He then took a moment to examine the crimson image of Edward Plainfield's hologram.

"I'm very surprised that you don't know, doctor," Klane said.

"Why should *I* know what this is?" was the doctor's response. "I've never seen anything like it before in my life. I don't even remember reading about them."

"And you haven't searched your data banks yet?"

"If the Man had any information about these structures," Bladestone said, "I would have found it. But he doesn't."

"This is curious," Klane said. "I can't imagine why the Elders would not provide you with information about them. They are perhaps the most significant advance in human physiology augmentation."

"But what's this got to do with me?" Hutchings asked.

"You invented them." Klane then considered the Raians assembled in the ward. "What about the rest of you? I take it that no one remembers, either?"

It was clear that no one had.

"So what are they?" Pablo Ramirez asked.

"Intelligence augments. Enhancers, if you will. They are more formally known as Strathclyde traces, named after a private research college where they were developed in New York. Nearly everyone in the solar system of adult years has one. And you don't know *anything* about them?" This last was directed at Hutchings.

"You've just told me everything I know about them," Hutchings said.

"You say they enhance intelligence?" the doctor asked.

"As I understand it," Klane said. "My own memory stops about the time I had mine installed. The Wall, as you call it, starts then. But they are definitely the prodigy of Major Hutchings's genius. He designed them and he also devised their installation process."

"No, I didn't," Hutchings said.

"Yes, you did," Klane persisted. "I also have a faint recollection that you were to be up for a Nobel prize in biochemistry because of them."

Everyone looked at Hutchings and the big man was, for a moment, rendered speechless by this bit of information.

"Ian?" the doctor asked. "Can this be true?"

Hutchings hesitated. His bold denial just seconds ago, in fact, might not have been entirely correct. The nanoneural machines he'd been secretly designing and ingesting the last three years in an attempt to get his memory back *might*, in fact, have come from his knowledge of the structure hovering in its 3-D hologram projection. However, he couldn't admit just yet that he'd been experimenting on himself.

"I don't know," Hutchings admitted. "They do look like nested nanobot colonies."

"I want to hear more about the intelligence-enhancement angle," Ramirez said to Klane. "How's that work?"

Klane's brow furrowed in thought. "I do have a faint notion that one of their features is to promote a kind of artificial telepathy, particularly in humans traveling among the outer colonies."

Klane returned his scrutiny to the silver-gold trace on the monitor screen that was languishing in Edward Plainfield's brain. "I do recall when I obtained my trace. I was unusually young for the implant. I was quite the troublemaker, even then. Perhaps that's why the authorities insisted it be done at that time."

"Go on," Hutchings said.

"As part of a parole arrangement, the Ward president decided that if I had a trace, I might feel more empathy for others. I had just turned seventeen. I did not like the idea of something like that growing in me."

"It was grown in you?" Hutchings asked.

"There is no other way to install them. That is part of your ingenuity. Do I need to tell you this?"

"You need to tell me as much as you possibly can," Hutchings said, "because I did *not* invent those things."

"You said they're grown," Ramirez asked. "How?"

Klane said, "I was given a green liquid that tasted like paint. It was alive with the Strathclyde micromachines. Green death, my roommate called it. My roommate threw up all that first night. He was gone the next day. His name was Tommy Garner. I do remember that."

"Hugh? What do you think of this?" Hutchings asked the doctor. "Your memory is about as good as anyone's here."

"This is all news to me. It's got to be terribly recent. Whatever it is, it's a major leap in biotechnology."

"And we've got those things inside our heads?" Kristen Barron asked.

"There is probably not one of you who doesn't," Klane responded.

"He's right," came a voice behind them.

Everyone turned. Kate, standing in the doorway, had been listening to Mr. Klane's exegesis of the Strathclyde traces.

"We all have them," she said. "At least I do."

"You *do*?" Hutchings responded. "Why didn't you tell us before this?"

"Because I really didn't know much about them until now." Kate pointed to the 3-D image of Plainfield's trace. "I don't know anything about them specifically, but I know that I *dream* about them every night."

She went on, almost in a haze of enthrallment. "Those colors . . . the silver and the gold . . . even that blue. The saddle horns are blue, probably a burnished cobalt. Maybe iridium. And the stirrups have some emerald in them, that same copper-green color."

"What, the horses in your dreams?" Hutchings asked.

"Not the horses. Their *saddles.* That's how I know about them. They're in my dreams. And they *are* called 'traces', by the way. I don't know about the Strathclyde part, but they are called traces by everyone else."

Kate stepped behind Hugh Bladestone to get a better look at the monitor. "With a little imagination you can see a saddle. And those parallel channels extending down either side of the brain stem . . . to me those look like stirrups. They lead upward to a saddle which cradles the brain."

She then said, "And I think it communicates with me in my dreams in some way. Letting me know it's still there—"

Hutchings felt as if someone had just whacked him over the head with a mallet. It didn't take much imagination to see how Kate's dreams might be the subconscious resonation of a presence in her head. *But what did the damn things do?*

Hutchings stared at Klane. "You said that these things are intelligence enhancers?"

"From what I remember," Klane confessed.

The doctor in his chair rubbed a black hand across the top of his head. "Mr. Klane, the electrical output of the human brain isn't strong enough to transmit any sort of signal beyond what is required chemically to boost neurons from one synapse to another. The work the Russians did with psychokinetics on Project Brainfire is well known. It took Mother Nature billions of years to evolve the biological circuits we *do* have in our brains. I don't see how any of this can be done."

"Unless," Ramirez said, "there was some sort of exterior attachment, such as an amplifier or relay transmitter. A person might be required to carry one in order to boost the signal. If that's true, then the traces might be useless over great distances without a signal booster."

"Which," Diane Beckwith added, "would render them useless if the System Assembly deprived us of those devices. We *could* have some sort of vestigial telepathic abilities left."

"I would concur," Klane said.

"You would? Why?" Hutchings asked.

"Do you recall when we had to rescue Mr. Plainfield from your Forbidden Zone territory yesterday?"

"It's not something I'd forget," Hutchings said.

Klane pursed his thin lips, then said, "I believe now that Mr. Plainfield might have communicated something to me while I was out on my walk. I simply 'felt' a need to be there."

"That was rather convenient," Hutchings quipped.

Klane nodded. "Perhaps 'convenient' is not the word. I cannot account for the impulse, otherwise. I daresay I probably wouldn't have gone down there at all on my own inclination."

Nobody said anything for a long moment as all eyes scrutinized the monitor image of Plainfield's brain.

"I don't buy it," Hutchings finally said. He pointed to the two stricken individuals before them. "Look, there's not enough room in the brain for any sort of alloyed structure to be installed, even if it is only a few microns wide. It would never be electrically efficient enough and the metal alone would offset the brain's normal chemistry. Something is definitely wrong with these people and I think we're looking at the reason why."

Kristen Barron turned to the doctor. "We should've done this when Lyle took ill. We might have been able to do something for him. Don't you think?"

The doctor, reluctantly, nodded.

Klane, however, dissented. The tall man said, "It is not likely that anyone's death can be attributed to their traces. The body simply dissolves them if they do not position themselves correctly when they're installed. And their polymer sheath prevents any of the metal alloys from affecting the brain's chemistry. The traces are as common now as college degrees."

Hutchings suddenly felt the full weight of his gold shackles hanging at the ends of his arms. He couldn't even begin to express his feelings—the inner turmoil now rising within him—regarding his possible role in the invention of the traces.

"But perhaps instead we should be using our time more wisely," Klane offered.

"What do you mean?" the doctor asked.

"You have survived this long with your traces. You should probably determine if they are the cause of the illnesses which affect these two people. I doubt that they are, but that is not for me to say. I believe that an informed medical opinion is called for."

"What do you suggest?" the doctor asked.

"That you examine every one of us in this room—

measure the size of the traces, measure their density, whatever. You need to get past this."

"I don't think we'll ever get past something like this," Hutchings remarked.

Still, they concluded that Klane's suggestion was a good place to start. They had to get at the truth and the only way was to do it as scientists, to do it the way they were trained.

And they decided to start with Mr. Klane.

16

Hutchings raged, he shouted, he screamed. In the meadow. Alone.

He cursed every god he could name and several he couldn't. He swung his gold-weighted fists around him hoping to connect with the demons from his eviscerated past, demons which he now knew were the Strathclyde traces. Their burnished silver came at him like flaming falcons beating their alloyed wings against the inside of his brain.

The traces. His very own merchants of disaster. They were *precisely* the sort of thing he could have engineered, and quite easily, too. This was all the proof he needed that indeed there might have been a way to kill a billion people upon the Earth. The Strathclyde traces *had* to be the agent of his crime.

Moreover, every Raian had one, just as Klane had said. The modified omniscanner in the infirmary showed Strathclyde traces in everyone's head, including his. The little Boys had them. So, too, the little Girls. Klane and Rhonda Barrie. Kate and Hugh. They all had traces.

Yet no one knew anything more about them beyond what they were able to see on their instruments. This also fueled Hutchings's anger. He was so close to the truth, yet so far away—thanks to the mental wizards who ran the System Assembly Penal Committee. The Wall of their amnesia still held back the facts regarding the traces and there was little Hutchings could do to penetrate it.

So he raged. He swung at tree limbs; he kicked up huge hunks of soil. He even tried to uproot a tree. Hutchings wrapped his arms around a stately birch and tried to pull it out with an application of every muscle in his body. He growled. He roared. But the tree didn't budge. Its densely packed root system clung to the soil with insensate obduracy.

"Son of a bitch!" Hutchings said, falling backwards with disgust onto the meadow floor near their small cemetery, his rage coursing through him like a giggling ghost, mocking every atom of his being.

So what the hell *were* the Strathclyde traces, anyway?

A voice came out of the ground. *"Are you through horsing around up there?"*

Hutchings lay back and spat out a bit of tree bark. The voice had come from a small aeration shaft next Lyle MacKenzie's tomb.

Hutchings looked at the concealed vent. "I guess," he groused. "What's the damage?"

The voice of Dr. James Tucker, the amanuensis for the Getaway Team, came out of the shaft. Doc Tucker said, *"It looks like you cracked one of the nutrient pipes. I didn't think that was possible."*

"Sorry, Doc."

"*It's oozing out of the ceiling,*" Doc Tucker said. "*And it smells like shit.*"

"That's because it is shit. Sorry."

Just below the meadow was an extension of artificial caverns. The Underworld boasted a sophisticated irrigation and root-support system with gloomy and winding tunnels of cool, compacted artificial earth. They even had a small underground stream used primarily for drainage that coursed down one hallway and was recycled back into the Environmentals network.

The Underworld was also the chosen home of the Getaway Team, a curious mix of military engineers, historians, and scholars who had long ago taken on the task of figuring out how to get off the Hot Rock.

"*While you're there,*" Doc Tucker said, "*we've come up with a couple of items that might be of interest. Are you in any sort of mood to hear about them?*"

"Might as well be," Hutchings said. "Go ahead."

"*Did you notice that all of the parolees except Janice Koetzle seemed to have some sort of military background? That could be significant. In fact, it probably is.*"

"I'm supposed to be a major."

There was a pause. "*That's news to us.*"

Hutchings said, "It was news to me. Klane called me 'Major Hutchings' yesterday. I let it pass."

"*Are you a major?*"

"Hell, I don't know. If I was, I'm sure I wasn't too happy about it. I don't like taking orders much."

Which probably explained his exile on a place such as the sun. . .

Doc Tucker then said, "*We've gone over the text of*

the Ward Judge's message. He said that Kate was a lieu-
tenant. Has she ever spoken to you of her military
experience?"

"No," Hutchings said.

"Could you ask her about it?"

"I'd rather not."

"Why?"

"She's seems to be preoccupied at the moment."

"We hear she's not going to leave. Is that part of it?"

"Who told you that?" Hutchings asked. He sat
bolt upright.

"The Tonkas. They got it from the little Girls. They're
quite happy about the prospect. The Girls, I mean. Now
they're all trying to keep it a secret."

"Those women. Can we talk about something
else?" Hutchings asked. "What do *you* guys make of
this military business?"

Tucker responded. *"We're starting to think that this*
might be a military prison, not a civilian prison. We don't
know what that means, exactly, but it must be
significant."

Hutchings looked wistfully at the New England
sky. "Maybe we got access to some sort of secret
military weapon. One of those Camoin planetbusters.
Maybe we blew the shit out of something big. Taiwan, maybe."

"There aren't a billion people on Taiwan."

"The collateral damage alone would be enough.
Most of Southeast Asia would be effected."

"But that's more than a billion people. You only took
out one billion."

"Maybe the Screws stopped counting after a
while."

Doc Tucker thought about this for a second or two and then said, "No, I remember you telling me that the Vapor was very emphatic in making sure you knew the magnitude of your crime. A billion counts of felony murder."

"I know, I know," Hutchings said with exasperation. This argument was part of an old, *old* tape loop running in his head, one he'd played to himself a thousand times over.

"Matt White was a captain at junior grade, Lorraine a sergeant, Kerry Harland a corporal. You think there's some sort of war going on out there that we don't know about?"

"Might be. Perhaps we're POWs."

"Ian, we'd like you to interview the new people in the presence of a Tonka. We need to know if there's a war going on out there. Woodfield and Balter think that our metal shipments to them may have military applications. We've sent them enough titanium and iridium for a fleet of space vessels. Remember, we're sitting on the mother of all mother lodes in the solar system."

A *war*, Hutchings thought. "That's a possibility."

"And remember," Doc Tucker added, "there was talk of using the Renner-shield technology to build the first interstellar vehicles. Perhaps someone in the System Assembly is planning on leaving town."

Hutchings shook his head. "Only if they've figured out a better way to power a Renner shield. We're here because we've got the sun to draw plasma from. It takes a lot to sustain a Renner shield, of any size. Even at that, a Renner shield compresses time on the inside. Lord knows if they've figured a way around that."

"We've thought that, too. We're working on the equations for just how much power they'd need to go from our system to another system."

Hutchings said, "I can talk to Rhonda Barrie. She seems to be the most cooperative. I'd ask Klane, but getting information out of Klane is like dealing with the devil. I'm watching him."

"Keep an eye on Dylan Oaks, too," Tucker added. *"The Tonkas are reporting him just about everywhere in the station. Hydroponics, the Suncup, he's even been to the monument at Eddie's airlock on D5. He's fascinated with the story of your expedition outside. He's even tried working the lock."*

"The computer has the lock codes. I don't think he can get past that. I wouldn't worry about it."

"Has anyone figured out how old Oaks is?"

"Three or four," Hutchings said. "He must have been a terror when he was a kid. A real kid, I mean."

A pause drifted between them. "Anything else on your mind, Doc?" Hutchings asked.

Tucker was hesitant. He then said, *"Actually, I was wondering if you could get a bedmate for me."*

"You don't need my help to get a bedmate. They're there for the taking. Just ask around."

"I was thinking about Cloris. You know her, don't you?"

"Pablo says that Constantine Rachbauer took her just the other day. We haven't seen either of them for at least forty-eight hours."

"Well, then, how about one of the little Girls? I was thinking about Bebe Wasson—"

"Doc, she's only three."

"But she's—"

"Let's see if we can get somebody your age."

"*Okay.*" The disappointment was evident in the man's voice.

Hutchings sat at the edge of the meadow, next to the grave of Lyle MacKenzie. The wind had ceased and the glade around him seemed unnaturally quiet.

But something was amiss.

Enormous patches of the sky seemed shorn of clouds as if the planetarium's daytime program had succumbed to the agents of entropy and had ceased working.

Hutchings found the game trail that led back to the spook hole's secret entrance to the meadow. Almost immediately he was poked in the eye by a tree branch which he didn't see.

"Jesus," he whispered, rubbing his right eye. First his nose, now his eye.

Just then the com-chime sounded beside his right ear and a voice said, "*An announcement.*"

The voice was mechanical, that of a Tonka. The AI circuits in the boys had initiative trips that allowed them to summon the attention of the nearest human if the need ever arose.

"Hutchings here. Go ahead."

"*An unauthorized person approaches the gazebo,*" it said.

Hutchings turned around. He was at the southern edge of the meadow, hidden in the trees. But the gazebo was only about forty yards distant. He couldn't see anything.

"State your location," he whispered.

"*Approximately twelve yards south, southeast of the gazebo. We are opposite this person.*"

Someone moved in the brush at the far end of the meadow, just opposite the gazebo. It was probably one of the little Boys—Bobby or Matt—even though they had been given strict orders to stay out of the meadow. Such orders, however, were often open invitations to defiance.

Hutchings walked out onto the meadow, right into a spongy pile of newly applied soil and he almost lost his balance. The stuff was everywhere and it stank to high heaven.

"Those assholes!" he said out loud.

He raced to the gazebo and stepped around it to where he could see their interloper.

It wasn't one of the little Boys.

"Rhonda?" Hutchings said.

The woman was standing alone surrounded by a patch of grass. She had apparently walked through the brackish goop, for it painted her legs halfway up to her knees.

She also wore no clothes. Those lay in a pile off to one side.

She turned to him, coming out of some kind of woozy trance. "I was hoping I'd find you here."

Now *here* was trouble.

17

Rhonda Barrie had been standing ankle-deep in a dark, manurelike substance and staring at the exposed planetarium ceiling. Hutchings had disturbed her reverie, but he then realized—too late—that she'd wanted that reverie disturbed, more specifically, by him.

Barrie's arms wrapped around Hutchings's neck and he felt the warmth of her breasts press through his jumpsuit. "I didn't know if you'd come or not. I thought you might."

Instinctively he put his hands to the woman's waist, feeling the very human warmth of her body. "Listen, I think you'd better get your clothes on—"

"Those things in our heads," she said. "They're going to kill us, aren't they."

It wasn't a question. It seemed to account for why the woman appeared to burn with a desperate, sexual energy.

"We don't know that," Hutchings said. "We don't even know what they are yet. Listen, it's cold up here. I think something's wrong with the arboretum program. Let's go down below."

"No," she said. "I'd rather not."

"Excuse me?"

"If we're going to die, I'd rather go out in the arms of a lover," Barrie said.

"Nobody's going anywhere yet. At least not while I'm around."

"Make love to me," she whispered. "Here. Now."

Hutchings felt like a thirteen-year-old. Barrie's breasts against him were very firm, her nipples hard with excited passion. They were, he noticed, the breasts of a woman who had not yet suckled a child—breasts ripe for the picking. Hutchings began to sweat.

"Have you ever made love on the gazebo?" she asked. "Have you taken one of your bedmates up here?"

"Actually, it's never occurred to me."

"I heard you talking to your friend. You have several bedmates, don't you?"

"Some of us do, yes. But—"

She wore a tantalizing perfume that, mixed with her body's natural musk, was beginning to make him a bit woozy. Her lips, full and inviting, hovered like a hex before him. All he had to do was *lean* into it.

She looked up at him. "Make love to me, Ian."

This, from Rhonda Barrie whose initial reaction to him had been the most expressive of the six. Now she wanted him to have his way with her.

Hutchings attempted to step back from the woman. But when he did, his right foot snagged a hidden divot and he fell backwards. Barrie, still clutching him, followed him down with a girlish laugh.

Her moist lips pressed against his and her saliva had a slight metallic tang to it. It was in no way unpleasant, conjuring memories of high school he thought he'd lost forever.

"Rhonda, please," he said, struggling under her. "There's something you need to know. It's important—"

Barrie's hands began exploring the terrain of his body. She found the zipper at the collar of his jumpsuit. It began heading south in a seductive, surrendering snarl.

Hutchings nearly jerked himself into a sitting position. Barrie rolled back onto the grass, her legs slightly apart. The aroma of her arousal was quiet intense. He hadn't experienced *that* in quite some time either.

"We have to talk," he said firmly.

The woman blinked at him, trying to figure out his behavior. Then it came to her. "My God, you're gay. You don't like women."

"I'm not gay," he said, almost laughing. "That isn't it."

"You're married, then."

"Not that I know of."

"Then what is it?"

Hutchings's right hand had landed next to her discarded jumpsuit. "I take it you haven't felt it yet." He passed her the suit.

"Felt what?"

"We don't know what it is, exactly, but you'll feel it in a day or so. At least that's how long it took for us. We were just too stunned to do anything about it in those first hours."

Puzzled, Barrie said, "I don't—"

Hutchings went on. "We think it's part of the mind-wipe. Evidently several key hormones in the brain pertaining to procreation are rendered inoperable."

"Inoperable? What do you mean?"

"It . . . well," he swallowed. "The fact is, we can't have sex."

"You *what*?"

"We can't have sex. At least the men can't. Women can get aroused to some degree, but men can't get excited at all."

"You're joking."

"That's why no one's been raped here. No one's even tried to rape anyone. I couldn't have sex with you even if I wanted to."

He did not elucidate that last remark. He was thinking of Kate as well as the vigilant Tonka hiding in the grass.

"But how is that possible?" Breasts dangling, Barrie slowly began climbing back into her jumpsuit.

"I don't know," he admitted. "But what I've seen today in the infirmary gives me a few ideas."

Barrie's voice was heavy with disappointment. "They told us we'd be raped first thing when we got down here—all of us, I mean, the men and the women."

"It's never happened. We get along fairly well."

"What about those bracelets you gave us? I thought you said the parrys were designed to protect us from physical attacks?"

"And they will, if that's what you want them for. Mostly if they're worn at all, it's for their beauty."

"Then what's all this talk about bedmates?" she asked.

"Someone to share a bed with. It's one of our few pleasures, sleeping next to someone you care for. Unless, of course, they snore or hog the covers or wet the bed."

"Wet the bed?"

"Our Children wet the bed. We haven't figured that one out either."

Barrie struggled with this new information. "Then why do I feel this way . . . toward you?"

"It'll go away."

"I don't want it to go away."

After a pause, she then said, "When I saw you yesterday in the Roughhouse . . . you don't know what that did to me."

"I thought it scared the hell out of you."

"It scared Arliss—it *surprised* me. I didn't know you people were able to change your internal gravity from floor to floor."

"Only in the Roughhouse, by design."

Barrie slipped into her boots. She stood up slowly. "They told us to expect the very worst down here, that you'd be difficult. Some of us would even die."

Hutchings, now having the higher ground, spoke. "The Children get into trouble now and then, but beyond that, nothing much happens here. We try to keep ourselves occupied with station maintenance or hobbies, but that's about as extreme as it gets down here."

Barrie seemed haloed with acute frustration. "You people don't seem . . . human anymore."

"There's more to the human experience than sex."

"Not much more."

"You'd be surprised. Sobriety and equilibrium count for an awful lot."

"Not where I come from."

"That's probably what got you into trouble," Hutchings said. "In fact, it's what gets most people into trouble, at least, from what I remember before the Wall."

At that point the silver surface of their artificial pond slid aside. The main meadow lift was bringing someone up into the arboretum.

Lorraine Sperry's head appeared and she gazed around her while the lift locked into place. "Bloody hell," she said. "What's that stink?"

Hutchings walked over to her. "Someone dumped a load of shit on the meadow."

"And the air's stale," Sperry added.

"I noticed that, too. So what brings you up here?" he asked.

Sperry's glance took in the presence of Rhonda Barrie, but in a typically British fashion, she seemed indifferent to what that presence implied. "Have you seen Matt White?"

"No. Why?" Hutchings said.

Sperry's surveyed the meadow. "One of the 'stiffs made it into common room six and overheard Oaks and White. He said they were going to hide up here."

"They were going to hide? Why?" Hutchings asked.

"They were playing with several computer programs in the Brains."

"They were?"

Sperry looked up. The actual ceiling of the planetarium was clearly visible. She nodded. "They got into the planetarium programs. One of them wiped out Larry's comet and half the constellations are gone. Looks like they wiped out part of the day program as well." She pointed. "No clouds. No blue sky."

"Who was on duty in the Brains?"

"Larry," Lorraine told him. "But when he stepped out to use the restroom, those two Boys got into the integrated programs for the entire meadow—the planetarium, Environmentals. Oaks wanted to learn about the meadow and I guess Matt thought he was the one to teach him. They're quite a team."

Hutchings scowled. "Those little shits. I'll kill them both."

"Larry tried calling you, but the Boys apparently took out half the com system as well. Larry and Elliot both are now trying to get the system back up before the Man downstairs takes some of the overload."

"Christ."

"Ian," Lorraine said carefully. "We can't have any more glitches, not with the parole Shunt coming. I think we should lock those two up until the parolees are safely off."

"And they're supposed to be up here somewhere?"

Sperry nodded tersely.

Hutchings walked across the meadow, searching the dense forest for the two little Boys. He was now troubled by the possibility that they might have witnessed Rhonda Barrie's come-on and might tattle to the rest of the Children. That rankled him even more than their potentially destructive, if completely understandable, deviltry.

Mad eyes scanned the trees. "Matt! Get your ass out here!" He heard a branch break. *"Matt!"*

"No!" the little Boy said from behind a tree.

Hutchings dove into the forest and found him. Though the tawny-haired Boy was an adult of average height, he only had the physical skills of a kid. He was no match for Hutchings.

"Lemme go!" Matt White protested. "Lemme go!"

"Where is Oaks?" Hutchings demanded.

"Lorraine! Ian's picking on me! *Help! Help!*"

Hutchings grabbed the little Boy with both hands and shook him like an Apache Indian's ceremonial gourd. "I told you this place was off limits!"

"What about them?" Matt said, indicating Barrie.

"What about them?" Hutchings asked.

"They're up here all the time, hanging around the gazebo. You let *them* come up here but not *us* and we were here first!"

The former pilot managed to take a swing at Hutchings but Hutchings caught the Boy's fist in midtrajectory.

"Stop it!" Hutchings demanded. He thrust the Boy backwards into Lorraine Sperry's arms.

"I hate you a thousand times!" the little Boy shouted. "You make up your own rules and do what you want all the time. You're such a *cheater!* That's what you are! A big fat *cheater!*"

"This is the first time *I've* been up here," Rhonda Barrie said in her defense. "I don't know about the others."

"Oh, yeah?" the little Boy countered. "*I* think you're waiting for the Shunt to come back! Me and

Bobby have been watching! You're gonna escape and leave the rest of us here!"

"I don't think any of us are going anywhere," Barrie told him, then looked at Hutchings.

She then walked off into the woods, heading for the maintenance tunnel that she'd used originally to climb into the meadow.

"Is there something going on between the two of you I should know about?" Lorraine asked when Barrie had vanished. "For security reasons, I mean."

"When I find out, I'll let you know."

"You're a bully!" Matt White blew a noisy raspberry in Hutchings's face.

Hutchings grabbed the little Boy and lifted him off the ground. "Listen to me. Do this again and I'll personally hand you over to the Spanker. He'll paddle your sorry ass *flat!*"

The Boy wet his pants.

"Let's get down to the Brains and straighten this out," Hutchings then said.

He dragged the Boy over to the main meadow lift with Lorraine close behind them. The Tonka watching the whole episode never did come out of hiding.

18

Hugh Bladestone desperately needed sleep, real sleep, not the vicious narcoleptic trances of quick-sleep.

He was deeply troubled by the discovery of the traces, more so than he had let on to Ian. The mere fact of their existence staggered him. He felt he should have remembered *something* about them, but he couldn't recall a thing. *They* had taken it from him, that awful dynasty of prigs called the System Assembly.

However, Bladestone's deeper intuition told him that something more dreadful than ignorance was behind this discovery.

That fear could have accounted for his sleeplessness. He and Kristen had gone to bed hours earlier, leaving Diane on duty. But he remained riddled with restlessness.

Kristen rolled over in her sleep, facing him, and he tried to focus on the susurration of her breath. It reminded him of twilight snow—snow falling through bare trees along the streets of the Chicago neighborhood where he grew up. In his mind he could visualize a bus pressing through the storm. His father rode the bus to and from work. And Hugh, as a little boy, loved to play in the street with his friends, waiting for his father's arrival at dinner time. *Dear God in Heaven, what in the world are the Strathclyde traces?* The holographs of the fifty or so scans they'd made that afternoon merged in his mind. Each had the silver sheen of the bus his father rode home at night . . . the sheen of armor . . . gray armor of the knights he used to read about in school.

Knights . . . armor . . . armored siege machines . . . warfare . . .

Almost immediately he began dreaming.

He is riding in the back of a large EMS vehicle which has been suddenly dispatched into the city. He seems to be the only medical person on board. With him are a dozen other men and women, some of whom he recognizes, others he doesn't. Everyone seems to be wearing military uniforms and each carries a powerful rifle. The deadly ornaments of grenades cling to their vests and belts.

This can't be right. I'm no soldier. I'm a resident of Chicago Mercy, a doctor in a hospital. What's going on here?

For some reason which he cannot grasp, he, too, is wearing the chitin of body armor. He also wears a breathing apparatus to protect his lungs from the dangerous silver air.

Through a side window of the EMS vehicle, he sees that the century's worst snowstorm is continuing unabated. He wonders: How can bullets effect the fall of snow? How can a military expedition push back the new Ice Age?

"*It's not the snow,*" someone says to his unasked question. "*Snow we can handle.*" He looks across from him and sees Eddie Brickman armed with a grin and a powerful Eberly automatic rifle. "*It's the goddamned dust we're after, man. Fuck the snow.*"

The city appears blanketed with blowing silver dust. Cars and trucks are covered by it, their human owners cocooned inside. The EMS vehicle effortlessly glides above the tragic landscape, its engines powered by a small fusion reactor that could operate practically forever if it had to. The craft even has a simple food processor. They have power, food, and medicine and they are on a mission. But the man who pilots the vehicle acts like a little Boy and wants to go home. His name is Matthew.

The Grown-ups in the vehicle, however, are there to engage the enemy.

What enemy?

Rocking back and forth in the gentle motion of the vehicle, Bladestone looks closer at another man sitting across from him. It's Lyle MacKenzie. And beside him sits Ian Hutchings. Ian is without his shackles. How very strange! Beside Ian sits Lorraine Sperry. She clutches a Mills concussor, one of the nastiest pistols ever invented. It doesn't just maim and wound. It blows the shit out of everything it's trained upon.

Everyone in the vehicle stares ahead as if they've come to do battle with the Devil himself. None of this makes any sense.

But then this is not a dream, something tells him. This is a memory *disguised* as a dream.

They have been summoned to the Ostermann Hotel on North Michigan Avenue. Racing sixty to seventy feet above the snowbound streets they pass dead signal lights that swing in the air above the intersections like hanged men. On the sidewalks are silver statues, people captured in midstride where they had been taken by the blizzard.

"Shouldn't we be doing something for them?" Bladestone asks. *"At least we can get them off the streets."*

"It's too late, man," Eddie Brickman says. *"We're taking the show straight to the enemy himself."*

Bladestone doesn't quite understand what Eddie Brickman means, but Eddie seems to know what he's talking about—Eddie Brickman, the most reckless individual Bladestone had ever known.

But isn't Eddie dead? And Lyle. . .Lyle MacKenzie died two years ago and they buried him in the meadow.

The meadow? What meadow?

The hover car soars down the abandoned Magnificent Mile, heading toward the Ostermann Hotel, the once-proud flagship of the Chicago Ostermann family. Now the Ost is little more than a black edifice of fragile, granitic ice.

He and his armored companions pile out the back of the personnel carrier in their specially insulated suits as if they were Marines hitting the beach of a faraway shore.

"Over here!" someone hails them at the hotel's entrance.

Ice crackles beneath their boots as they enter the

hotel lobby. Inside, people are immobilized everywhere Hugh looks. It is a frozen statuary.

The team separates.

"Hugh, over here!" calls an armored figure at the door to one of the stairwells.

There, two men bear a stretcher between them. On the stretcher is a beautiful woman of elegant African-American lineage. But she is dressed very strangely, considering the time of the year, *considering the circumstances.* She is wearing a black evening gown with traceries of bright sequins and small pearls around her low-cut collar. A brittle layer of ice, just millimeters thin, covers her.

The woman is beautiful. And nearly dead.

She manages to open her eyes and a few words escape. "Don't leave me, darling, please don't leave me. . . ."

The horror has frozen him in place.

The woman is his wife.

And they are much too late.

"Hugh?"

Bladestone sat upright in the darkness. Kristen, still in her nightgown, stood alone, silhouetted in the doorway to their room. She looked quite frightened.

"I'm up. What is it?"

"It's Mr. Plainfield," Kristen said softly. Her eyes were filled with an infinite sadness. "He's gone."

"Gone?" Bladestone flung back the covers, flinging back the nightmare of his dying wife in that icebound hotel. "Has he wandered off again? Where did he go?"

"No," Kristen intoned. "He's dead."

"He's what?"

"We tried everything we could," Kristen said. "But it happened so fast."

"Why didn't you wake me?" He grabbed his bathrobe.

"You were sleeping so peacefully."

"You should have awakened me immediately."

"We thought we could stabilize him."

The two raced from their bedroom and stepped into the special ward. There, they found Diane Beckwith hovering over the vessel that had once held the spirit of Edward Plainfield. "What happened?" the doctor asked.

"I don't know. He just . . . shut down," Diane told him.

Bladestone checked the monitors above the old man's bed. Flatlines everywhere.

"He went into full cardiac arrest," Diane went on. "The monitors caught it and we were in here in seconds."

"Did you try CPR?"

"Yes," Diane nodded. "But his jaw is locked shut."

"Did you try giving his heart a shot of adrenalin?"

Kristen Barron answered in her stead. "I tried. But I couldn't get a cardiac needle into his chest."

"What?"

"It broke. He's gone completely stiff throughout his entire body. The needle wasn't strong enough to penetrate his skin."

Bladestone tried checking the old man's eyes, but Plainfield's eyelids were locked in place. It was as if rigor mortis had instantly set in.

"Did you try electroshock?"

Kristen said, "That's the last thing we did. We gave him a standard jolt but he didn't move. No muscular reflexivity at all. He's like a piece of wood."

"I'm sorry, Hugh," Diane said. "I should have gotten you immediately. You were just across the hall."

Hugh examined Clarissa Pickerall on the bed beside the old man. Her vital signs on the headboard monitor appeared to be stable except for the one-degree elevation in her body temperature. Everything else was normal.

But what did that mean anymore?

"Hugh?" Diane asked.

He looked at both his attendants. They were—or at least had been—trained EMS technicians in their former lives. They were also among his very best friends, second only to his wife. *His dead wife.*

"It's all right, Diane," he said softly. "It's what I would have done. You didn't have the time to waste."

"You were sleeping so soundly, we thought that—"

He managed a forgiving smile—not that forgiveness would bring back a dead man. "It's okay."

"Hugh," she said uneasily. "This happened to Lyle. It was like this."

He nodded. "Kristen, you'd better get Ian down here. Don't use the com. If he isn't in the meadow at this hour, he's probably in his laboratory. But don't tell anyone what's happened. All right?"

"Hugh?" Kristen breathed. "What is happening?"

Bladestone tried not to show his own worry. "Just get Ian down here. Fast."

19

Hutchings and Kate spent what was supposed to be their last night together arguing. She just could not be persuaded to leave. There was nothing in-system for her to go back to. The only meaningful life she had was on the sunstation, she said, and that was that. Hutchings couldn't convince her otherwise. Eventually, Kate rolled over and went to sleep, leaving Ian staring at the ceiling.

The hours went by. Unable to sleep, Hutchings decided to take his frustrations down to the Roughhouse where he jogged in a gravity field close to that of Uranus. Hundreds of burned calories later, he collapsed on the track and listened to the sunstation's Environmentals hum. There, he managed to get a little sleep.

He was in common room three, mulling over a bowl of strange-tasting oatmeal—the coffee didn't taste so good either—when Kristen Barron found him and told him that Edward Plainfield had just died.

When Hutchings and Kristen returned to the infirmary, they found that Bladestone had become greatly depressed. As he informed Hutchings, the old man's death went beyond anything he knew about human pathology.

So Hutchings decided at that moment that they had to take two courses of action. First, they had to know more about the traces. Bladestone wanted technical specifications and proof that the augments were not responsible for the deaths of Plainfield and, perhaps earlier, that of Lyle MacKenzie. It was time to demand some answers from the System Assembly.

The second course of action directly involved the Fiddlers. Remembering that they had kept Lyle Mac-Kenzie's body in a small stasis chamber until the meadow was completely built, Hutchings came up with the idea that they might put Clarissa Pickerall in Lyle's former chamber. They could keep her preserved in suspended time until they could figure out what was wrong with her, based on the assumption that Pickerall had whatever it was that killed Edward Plainfield. Lyle's stasis chamber, like their parry bracelets, operated on Renner-shield technology. Given enough power, the chambers could compress time within the chamber for days, weeks, perhaps even years.

So while the Fiddlers got Lyle's stasis chamber out of mothballs, Hutchings composed a letter detailing their problems. He also included a statement complaining of the basic inhumanity of their incarceration. He demanded an outside hearing of their case with Amnesty Interplanetary's Supreme Council in Geneva, Switzerland. If mammals had been afforded "human" rights by the AI Protocols of 2023 C.E. and were to be treated with compassion and decency, then the men and women of Ra deserved the same.

In affect, the Raians were staging a modest rebellion. They had nothing to lose. The wrath of the System Assembly could not possibly match the wrath of the sun they faced every day.

When 11:00 hours came, Hutchings took the main lift up to the meadow with Cpl. Steven Welch, the only one of the nine parolees who had decided to accept his reprieve. Welch's was a particularly interesting case. The man had become a bindlestiff about nine months ago, rendered helpless by sudden onslaughts of quick-sleep. What also plagued the man were recurring nightmares of disjointed seminar implants that were breaking down in his brain.

Welch's last memories were of working on a second doctorate, this one in English, at UC Berkeley and he had, at that point, about a hundred college hours of literature sems. However, quick-sleep did something to the sems and his dreams became filled with characters from the works of one specific writer, works Welch characterized as written in a style of reverential narcissism. As Welch's bouts of hypernarcolepsy got worse, so, too, the nightmares. Indeed, in his dreams, the characters from those books—children, mostly—would come alive and lecture him with mature wisdom as they lectured the adults in their original literary settings. Welch would wake up in his flop, screaming. He eventually turned to Ian for help.

Hutchings was able to devise a modest Critic, a biotech armada that simply disengaged the implanted sems causing the trouble. It seemed to work. Within days, the lecturing children faded away. Unfortunately, Welch lost all of his other sems as well, including those relating to his first Ph.D. in linguistics. But the man did appear to sleep better.

When they rose into the meadow's small pond, they were greeted by Lorraine and Elliot. The meadow was otherwise cleared of unnecessary personnel. Kate had chosen to wait out the appointed hour with the little Girls. There was a strong possibility that after Welch's molecules raced up the Renner-shielded monopole corridor, liberated from the fiery menace of the photosphere, the System Assembly would simply vaporize the Kaians for their disobedience. Everyone else was at their duty station, waiting.

The four approached the gazebo. The day program with its New England clouds was still patchy, but there was plenty of light to see by as they walked across the grass.

Hutchings put a large hand on Welch's shoulder. "You don't have to do this. We can send the message up by itself. We don't know how they're going to react. They could take it out on you."

Welch's thumbs dug into the straps of the backpack which contained his flop and the few possessions he owned. The look in his eyes was still that of being trapped in the land of dreams.

"I owe this to you," Welch said. "You took care of me when I needed it."

"All we did was make sure you had three squares and a flop," Hutchings said.

"Well, there's that," Welch said. "But it was those

goddamned lit sems. The children in those novels were always wise, always so damned special."

"There's no accounting for taste, I suppose," Hutchings said.

"There's that. But I remember this five-year-old kid lecturing a seventy-year-old mountain man on the ways of the world. It's that kid that was in my dreams." Welch shuddered. "That writer should have known our Children."

"I'm just glad there was something I could do about your nightmares," Hutchings confided. "It's one of my few real accomplishments here."

Welch shook Hutchings's hand. Welch then said, "They're dead wrong about you, you know. The Screws, I mean."

"That's what I tell myself."

Welch then took the diplomatic pouch that contained the letter Hutchings had composed. He stepped onto the gazebo.

"Good luck, up there. Stay out of trouble," Hutchings said. Lorraine waved and Elliot gave him a thumbs-up.

Over Ian's com came an announcement from Larry Voorhees who was down in the Brains: *"I'm tracking Bold Charon at a million miles out. Monopole corridor alignment has been established and we've got a firm homing signal, Ian."*

"Stand by," Hutchings said.

A few seconds passed. Voorhees's disembodied voice then announced: *"Transmission lock confirmed. We're holding steady. Monopole stream reversal has begun. Stand by!"*

Hutchings stepped away from the gazebo as the

Shunt mechanism began to hum from deep within the stage. Corporal Welch looked both expectant and fearful. He gave them his bravest smile.

Hutchings knew they would never see him again.

"It's showtime!" Voorhees said.

Welch vanished from the stage.

A thick, hovering mist made from the sudden condensation of water molecules in the wake of the transferred man floated above the stage. This quickly dissipated in the wind drifting across the meadow.

"Now what?" Shoemaker asked in the silence that followed.

Hutchings said, "Well, not knowing what the time-dilation effect is on the Outside, I suggest that we go about our business. Larry will signal us when Screws reactivate the Shunt from Topside."

"If they decide to respond to us at all," Shoemaker said.

"I think they will."

"You have too much faith in them, Ian," Lorraine commented.

"Maybe."

Hutchings turned and headed for the mirrored surface of their small pond, wanting to track down Kate. He had a need just then to be with her, that old heartache he thought he'd forgotten from his days in-system. If the System Assembly disapproved of his message, they would all be targets for death. And easy ones at that.

"How long do you think it will take for them to answer?" Lorraine asked, standing near the gazebo.

Hutchings shrugged. "It's their game. They might not answer at all."

"You really believe that?" Elliott Shoemaker asked.

"No, not really," Hutchings said. "They're having too much fun with us. Call me when you guys hear from them."

20

Barely an hour had gone by before they received a reply. In fact, *Bold Charon* was inside the monopole corridor above the sunstation at a million miles out and gone before Larry Voorhees had the time to acknowledge its presence. But the relay ship safely teleported a diplomatic pouch which landed on the gazebo stage and both Elliot and Lorraine were there to pick it up.

The pouch did not have a letter inside it, however. Instead, a lone data tile rattled out into Hutchings's large hand. Leaving Lorraine to guard the gazebo, Hutchings and Shoemaker went to the Brains where an anxious Larry Voorhees waited to see what the System Assembly had to say.

Hutchings handed the tile to Voorhees. "Let's patch this into the rest of the station. There's no sense in keeping something like this a secret. If we're going to get crisped, everyone might as well know why."

Voorhees and Shoemaker sat at the control console before the Big Board and quickly brought the rest of the station on-line. Hutchings stood behind them, eyes fixed on the main video screen on the Big Board.

The contemptible crest of the System Assembly's Corrections Ministry appeared first, and it lingered in place for thirty long seconds. This was also accompanied by the faint hissing of static, which was highly unusual. It had a curious melodic cadence to it, as if pleasantly warped by the Shunt's reassimilation process.

"Music for our dining and dancing pleasure," Voorhees quipped.

To Hutchings, it had the quality of arctic gales, arpeggiating up and down ethereal scales barely audible to the human ear.

"Could be background scatter that might have gotten scrambled in the transfer," Hutchings said. "We'll get the Fiddlers on this later. It'll give them something to do."

The crest hovered on the screen and Voorhees rocked back and forth in his chair. "Come on, you sonsabitches," he whispered. "Let's get on with the show."

The screen gave way to a hard-featured, severely disapproving man. The static, though, continued, if diminished somewhat.

This was not a Ward Judge. It was someone much higher up in the System Assembly hierarchy. That he didn't wear the green hood of the Quorum was significant in itself. Fiftyish, he wore a crisp, cerulean blue uniform with silver trim at his collar, every inch the stern authoritarian, his face molded by the Law. His short silver-gray hair bristled like needles or nails—a man whose very moral fiber was probably made of metal.

"I am High Councilor Davis Whitehall."

"Jesus," Voorhees breathed. "They sent our message all the way up to the Council!"

"Shh," Shoemaker hissed. "I want to hear what this poltroon has to say."

The Councilor's lips hardly moved. To Hutchings the man could have been a ventriloquist's dummy, a shill for the System Assembly's high and holy Council of Thirteen.

"We have received your communication and have considered it fully," the Councilor said. "Our regard for your humanity requires us to address the contents of your message in no uncertain terms."

"Oh good," Voorhees said.

"Know this: We are not responsible for the malady you report among your colleagues and we are outraged that you would even suggest that we would resort to such tactics. You were screened for illnesses before you were sent to Ra. We would *never*, I repeat, *never* treat you with such barbarity. To think such a thing is absolute blasphemy."

"Now we're guilty of blasphemy," Voorhess said.

"Quiet," Shoemaker said.

The Councilor continued. "It is our belief that you are lying about the illness which currently afflicts you. You were in excellent health when we sent you to Ra eleven years ago. If anyone has perished, it is no fault of ours. We cannot take any responsibility for what happens to you once you've arrived at the prison facility. Our obligation ends there."

The emotionless Councilor did not blink, he did

not exhibit a scintilla of human emotion. Hutchings wanted to punch the face on the screen.

"We believe that your medical facilities are sufficient to find a solution to any medical problem that may arise, barring death. At the very least you can effect temporary relief to those who you say are ill. However, do not attempt to send any of your sick on the Shunt designed for the parolees. Unauthorized transferees will be destroyed regardless of their condition."

"Assholes," Hutchings whispered.

The Councilor continued his harangue. "However, decency dictates that we provide you with some information regarding the augments which you claim to have only now discovered, the Strathclyde traces."

Whitehall's image on the screen was replaced by a 2-D representation of a human brain containing what appeared to be a fully developed Strathclyde trace.

Hutchings was stunned at what he saw. The augment had tendrils and filaments twisting through the brain down pathways that Hutchings thought could not be traversed, even at a microscopic level. Its metallic blue, crimson copper, and fine gold wiring resembled the circuitry of a very sophisticated computer. Every channel of the brain was bolstered by the traceries of an incredible complexity.

"Wow," Shoemaker breathed. "Will you look at that?"

The Councilor's visage reappeared. "What you have found in your brains are the anchoring templates of the intelligence magnification assemblies developed by Dr. Hutchings. Yours have been decommissioned and reduced and will never again by of any use to you. I wish to emphasize, however, that the traces have no bearing on your current situation. We suggest that you forget about them and turn your attention to the crisis at hand, if indeed it is a crisis."

"Remind me to kill that guy someday," Hutchings said.

"I can do that," Shoemaker replied.

Whitehall's voice became colder. "Now the matter regarding the prisoners to whom we've granted parole but who have decided to remain on Ra. Their refusal is absolutely unacceptable. All parolees will be lifted up in forty-eight hours your time from the time of the previously scheduled Shunt. Should you refuse to comply, you will be destroyed. Your refusal today to send all parolees is a Vapor Injunction, your first. If you do not send up the rest in forty-eight hours, that will be your second and you *will* be released from the Anchor. This is nonnegotiable."

"Swell," Shoemaker breathed.

"Moreover, we demand that the parolees bring up proof that those who have died have been properly recycled. The food processor is programmed to register the recycled remains of deceased humans. We insist that this information be sent to us as proof that nothing has gone to waste. This is as we say."

The image vanished from the screen and was replaced by the crest of the Corrections Ministry. Seconds later, it vanished into absolute darkness, taking the strange static with it.

"Nice person, that Whitehall," Voorhees said. "I wonder how many babies he eats for breakfast?"

Shoemaker turned and looked up at Hutchings.

"So, those things in our heads really are intelligence enhancers?"

"Search me," Hutchings said.

"Anchoring bases," Voorhees said. "That's what he said. They're the remains of the anchoring templates from which they're grown."

They would be hearing, and soon, from the other adult members of the prison; but for now, the three men stood thunderstruck in silence.

Then Shoemaker spoke out. "They want us to send up proof that we've recycled our dead. How are we going to do that? There's nothing left of Kerry and Melissa, or Eddie."

"I'm thinking about Lyle," Hutchings said. "I don't know what we're going to do about Lyle."

"Are we going to have to dig him up and *then* recycle him?" Voorhees asked.

"Not while I'm alive," Hutchings said.

"Ian, there isn't a single reference to recycling anybody, dead or alive, in sunstation protocols," Shoemaker said. "I know there isn't because I've looked."

"They seem to be making up the rules as they go," Hutchings said.

Larry Voorhees leaned back in his chair. "Those people need to be taken down a few notches," he said.

"We're the just ones to do it," Hutchings said.

Shoemaker laughed bitterly. "Oh, right. A lot of good we can do."

"We'll do what we can," Hutchings said. "We're not going to let those bastards bugger us and expect us to smile about it. Larry, make sure Doc and the Getaways get a hard copy of this message. Also have them make some sort of background separation of the static we heard. There might be something imbedded there we can use."

"Done," the lanky Oklahoman said. "What else?"

"Let's convene the Meadow Council. At the very least, we're going to have to decide what to do about Lyle."

"Right," Shoemaker said.

Voorhees looked up at Hutchings. "Listen, what does it matter to them if our parolees stay or go? I mean, if they'd Shunted down a hundred or so new people, then it might make sense, just to make room. But, hell, we can hold at least three hundred people here. What are they thinking up there?"

"We have to figure that out," Hutchings said.

"Forty-eight hours," Voorhees said. "That doesn't give us much time."

Shoemaker nodded. "Maybe we can *fake* Lyle's recycling somehow. Pablo might be able to get the Sally to think Lyle and the others have been recycled."

But Hutchings wasn't thinking about what to do with Lyle or how to go about fooling the Sally.

"What we really need is time," he said. "This could take us days to puzzle through. Weeks, maybe. And weeks we don't have."

The com-chime in Hutchings's right ear sounded out. "I'm here. Go ahead."

"Ian?"

Everyone there recognized Kate's voice.

"I'm here. What's up?"

"Something's happened to Bebe."

Hutchings blinked. "What's happened to her?"

"Bebe won't wake up."

"Is it quick-sleep?'

"I don't think so. She's burning with fever. Not only that, she's gone completely stiff, Ian. I can barely bend her arms."

The three men looked at one another.

Shoemaker said, "Plainfield and Pickerall."

"And Lyle," Hutchings added.

Kate had heard their words. *"Yes. I think so."*

"I'm on my way," Hutchings said to the com. "Out."

He then pointed to the console. "Break the message down. Get a copy to Doc and the Getaways. Also, have Pablo send four of his best people to my laboratory. I'll be there in twenty minutes."

Shoemaker and Voorhees set to work.

21

Hutchings bolted from the command center and ran to the spook hole. Shooting up three levels in less than two seconds almost launched him into unconsciousness, so massive were the lift's accelerative forces.

Emerging into the corridor that led to the dorms, he found toys scattered everywhere, including several Tonkas. In fact, he almost tripped over one.

"Goddamnit!" he shouted. Everywhere lay crayons, construction paper, bottles of glue, wooden blocks, inert lumps of molding clay and a trail of spilled glitter. The glitter was so fine that some of it even hovered in the air.

Coming from the opposite direction were Hugh Bladestone and Diane Beckwith who had been contacted by Larry Voorhees the instant Hutchings had left the Brains.

Hutchings pointed to the artifacts out in the hallway. "We don't need the Vapor," he said. "A person could get himself killed right here."

In the Girls' room, Hutchings found the gathering

of initial witnesses. Junie Russell and Lisa Anderson huddled next to each other, confused and frightened. Kate, wrapped in a bathrobe, hair dripping wet from a shower, was kneeling at Bebe Wasson's side.

"I *tried* to wake her *up*," Junie Russell said. "We were going to have pancakes today. Bebe likes pancakes."

Kate rose from Bebe's side and Hugh Bladestone took her place. However, Hutchings could see from where he stood that the little Girl was seriously ill.

"It's definitely not quick-sleep," the doctor said. He looked up at the other two little girls. "How long has she been like this?"

"Long time," said Junie.

"Was she like this when you went to bed last night?" the doctor asked.

"I don't know," Lisa said.

Then Junie added, "Bebe *snores*."

"She snores?" The doctor could not make the connection.

Kate, however, made the connection. "Bebe didn't snore last night. Is that what you're trying to say?"

"She snores *loud*, too," Junie asserted. "Bebe *wakes* us *up*. Lots."

Lisa nodded.

Kate faced Ian. "Bebe's got an upper nasal problem, probably a deviated septum. It's not a snore so much as a whistle. I would have known if I had spent the night with them. I would have heard it."

"This isn't your fault," Hutchings said.

Kate disagreed. "After you left last night, I should have come here. I *knew* something wasn't right."

"Kate," Hutchings started.

"Why didn't you wake me when you left? How could you let me sleep in like this? I just woke up."

"You did?" Hutchings was truly surprised by this. "When?"

"About half an hour ago. I slept like a rock."

"Bebe's sleeping like a rock," Lisa Anderson pointed out.

Hutchings considered the doctor. "What do you think?"

Bladestone pressed his hand to Bebe's forehead, then felt the sides of the little Girl's face. "It appears to be what the others have. Or *had*," he said, correcting himself.

Hutchings recalled what Councilor Whitehall had so righteously told them. "That son of a bitch Whitehall said that we're *imagining* all of this."

"Or that we're lying," Bladestone said. He stood and wiped the palms of his hands on his pant legs. "Look, I don't know what's going on," he said. "But we've got a major problem here. This isn't like anything I've seen before—at least, it's not anything that I can remember. I ran the symptoms through the computer in as many different configurations as I could think of and even it doesn't know."

"What did it come up with?" Hutchings asked. "Anything?"

"Yes. It said it's either epilepsy or the flu," the doctor told him.

"The flu?" Hutchings responded. "That's all the computer could come up with?"

"But it's not influenza and it's most definitely not epilepsy."

The doctor paused as if daydreaming. He then

said, "Even if we can identify it, I don't know if there's anything I can do to combat it. Our facilities are limited here. But that could be part of their plan, too."

"The System Assembly built this place," Diane said. "They *know* we can't do anything major. We're lucky to have access to the pharmeceuticals we can get from the Sally."

"Could this whatever-it-is be too small for your computer to screen?" Hutchings asked.

Bladestone nodded. "It's either that or the Screws have come up with something my computer doesn't recognize as either anomalous or inimical. It looks like they expect us to die."

When Kristen appeared with a hover-gurney, Hutchings got the stricken little Girl onto it.

Kate covered her mouth with her hand, on the verge of tears. "Ian, look at her," she said softly.

"You'd better get dressed," Hutchings told her. "We've got a lot to do in forty-eight hours. At the very least we're going to give you some sort of message to take back. That and copies of Hugh's diagnosis to prove to those bastards that something is really happening to us down here."

"What are you talking about? I'm not going anywhere."

"I take it that you didn't hear the message."

"What message?" Kate's brown eyes were wide with alarm.

"You guys evoked a fully fledged Vapor Injunction by not going. Our first. If the rest of you don't go back in forty-eight hours, that'll be our second injunction and they'll drop the Anchor out from under us."

"It's more than that," the doctor added. "They want proof that our dead have been recycled through the Sally."

"That can't be true," Kate said, aghast.

"Every bit of it," Hutchings said. "There's a program in the Sally's software that is apparently designed to register the passage of humans through the recycler. They want proof that we've been following the rules. Or it's adios."

"But, Ian, there isn't anything left of Eddie or Marlissa, or—"

"Or Kerry. I know. The problem is that we didn't tell the System Assembly *how* they died. We didn't tell them that we were outside on the vessel's hull when Eddie fell or that Marlissa managed to get into the 'cup and gut herself in an alloy Shunt. If they get wind of how clever we are, they'll probably drop the Anchor just for good measure."

Kate's shoulders drooped in the face of the facts of their predicament. They were at the mercy not only of the mindless monsters who put them there, but the sun's golden peril as well. They were besieged from all sides. Hutchings saw the defeat in Kate's eyes and he wanted to hold her forever. But the odds were entirely in favor of the System Assembly. It was their ball, their game, their playing field. The officials were corrupt, the game rigged. It was all over but the crying.

"We're holding a meeting of the Meadow Council in one hour," he said. "We've got a lot to discuss. Have you eaten yet?"

Kate shook her head. "I'm not hungry."

"You'd better get something. The meeting might be long."

"They've got us, Ian. They've won."

"Not yet, they haven't."

Kate closed her eyes. When she opened them, tears had appeared. She gazed deeply at him. "What about you? What are you going to do?"

Hutchings forced a heroic smile and hugged her. "At the moment I'm going to have a talk with Klane and that pet monkey of his. I've got a feeling that they know more about this than they're letting on. If I find out that's true, I plan on stuffing *them* into the Sally."

When Hutchings left Kate at the door to her private suite to finish getting dressed, he stalked out into the corridor raging with more anger than he'd ever known before in his life. He kicked a Tonka clean down the hallway. Then he said, "Com, open, Klane."

In the air next to Hutchings's right ear, Newsome Klane's spectral voice appeared. It bore its usual note of indifference.

"It is Mr. Hutchings, I believe."

"Where are you?"

"I am in common room six, where you earlier ordered me."

That meant that Klane had been just a few doors down from where the little Girls lived, where Bebe had taken ill.

Hutchings said, "Stay right there. Is Oaks with you?"

"At the moment he is. Five minutes from now, who knows?"

"Don't move. Out."

Hutchings walked briskly down the corridor, fairly trembling with rage. But he found Klane and Oaks where Klane said they'd be. They were seated at the end of a long table in the main common room, calmly eating their lunch.

Dylan Oaks saw Hutchings walk in. He jumped up. "Hey, it's Mr. Hutchings! Mr. Hutchings, guess what we found out!" Oaks came scurrying around, eager as a pup.

Hutchings saw that Oaks wasn't wearing his parry. He clamped a steely hand around the small man's surprisingly well-developed arm. "I want to talk to you. Both of you."

"Ow!" Oaks exclaimed.

"We've just lost Edward Plainfield, and Clarissa Pickerall is very sick. Now one of our little Girls has taken ill and I think *you* guys have something to do with it."

"I haven't the slightest idea what you're talking about," Klane said in protest.

Hutchings drew up a chair, straddled it backwards and leaned into Klane's face. "Let me put it this way. With a couple of exceptions, we're a healthy crew. Then, you people show up. A few hours later one of you dies. A little later on, another of you collapses. Then a little Girl who hasn't been sick in years goes into some sort of seizure-induced coma. You tell me, Klane. What are the odds of those things happening all by themselves?"

Klane was nonplussed. "What are you suggesting?"

"I'm suggesting that you or your pet squirrel here brought something down. I'm suggesting that you're part of an effort to kill us off."

Oaks's eyebrows shot up at the reference to a squirrel. He seemed pleased by it, not insulted by it as Hutchings had intended.

Klane's eyes, however, were faraway blue suns. "You think that I would willfully accede to a plan to carry a disease of some kind that might kill me as well as any of you?"

"You might if you were inoculated against it."

"Your troubled physician ran several tests on us. Remember? You were there. He found nothing."

Hutchings pointed to Klane's head. "He found that *thing* in your skull."

"He found a similar *thing* in your skull as well," Klane said. "Which, I might add, *you* created."

Hutchings's eyes narrowed. "Whatever they are, we've lived with them peacefully down here for three years. Our present crisis began when *you* people showed up. It all comes down to you."

"Have you consulted with Ms. Adamson and Ms. Barrie on this matter? They could be the agents you seek."

"Somehow I think you're behind this, Klane. You've got the look."

"I recommend that you consult with the other two women before you start throwing around accusations, particularly at me. They might be afraid of you, but I am not."

"I'll consult them later," Hutchings said. "*After* I take you apart."

Klane sipped his tea. "Yes, I was told that you would probably behave this way."

"Hey, I killed a billion people," Hutchings said. "I don't think it'll matter if I kill one or two more."

Klane folded his hands before him on the table. "Perhaps I should remind you that I was instrumental in rescuing Mr. Plainfield from your Forbidden Zones. If I wanted Mr. Plainfield dead, why did I assist in his rescue?"

"Perhaps," Hutchings said, "to make sure he stayed around long enough to infect everyone else. He might have been the carrier, too."

"Yes," Klane pointed out, "but poor Mr. Plainfield had no opportunity to mingle with your crew the way Mr. Oaks and I have. It's been a couple of days now. You're still alive and I'm still alive. Even Mr. Oaks is still alive."

Oaks nodded enthusiastically.

"You're immune and he's immune," Hutchings countered. "That's why it all comes down to you."

"Or Ms. Adamson or Ms. Barrie."

"No," Hutchings said, glaring. "It's you. I feel it in my bones."

"I heard a rumor," Klane said slowly, "that you and Ms. Barrie had a few intimate moments upstairs in your forest. Perhaps she has 'persuaded' you that she might not be to blame when she very well might be."

"This isn't about her."

"You are such a clever man."

Hutchings knew that he wasn't about to get anything out of Klane, short of torturing him. "Listen to me. If I find out that you *are* part of this," Hutchings said, "I'll crush your skull with my bare hands."

"Then I believe I shall have to start wearing that bracelet you gave me," Klane said, utterly unaffected by Hutchings's words.

Lorraine Sperry and two deputies appeared in the doorway to the common room. The Tonka Hutchings had booted down the hall had apparently sent out a distress call.

"All right, gents. Fight's over. Back to your corners."

Oaks blinked, looking from one Grown-up to another, not quite comprehending what was happening.

Hutchings stood up. "We're going to reexamine all of you, from top to bottom and we're going to get some very definite answers to this."

"Ian," Lorraine said. "Back off."

Hutchings held his fist, a boulder of pink gristle, in the tall man's face. "Don't fuck with me, Klane. If any of my people die, *you* go with them."

With that, Hutchings left the common room.

22

As a result of the Vapor Injunction, Kate found herself extraordinarily depressed, her very soul had gone cold with despair.

When the Meadow Council met that afternoon near the gazebo, a rainless storm blustered above the forest—Ian's idea. He wanted something to mirror his mood. For Kate, however, the storm only dampened her spirits. She didn't know how much more she could take.

"Some storm," Elliot commented. The clouds above moved visibly fast, each one a distinct digital projection that looked as if it could chuck actual bolts of lightning or pummel them at any time with golf-ball-sized hail.

Kate shivered, but she didn't think it was from the weather. All morning she had felt feverish. It was almost as if her mind had been processing like a supercomputer, searching furiously for a way—an excuse, a reason, a ploy, *anything*—to remain on the sunstation.

But what if she *was* ill? Didn't Councilor Whitehall

say they would destroy anybody who rode the Shunt who happened to be ill? Yet, she *was* one of the parolees. Would they make an exception in her case?

Kate couldn't think straight. She needed sleep—about a thousand years of it, away from the living fire menace of the sun.

Ian put an arm around Kate's shoulders where they sat in the grass near the gazebo. "Are you all right?" he asked.

"No."

"We'll fix that," he said, and hugged her. She managed a thin smile.

"Who's minding the store?" Lorraine asked as she approached the group. She had come up through one of the maintenance tunnels, making sure there were no little Boys eavesdropping on the Meadow Council.

"Larry is," Elliot said, leaning back. "I can't tear him away from the Man. He's really pissed off."

"Larry or the Man?" Lorraine asked, sitting beside him.

"Larry. When Matt and Oaks wiped out his comet, they accidentally took out most of the planetarium's programs. Oaks apparently didn't like the comet and wanted to rewrite it."

Lorraine looked up at the blustery sky. "The day program seems normal now."

"It was in a separate directory," Elliot said. "Those two are going to be a lot of trouble."

"We're lucky they haven't already vaporized us," Ian said.

"Anyway," Elliot went on, "Larry wants to make a few improvements in the comet."

"What sort of improvements?" Pablo Ramirez asked.

Pablo Ramirez was sitting on the gazebo steps just a few feet away, fiddling with what appeared to be a spray device—a canister and nozzle mechanism— Ian had asked him to work on.

"He's thinking of making the comet look like a space ship," Elliot said.

"He wants it to look like a *space ship*?" Pablo asked.

Elliot shrugged. "He got the idea in a dream last night. He wants the comet to look more . . . artificial, I guess. You know—windows, doors, tail fins, dual overhead cams, twin exhausts, chopped and channeled. Don't ask me. Ask him."

"He sure has strange dreams," Pablo remarked.

"We *all* have strange dreams," Kate said.

Hugh Bladestone was the last of the Council to arrive. He came up through the meadow pond. "Sorry I'm late, people. I wanted to make sure that Bebe and Clarissa were resting well."

"How are they?" Kate asked.

"The same," the doctor reported. "But we're going to have to do something about it, and soon. We just can't let them die."

"That's not going to happen," Ian stated. The doctor, however, did not appear to share Ian's confidence. He looked thoroughly exhausted. In fact, he *looked* as tired as Kate *felt*.

Kate glanced around the meadow. "Too bad Larry can't write any life to this place. Squirrels and birds. Children playing games. Real children, I mean. Life."

"Lately it's been getting quite a lot of life," Lorraine said.

"Who?" Ian asked.

"Klane, for one," Lorraine said. "And Arliss Adamson has been up here a lot."

"That explains why we don't see much of her," Elliot said.

"What do they do up here?" Ian asked.

"Klane wanders about. Adamson mostly watches the gazebo."

"I've given orders for everyone to stay away from the gazebo," Ian said. "That goes for the new people too."

"So far," Lorraine acknowledged, "neither of them has approached the gazebo. They just mill about."

"That's what *I* did," Pablo said. "I hung around here for months. I thought that if the Shunt platform was going to start back up, I wanted to be here."

"I think," Hugh said, his mind on another track entirely, "that we made a major error in not putting the new people in quarantine. It was stupid and careless."

Kate took hold of Ian's left hand and their fingers interlocked like the roots of two trees . . . *like Ian's silver birches . . . Bebe's cactus plants in the desert.*

The meeting had more or less begun, now that they were assembled. No one needed to pound a gavel to make things official.

"I'll say it again, Hugh," Ian said emphatically. "What's happened is *not* your fault. We had no way of knowing that the System Assembly would send us sick individuals."

"We should have anticipated it," Hugh countered. "At least I should have."

"We played by their rules," Ian said. "We were told to expect new prisoners every three years our time and we were ready to accommodate them. Not one of us has done anything wrong."

"And I double-checked the first scan I made when I Gleaned them," Pablo said. "They weren't harboring anything on the inside or anything on the outside. They were completely clean."

Elliot added, "The supplies in the transfer crates that came down with them have also checked out all right."

"Perhaps it's just something we can't detect," Kate said. "Ten to eleven years have gone by on the Outside. They could have made a pathogen we can't detect. They know our technical abilities down here. We're at their mercy. They can do anything to us they want."

Lorraine looked at Ian. "Is it possible that the System Assembly's gone back to the old blood-atonement policies of the last century? Maybe they now *want* to execute us."

"That's one possibility," Ian admitted.

"But why would they offer parole to some of us?" Kate asked.

"Perhaps because they can still use you," Ian said. "At the very least they don't waste good food."

"That's an awful way of putting it," Kate said.

"Well, it's true," Ian countered. "Think about Steve Welch. He *could* speak seven languages and he had a doctorate in computer and machine languages from Stanford University. The System Assembly would be stupid to squander such a valuable resource."

"What about the sunstation itself?" Pablo asked. "Ra's a damn good resource. It's only a question of time before the Renner shield fails and we go *phfft*!"

"I think they do want it back," Ian said.

"Didn't your U.S. cavalry give the Sioux Indians blankets laced with small pox in the 1880s?" Lorraine asked. "You think that's what they're doing here?"

"That's unconscionable," the doctor said.

"Humans have long done the unconscionable," Ian countered. "I don't think that's ever going to change."

"Yes, but the question is, do you think Klane and the others are in on it?" Elliot asked.

Ian shook his head. "Not willingly. I think Klane's a true sociopath. He doesn't care for anybody's interests but his own. Oaks I haven't figured out just yet."

"He's just a little Boy," Kate said.

"A little Boy who can get us killed," Lorraine added. "If we're not careful."

"Oaks has been roaming the entire station," Elliot said. "Maybe he's carrying the agent."

"I think we should assume that they all are carrying the agent, whatever it is, even if they're unaware of it," Ian said.

"That seems the most likely," Hugh said.

Kate, though, felt terribly withdrawn. She lowered her eyes and stared at the grass. "They're going to win. They hold all the aces."

"And they cheat," Pablo added.

"Well, we're not licked yet," Ian said.

"So what's on your mind?" Elliot asked.

"The traces," Ian said. "That's what's on my mind. I don't think the Screws ever intended for us to learn about them."

"It was an accident we found them at all," the doctor admitted. "Blind, dumb luck."

"Dumb or not," Ian said, "I think we can use them to our advantage."

"How?" Hugh asked.

"Let's put aside who might have invented them, because I haven't figured that one out myself. Let's look instead at what they're supposed to do. Klane said they're intelligence *augments* and Whitehall said they're intelligence *enhancers*, which seems to me to be the same thing."

"Okay," Elliot said. "So what do we do?"

"We rebuild them."

They stared at Hutchings, even Kate. Ian continued. "What we have in our heads now, according to Whitehall, are the anchoring templates. So I say we reconstruct them. I say we build directly onto those templates and see if we can *re*commission the traces."

"You mean you want to make us smarter?" Elliot asked.

"That, if that's what they're for," Ian said. "I'm more interested in getting our memories back."

"You think we can get them back?" Elliot asked.

Ian nodded. "And whatever advanced cognitive abilities come with them."

"So you *do* think you invented the traces," Elliot said.

"Hell, I don't know. Nowdays a college senior can make any of a hundred different nanocomponents at any decent university."

"What you're proposing is risky, Ian," Hugh said. "Not only is our amnesia a mystery to us, so are the traces themselves."

"One might have to do with the other," Ian argued. "We won't know until we start looking into it."

The doctor nodded slowly. "It is possible that a decommissioned trace could cause epilepsy or ana-phylactic shock, if the brain had gotten used to a full trace."

"So what can we do?" Kate asked. *We.* How much longer would she be using that term?

Ian said, "If the traces *are* intelligence enhancers, then we should do everything we can to reconstitute them. With our combined knowledge we could even be able to figure out what these seizures are and how to deal with them. Maybe the *lack* of the traces is the cause of the seizures. Who knows? We won't know until we start digging around."

"In the meantime, what do you want to do about the new people?" Lorraine asked.

"We'll leave them out of the loop for the time being," Ian said. "We don't know yet what their role in this is. Besides, we're a little ahead of the game with the System Assembly and that's an edge I want to keep."

"What do you mean that we're ahead of the game?" Elliot asked.

Ian rose to his feet. Kate rarely saw him this ex-cited. "I've been trying to find a biotech solution to our amnesia for some time. I've managed to achieve some minor processing enhancements related to elec-trolytic functions in the limbic system in my own brain."

"What?" Hugh said.

"So far, all they do is keep me awake for long periods of time. But now that I've seen the anchoring templates, I think I know what's behind our memory loss."

"Wait a minute. You've been experimenting on *yourself*?" Hugh said.

"Yes. Anyway, I've—"

"How long have you been doing this?" the doctor asked. He also rose to his feet.

"About a year, year and a half." Ian waved away the doctor's concern. "Look, we have something specific to target now. One thing we can do is analyze the different permutations of the traces in each one of our brains. If the computer can construct a composite, we might be able to see where we can build upon the anchoring platforms."

Ian paced back and forth. Kate yearned for a fraction of his enthusiasm and energy. Even a bit of his anger would have fueled her.

He said: "In fact, I've got some of Pablo's boys down in my laboratory right now."

"I wanted to ask you about that," Pablo started, gesturing with the gizmo in his hand. "And this thing here—"

Suddenly, Kate felt the meadow rise from underneath them. It was a definite swell and it caused Ian to lurch forward suddenly.

"Whoa!" he said. "What was that?"

"What was—?" Pablo started.

"I felt it, too," the doctor said, his hands out for balance.

The earth moved beneath their feet and, this time, they all felt it.

"Something's happening to the ship!" Lorraine said.

"That feels like the Anchor!" Pablo said.

The meadow beneath their feet seemed to rise then sink as if they were a cork on an ocean swell.

Kate jumped up and held onto Ian. "Oh, my God," she said. "Oh, my God!"

Elliot took hold of Lorraine as a spin of vertigo filled the stomachs of the Meadow Council.

Then, without any further ado, the storm overhead ceased, the clouds disappeared, and the lights went out.

"Ian!" Kate said. "That was the Anchor! They've dropped the Anchor! It's happening! *It's happening!*"

23

The meadow became deathly still. However, the red terrors of the sun didn't come crashing in on them. At least not yet.

"We've still got our internal gravity," Ramirez noted in the darkness. "That's a good sign."

"Either auxiliary power switched on or main power didn't entirely go out," Shoemaker said holding Lorraine close to his side.

Hutchings found the main meadow lift, their small "pond", but it did not respond to his pressuring of the lock hidden in the grass.

"Main lift's out," Hutchings told them. "We'll have to climb down. There's a secondary maintenance tunnel approximately forty feet from where I'm standing. We'll take that."

"I can't see a thing," the doctor said loudly.

"Follow me, then. I'll make as much noise as possible. I know exactly where it is."

However, Ramirez, who had been rummaging through his various utility pouches, managed to find a pencil-sized flashlight. This he pulled out and projected a crystal lance of white light across the meadow, pointing the way.

"Where is it? That way?"

"Yes," Hutchings said. "It's over there. In those ferns."

Ramirez's powerful beam cut a clear path to the nearest maintenance tunnel.

Hutchings reached the grate and pulled it back, its hinges complaining. Pablo was the first member of the Meadow Council over the rim.

"What I want to know," Elliot said to Hutchings, "is why we aren't dead yet."

"I hope we live long enough to find out," Hutchings said.

"Did we lose the Anchor?" Kate said.

"I don't know. But *something* happened to the Anchor," Hutchings said. "If it swung sideways a fraction, that might account for the rolling motion we felt."

Below them in the tunnel Ramirez held his flash-beam up so they could see where they were going. The doctor was next over the rim of the tunnel.

Hutchings turned to Lorraine. "I think you'd better stay and watch the gazebo. If anybody comes up here, shoot first and don't ask any questions."

"I don't want to die alone up here, Ian," she said.

Elliot, part way into the tunnel, climbed back out. "Sounds good to me."

"Right," Hutchings said. He swung over the rim and descended into the Underworld.

Auxiliary power in some parts of the sunstation had, indeed, kicked in. Tiny guide lights on the floor of the Underworld met them when they appeared.

So, too, did Doc Tucker and some of the Getaway Team.

They had apparently made quite a lot of noise clambering down, for when they got to the bottom, Tucker was waiting for them amid an inverse forest of artificial stalactites.

Doc Tucker had grayish blond hair and stood in his purple jumpsuit with a slight stoop, a crimp that came from years of pouring over microfiche libraries, looking for a way off the Hot Rock. "Any idea what happened?" Tucker asked.

"We think the Anchor moved, but we're not sure."

Hugh and Pablo moved past Hutchings, but Kate lingered. Tucker held Hutchings back. "We've got something to show you."

"What?"

"Alan!" Doc Tucker called out to a figure at the other end of the hallway. "Bring it."

Alan Holly, another purple-clad Getaway, came hustling forth with several sheets of paper in his hand. "You might want to look at this, Ian," Holly told him.

"Can it wait? I'm in a bit of a hurry."

Doc Tucker pointed. "We think it's important."

The sheets were scrawled with music notation, computer-generated.

"Okay," Hutchings said. "What's it mean?"

Holly told him. "I sifted through the background static of the Councilor's message, running it through a stochastic static-elimination program. It's definitely music."

"Are you sure?"

"It's some sort of serial composition with repetitive

motifs, rhythmic overlaps, and extended phase-shifts. It's music, not transmission details gone bad."

"Why would they send us music?" Hutchings asked. "Were they listening to it in the background?"

Holly shrugged. "I can't say, but if they were, it'd make sense. This music is depressing as hell. Makes you homesick. At least it made me homesick."

Hutchings handed the script back to Holly. "Can you orchestrate this through your computer? Something simple?"

"We were doing that when the lights went out," Holly said.

"When you get it, I want to hear it."

"If we don't die first," Holly remarked.

"We're working on that."

Hutchings reached the primary tunnel where Kate waited. Pablo and the doctor had already disappeared into it.

"Kate," he said, holding her back for a second. "What's in the Suncup?"

"A load of plasma."

"How much?"

"Last I checked, about twenty tons, compressed."

"It's still hot?"

"Ten-thousand degrees Kelvin. Why?"

"We may have to use it to run a secondary power system and reroute it into the main grid if Larry can't bring the rest of the station on-line. See if you can set that up."

"What about you?" she asked. "What are you going to do?"

"I want to check something first."

He started to leave. "Wait!" she said.

With her feet perched on the top rung of the shaft, Kate grabbed the front of Ian's jumpsuit. She pulled him close and kissed him hard. "See you in the next life," she breathed.

"We're not through with this one yet," he said. With that, Hutchings spun around and shot past the huddled Getaways, running in the direction opposite the maintenance tunnel.

Guided only by the running lights along the floor and dodging the artificial stalactites, Hutchings found his spook hole. Hutchings long ago had programmed the spook hole's system to switch over to auxiliary, if, as was the case at hand, the power ever failed.

The door opened at his command and he stepped into empty air. "Brains!" he barked.

Hutchings plunged downward with dizzying speed and was extruded into the main corridor of Level G. His friends climbing the maintenance tunnel upstairs had yet to traverse even a quarter of the distance he had just traveled.

In the Brains, Hutchings found their computer wizard sitting at his console before the Big Board, fingers dancing over the keyboard like those of a concert pianist performing an impossible work: *Murder Melody for Three Hands. . .the Death Sonata in G.*

"What happened?" Hutchings demanded.

"Suncup," Voorhees said. "There was a full-system overload caused by one of the Suncup's backup systems. When the Man tried to compensate for it, several systems—Environmentals, the com system, everything—went off-line."

"Are we going to Pop?"

"Not if those people in the Suncup stop farting around with their system."

"Have you tried talking to them?"

"The coms are down and I can't leave the console here. Otherwise, I would've run down there myself."

"Kate's on her way there now."

"What about Engineer Bakondi. Is Sheila on duty?"

"I don't know. Why?"

"Because I can't imagine her doing anything this colossally stupid."

"Then it probably wasn't her. Pablo thinks the Anchor moved. Did it?"

"Yes," Voorhees admitted.

"Why?"

"*Why?* I want to know *how*," Voorhees said. "Nobody's ever been able to get the Anchor to move, and we've tried."

"What's its status now?"

"It appears to have stabilized in a new position."

"How much did it move?"

"It rose about twelve feet—which is virtually nothing compared to the tether's half-mile length. But it was enough."

"All right then," Hutchings said, breathing a bit easier. "First things first. Make sure all our extra power goes back into the Renner systems. Without the Renner shield we're dead. Everything else comes second."

"Unless we lose *all* power."

"Let's try not to think about that right now."

Hutchings left the Brains and returned to the spook

hole, heading, this time, for the Suncup another two levels below.

When he emerged onto the Suncup level, he found a scuffle in progress in the corridor. Several Suncup techs were wrestling with Dylan Oaks. Matt White stood off to one side. From his expression, Hutchings could tell that the little Boy knew that he was in a hell of a lot of trouble.

Hutchings dove into the pile of grappling bodies and started tossing people aside. He pulled Oaks out by the scruff of his neck. Oaks, in turn, swung his fists at him, but his arms were too short to connect.

"Lemme go!" he yelled. "Put me down!"

Hutchings then grabbed Matt White and dragged them both into main operating center of the Suncup where two engineers were frantically working at their monitoring station.

"What did they do?" Hutchings asked Engineer Bakondi.

Bakondi was a light-complected, frizzy redhead who was passionate about everything she did or said. She said, "Those little shits came in here and wanted to play with the station holograms. They said that they couldn't bring up the holograms in the common rooms, so they asked to use our secondary station."

Bakondi pointed to a separate computer room visible through a glass partition. "So, like an idiot, I said they could. Those little bastards almost evaporated us!"

"It was an accident!" Matt pleaded.

"It *wasn't* an accident!" Bakondi shouted, apoplectic with rage. "You tried to override the Man from back there! You could have killed us all!"

Hutchings's hand was like a steel clamp on Matt's shoulder. "I *told* you not to fool with *any* of the sunstation's programs!"

White squirmed in Hutchings's powerful grip. "You said I had to stay out of the Brains. You didn't say I couldn't play in the Suncup!"

"No one *plays* in the Suncup! This area is for Grown-ups only!"

"Dylan said I could."

"Have you lost your mind?" Hutchings said. "He can't give you permission to do *anything*! Who let you out of your room?"

"Dylan."

At that point Kate appeared from the maintenance tunnel. She slid into her chair at the control board beside engineer Bakondi. "Tell me what happened," Kate said.

Bakondi said, "Those two pulled up the hologram of the sunstation on the console back there. Somehow they got access to a sector in the Man and started 'exploring'. But whatever it was they tried to do, they needed a massive amount of processing memory. The Man had to halt all nonessential programming in order to give them the necessary RAM."

"How much memory did they divert from the Man?" Kate asked.

"About eighty gigs."

"*Eighty gigabytes?*"

"They pulled so much processing power that nearly all the systems in the free zones shut down. We lost seventy-three percent of processing ability in the Brains and may have suffered actual hardware damage. We were lucky we kept gravity and auxiliary power."

"What about the Man, down in the Forbidden Zones? What did it do to him?" Hutchings asked.

Kate, who was already making her own systems-check, didn't even look up. She answered for Bakondi. "It appears that they failed to penetrate the Man's locked sectors. But had they accomplished that. . ."

"That would have been the second Vapor Injunction," Hutchings interjected. "That would have been it."

Bakondi added, "We were lucky that the Renner engines never paused and that the main fusion reactor stayed on-line. We're goddamned lucky to be alive, no thanks to those two."

"But I'm a Suncup engineer now," Dylan Oaks insisted. "The Ward Judge said! I can do anything I want in here!"

Hutchings grabbed Oaks and Matt White and knocked their heads together. It made a sound like two pieces of dull wood. Both little Boys fell to the floor, crying.

"*Ian!*" Kate scolded.

"Listen to me, you little barbarian," Hutchings snarled down at Dylan Oaks. "You'll *never* be a Suncup engineer! I don't give a flying fuck what the Ward Judge said! He's not down here. And I'll fucking kill you if you *ever* step inside this room again!"

"And *you*—" Hutchings said, turning to Matt. "You know better than this!"

The Boy's chin trembled. "But Dylan said we could bring up the real flight deck on the computer. You know, the one down in the Forbidden Zone. He said we could put it into Pablo's hologram of the sunstation. Dylan said it was like the one I built in my room. I wanted to *see* it."

"Can it! This entire floor is off-limits to you for-fucking-ever. You understand?"

The Boy nodded tearfully, shaking terribly beneath Hutchings's reproach.

Hutchings stood next to the two women at their consoles. "Was there any damage to the computer in the Brains because of the power drain?"

"We'll have to do a sector by sector analysis," Bakondi said. "Those two had ninety-one systems applications up when the computer went down. All of the applications went down with it."

"Can we rewrite them?" Hutchings asked.

Bakondi nodded but wasn't too happy about it. "It will take us *days*, and that's if we work around the clock."

"We should be dead," Hutchings grumbled.

"Hey, our *atoms* should be dead," she fired back.

"What was that rolling motion we felt?" Hutchings asked.

"The Anchor was automatically adjusted by the Man when the power was transferred from the other systems to keep the Renner engines going," Bakondi said. "It had to adjust to any fluctuations in the inner shell of the shield itself, as it's programmed to do. The atmospheric buffer that surrounds the hull helped. We're lucky we kept it out there."

"That's good news," Hutchings said.

"Not really. When the Renner shield was adjusted

to the shift in the Anchor's position, it threw off the entire monopole's alignment bearing."

The room became quiet except for the whimpering of Matt and Dylan Oaks on the floor. Only the adults had grasped the absolute gravity of Bakondi's last statement.

Hutchings looked to Kate. "Is the com system up?"

Kate checked the board. "It's just gone back on-line."

"Com, open, Voorhees," Hutchings said. "Larry, are you there?"

"So far."

"What's the status with your computer?"

"Busy as hell. I didn't know it could process so fast. Why?"

"Are we going to implode?"

"If the Man breaks down. He's processing at the limit of his abilities right now, trying to get the monopole signal coordinates within the Renner corridor realigned. Did Sheila tell you that it's out of whack?"

"Just now. How far out of alignment are we?"

"Less than a tenth of a degree," Voorhees said.

"But it's enough."

"Damn tootin' it's enough. It's more than enough."

"How long is it going to take to get it realigned?"

"It would be nice if we had Bold Charon *topside to help with a realignment, but we'd have to be able to communicate with the outside to tell the System Assembly where to place* Bold Charon *so we could home in on their signal. But we can't talk to anybody until we get the signal realigned inside the monopole corridor. It's like my Uncle Fudd once said: You can't have your cake and eat it too."*

"Is this 'cake' something we can fix?" Hutchings said.

"You mean is this something I can fix?"

"Yes."

"I'm trying. But I don't like the Man working at this rate. It's processing at ninety-eight percent of its design parameters. It's only a matter of time before he breaks down."

"Will we at least be able to get the parolees off when the time comes?" Hutchings asked. But he already knew the answer.

"No. We have to reestablish an alignment signal and lock to it. Without it, nobody comes, nobody goes."

"That's just great."

"That's not all there is."

"You mean there's more?"

"Unless there's something wrong with my board. But it looks like the Sally is processing only at thirty-two percent of its capacity as well."

"The food processing system?"

"There's been some sort of major scrambling in the algorithmic sequences for much of the matter-translation software."

"Explain that."

"Most of the Sally's resident memory has been erased."

"Can we eat?"

"Not from the programs which have been scrambled. They're gone forever. We might be able to get a few basic proteins and amino acids to come out, but they'll probably taste like shoe leather or glue."

"Don't we have any backup files in the Brains?"

"Sort of."

"What do you mean, 'sort of'?"

"Those files are down in the Forbidden Zones. More specifically, they're stored in the Man. And the answer is 'No' to your next question."

"Can you access them?" Hutchings asked anyway.

Voorhees said, *"Not from here. We have to go down there ourselves and take off the systems-locks on every file in the Man. That's assuming that we can rewrite the systems applications for the programs."*

Hutchings clenched his fists and for the first time in his life—at least the life he remembered—he actually felt as if he *could* kill somebody.

Or *two* somebodies.

"We don't need the System Assembly to kill us off," Hutchings said. "We can do it all by ourselves."

24

For the first time since their incarceration, Hutchings feared that a Dark Age might beset them once again. The adult Raians didn't exactly run riot after the unprecedented power outage, but they were rattled. Some of the more unstable adults attempted to storm the gazebo, which Lorraine's deputies continued to guard. One of them waved her concussor at the unruly crew and they wisely backed off.

The unrest was symptomatic of a much broader problem. The events of late had so disrupted the normal sunstation routines that most of the adult Raians were becoming unmanageable. As such, Hutchings had never found himself so busy. He particularly had to reassure the Fiddler crew in his private laboratory. They were scared to death and they didn't think the large stasis chamber they were building for Hutchings would meet with the System Assembly's approval—or the Vapor's, for that matter. It took some efficient coddling by Kristen Barron and Diane Beckwith to convince the Fiddlers that it was all right.

Later that afternoon the Meadow Council gathered

in the infirmary, but not so much because Hutchings had called a meeting. They simply ended up there. The two comatose women—Bebe Wasson and Clarissa Pickerall—were at the heart of the crisis, and each of the responsible adults on the council had gravitated to the nexus of their concern: the new slow-sleep chambers under construction in a separate wing of the infirmary.

The Fiddlers were putting the finishing touches to the second slow-sleep chamber, the one that would house Bebe Wasson. The first chamber, the one built for Lyle MacKenzie, already contained Clarissa Pickerall. The chamber, a semicylindrical affair, had its own internal environment and its own set of Renner generators, one located at the head, the other the foot of the bed. A charcoal-black iridescence surrounded Pickerall: miniature Renner shields which slowed time on the inside to such a degree that, to those on the outside, Pickerall's condition would not worsen. It was the best they could do until they figured out what was wrong with her.

Hutchings stood at the large viewing window, the doctor beside him. "Did the outage affect the power to Pickerall's chamber?" Hutchings asked.

"No," Bladestone reported. "The chamber isn't connected to the station's power grid. Pickerall's effectively on hold for as long as the chamber's internal power lasts."

"How long will that be?" Hutchings asked.

Ramirez, sitting at a long table behind them, sipped a cup of strange-tasting coffee, a product of the broken Sally. "The gigacells can last for three months, our time. But it only takes a tenth of a second to recharge them. To do that, we'd have to lower the Renner shield that surrounds her. But only for a tenth of a second."

Hutchings nodded his approval at this.

Kate walked over to the shielded window and stood next to Hutchings. She had appeared lately to sink further into her melancholy, now that matters had worsened for them all.

"I'll talk to the System Assembly, when I go," she finally said. "I'll tell them about Pickerall and Bebe. And the Sally. They can't deny us—" She broke off for the briefest second—"they can't deny *you* the minimum necessities for survival down here."

Hutchings put his arm around her. "They seem to have done quite a lot in that regard already. We should have had full medical data on the traces, but we don't. We should have had access to all backup files for the food processor, but we don't. I don't think those idiots Up There give a shit about anything but themselves."

The doctor added, "And we don't know what they'll do to you and the others when you go. They might re-erase your minds when you get out."

"I've thought about that," Kate said.

Hutchings faced them. "Well, we've got a day and a half to figure a way out of this situation."

"Which situation?" Ramirez asked. "We've only got about six or seven of them."

"I'm thinking of all of them," Hutchings said.

"Where do we start?" Ramirez asked.

"We can start by trying to gain access to the Man's mainframe and see if we can restore the food software. We can probably do something about the monopole corridor's alignment as well, since the default settings are also in the Man. Of course, once we get there, there's no telling what else we can do. But for the time being, I think we should focus on basic survival priorities—the monopole corridor alignment and the Sally."

Only the soft humming of Clarissa Pickerall's slow-sleep chamber beyond the glass wall could be heard: Everyone there was stunned into a sudden silence by what Hutchings had suggested.

"Hey, man, all that stuff's down in the Forbidden Zones," Ramirez said. "Or have you forgotten that?"

Hutchings said, "It's there along with the main flight compartment, the main fusion reactor, the Renner shield generators, even the Anchor's mooring control facility is down there."

Lorraine Sperry, their cop, leaned forward at the table. "Don't even *think* of it, Ian," she said. "We've got one Vapor Injunction already against us. Even *attempting* to enter the Forbidden Zone is an injunction in itself. Two Injunctions add up to one big evaporation. I won't let you do it."

Hutchings absently rotated one of his shackles. "What if I told you that we've already *got* two Injunctions? What would you say to that?"

"What was the second Injunction?" Ramirez asked.

"When Plainfield entered the forbidden Zone on S6. Actually, that was the *first* Injunction. But Whitehall said that the parolees' refusal to take the parole Shunt was the *first* Injunction. Any penetration of the zones is *supposed* to evoke an Injunction. That information would have gone up the monopole corridor with Steve Welch. Either Whitehall didn't see it—

which I doubt—or it didn't exist to go up with the Shunt in the first place."

"If that's true," Shoemaker said, "then some Vapor Injunctions might not be injunctions at all."

"For all we know, there might not actually *be* any Vapor Injunctions," Hutchings stated. "The simple fear of doing something wrong, even doing something *accidentally* wrong, is enough to stifle anybody's behavior. It certainly works on the Children. They're scared to death of the Spanker."

"But you yourself *saw* the Vapor," Lorraine said. "He's definitely real, from what you said."

"The Vapor is real enough," Hutchings admitted. "But Vapor Injunctions themselves might not be. Think about it. Larry's computer is constitutionally too busy to be watching us all of the time. Downstairs, the Man has his hands full with the Renner shield and the main fusion reactor that keeps this place going. But the Man isn't so busy that he can't add."

Lorraine then said, "Ian, if the rest of the crew suspects that Vapor Injunctions aren't real, then we're in for a lot of trouble. We'd be courting disaster. It'd be worse than our Dark Age, those first seventy-two hours we got here."

"I agree," Hutchings admitted. "But no one has figured this out except us. Not even the Getaways."

"Still," the doctor said with a sigh of unmasked defeat, "we can't get into the Forbidden Zones, so there's little we can do."

"Actually," Hutchings said, "I think we can."

"How?" Ramirez asked.

"Two of us have already gone into the Forbidden

Zones and come out alive. Well, at least one of us has."

"Who?"

"Klane and Plainfield. They both entered the Zone on S6 and were mostly unaffected. We don't know what later killed Plainfield, but Mr. Klane is still alive, and he's no worse for the experience, as far as I can tell."

"Maybe it hasn't hit him yet," the doctor said. "The repellers in the Zones could affect each one of us differently."

"I don't think Plainfield's death had anything to do with the repelling forces down in the Forbidden Zones."

Ramirez was thinking. "You know, Matt White is absolutely convinced that the piloting facility is located on the floor below and slightly aft of the Suncup. If he even gets a fraction of his memory back he could fly us off the Hot Rock. . ."

Lorraine jumped up. "Stop it, you two!"

"I wasn't thinking that far ahead," Hutchings told Lorraine. "But everything we need is down in the Forbidden Zones. At the very least we'll have access to the Man and Larry can realign the monopole coordinates. Perhaps we *can* leave the sun. I don't know. I *do* know that we've got to realign the monopole transmission signal and we have definitely got to find the backup software for the food processor. We've still got to eat."

"You can't be serious about this," Lorraine stammered.

"Actually, I'm very serious about it."

Elliot was skeptical. "Ian, I'm with Lorraine. It's

too risky, even *if* you've figured out a way for us to get into the Forbidden Zones."

"That was *my* next question," Ramirez said. "How the hell do you plan on getting in there? We've only been trying to get past the repelling force for three years. And we've tried everything."

"Except the one thing we didn't know we had, at least until yesterday."

"And that was—"

"The traces," Hutchings said. "Remember, Klane and Plainfield came out of the Forbidden Zone virtually unscathed. The only thing they had that we didn't were somewhat more articulated traces. Perhaps some aspect of their chemistry blocks the effects of the repeller field on the brain."

"Is this something you remember from having invented them?" Ramirez asked.

Hutchings shook his head. "I'm just working on logic here, working on what I've seen, what *we've* seen."

"Are you suggesting we get Klane to go *back* there?" Elliot said. "I've only known the man for a day, but the one thing I do know about him is that he's not good at taking orders or working on a team."

"I don't think Klane could get any further than he did the last time," Hutchings said. "Remember, he came out with a headache, so that means that he's not immune. Besides, I don't trust him either. I have a better idea. Actually, I have two ideas."

"What are they?" Elliot asked.

"I think the traces are the key to everything. We need to build on them, expand them, put them to practical use."

"What's your second idea?" Ramirez asked.

"The traces surround the primitive parts of the brain, where all the basic human survival instincts are generated. Maybe the repeller forces work on the lower brain exclusively, in order to instill panic or fear."

"Hmmm," Elliot muttered. "Then how do we go about pulling this off?"

"I think that we should find out what the traces are made of, then process them into a metal alloy that can be painted onto environment suits. My idea is to walk into the Forbidden Zones protected by the alloy, the same way Klane's brain was protected by the traces' anchoring template."

"Ian, no," said the doctor gravely.

"Hugh, we know that Pablo's Gleaner can easily absorb and analyze the traces. That won't tell us what the traces can do, but it will tell us what they're made of. That's all we need."

"But how are we going to generate the alloy?" Pablo said. "The only metals the Sally generates are those that constitute nutrients in food. It would take us months to develop the programs that would be required to produce the amount of alloy you'd need."

"Not the Sally," Hutchings told them. "The Suncup. It can process a wide range of alloys. *You* figure out what the traces are made of, then Kate will manufacture it. You can then apply it to the E-suits. *That* will only take a few hours, at best."

Bladestone then said, "That means I'll have to do an autopsy on Plainfield."

"You people are out of your bloody minds," Lorraine said.

"Maybe. But it *might* work, Lorraine," Hutchings said. "And that's good enough for me."

The silence was broken only by the occasional clatter of a tool dropped by one of the Fiddlers in the next room.

"We've got to *try*," Hutchings insisted. "Otherwise, we're dead."

The doctor nodded grimly. "I'll tell you this, Ian. If you'd suggested that we do an autopsy on Lyle to get at his trace, I would have refused."

"Lucky for us," Hutchings said, 'we don't have to. They sent us Plainfield. He saved us from having to desecrate our dead."

"I still think you're going to kill us all," Lorraine stated.

"Probably. But I—we—won't go down without a fight."

25

Bladestone, back in his dream, wanders about the lobby of the Ostermann Hotel. Pablo Ramirez and his men have jury-rigged the elevators with independent power systems so they don't have to climb the thirty stories to reach the frozen victims in the hotel. Kate DeWitt and her crew are busy in the subbasement attempting to get the main fusion reactor back on-line so they can transfer a modicum of power to the other hotels along North Michigan Avenue.

He knows that none of this may work. Tiny granules of silver—a blowing insidious dust—seem to be everywhere. Ian Hutchings thinks the dust itself is the problem. Ian may be correct in his assumption. The air of the hotel has a tinge of living alloys—arsenic, iron, iridium. In fact, people seem to be turning into metal.

And it is Bladestone's job to revive them, if he can.

But I'm just an intern, he thinks. *They need more than just an intern. They need an entire medical corps, including all kinds of technical support—not what they've brought in their bags.*

Ian Hutchings, dressed in an arctic parka, comes running up to him. He resembles a giant adventurer in search of polar treasure. He carries one of the new Beatty omniscanners. He points a gloved finger at its readout screen.

"Look at this, Hugh!" Ian says. "The bonding structure can adapt itself to any surface—plastic, metal, wood, you name it. But you should see what it does to human tissue. It seems designed specifically for our chromosome pattern. But it can bond to anything. Carbon-based life-forms, silicon-based forms. Anything!"

Ian's excitement seems out of place here. But then, everything seems out of place here. He is out of place here. He's just out of med school and these people are soldiers.

Ian is still talking. "I found that it creates artificial monoamine oxidase enzymes that seek out only those neurotransmitters in the medulla oblongata. It seems to position itself at either receptacle end and appears to rewrite all neural messages according to its own preferential programming. . . ."

People are running to and fro in the hotel ballroom. Why is everyone carrying guns? he wonders. He has a handgun. Ian has a handgun. . . .

Then he looks closer. These are not guns, real guns. No. These appear to be dart guns. And the darts, he realizes, are filled with medicine. Everyone has them. Everyone but that crazy Eddie Brickman. He's on the roof of the Ostermann with a flamethrower, fighting the Holocene weather. A flamethrower! He said, "Fuck the darts! This'll show those sonsabitches!"

But how can Eddie Brickman be on the roof of the Ostermann Hotel? Didn't Eddie fall into the sun?

"Hugh, we can control it," Ian continues. "We can retard its growth or we can accelerate it. All we have to do is—"

Hugh's mind drifts off. There is so much chaos in the main ballroom of the Ostermann Hotel that he has forgotten why *he* has been called there.

He looks down as if from a great height. A woman lies beneath him on a cot which two medics have set up. She is extraordinarily beautiful. But she is also dead. The snow has gotten to her and he hadn't been able to revive her.

Hugh holds a hypodermic syringe in his right hand, a hand that is trembling. He is too late. The solution in the hypo, a product of Ian's biotech genius, could have undone the damage in the woman's brain, had it been delivered in time. He had been late by just a few minutes. *He* will survive because he has already taken the cure. But the woman before him is gone.

Sadly, she is not the first to succumb, nor will she be the last. She is just another casualty, a statistic, one of perhaps several hundred million human beings.

Cassandra Patrice Tourier Bladestone, however, was the one human being whose survival mattered the most to him.

"Cassie," he says in a soft whisper.

He is too late to save his wife.

"I think I might have killed my wife," the doctor said to Hutchings when he came for him. "I mean, I could have saved her, but I was too late."

"It was just a dream," Hutchings said. "We all have them."

"Criminal negligence. It's common in the medical profession. It had to be something like that," Bladestone said. "An act of carelessness on my part."

"You're not the careless type."

"Then why am I here?"

"You're here because the System Assembly is a bunch of assholes," Hutchings said. "Of all the people on Ra, you're the least capable of criminal negligence. It was just a dream, just your mind diddling with you."

The doctor rubbed his eyes. "Maybe. I did get one message in my dream that I'm sure of, though."

"What was that?"

"My wife's name. Cassie. And I remember that we met at a charity ball. It was at one of the best hotels in Chicago. It snowed like a son of a bitch that night. In the dream, she's there at the hotel and dying and I can't stop her. I had the unshakable conviction that I had killed her."

Hutchings knew the force of dreams. He was also able to recognize the onset of quick-sleep when he saw it. The distant expression locked in the doctor's eyes was that of a bindlestiff-in-the-making: the despair, the hopelessness, the rapturous desire to live in a world of dreams until death finally arrived.

"Perhaps we can make amends for whatever it was you did," Hutchings told him.

"How can anyone make amends for taking a human life?"

"Search me. But I plan on giving it a try and I have a longer way to go than you do. Unfortunately for you," he said, slapping the doctor on the back, "I'm taking you with me."

The doctor managed the ghost of a smile. "Now you're starting to talk the way Lyle did. He had the courage of ten men."

"We have our own reserves of courage," Hutchings told him.

The doctor rose from his desk. He took a deep breath. "So, you really want to do this? You think you can stomach a partial autopsy?"

"I don't think I have any choice."

"Nor do I. Let's get on with it, then."

While the doctor had been sleeping and Hutchings worked in his own private lab, Diane Beckwith and Kristen Barron had managed to convert a long metal table in the infirmary into a workable autopsy tray. It had stainless steel gutters and an efficient drainage system which would funnel blood and other debris immediately into the station's recycling system. This was done to appease the recognition chip in the computer, assuming there really was one. The two women also managed to locate surgical gowns, protective masks and tight-fitting rubber gloves and all sorts of surgical tools, none of which Hugh had had any use for until now.

Hutchings stood at the head of the table and watched as the doctor made several incisions in the back of the old man's skull. Plainfield had been placed face-down on the tray—which was elevated slightly at the upper end—with his head lodged between two padded blocks so the skull wouldn't move beneath the doctor's blade. Plainfield's entire backside was a bluish purple where his body fluids had settled in the twenty-four hours since his death.

The doctor worked carefully, tracing a large rectangular area that went down to the skull's base where it joined the neck. The doctor then cut away the flap of skin, exposing the underlying musculature at the base of the skull. Again, with professional exactness, he sliced through the muscles and tendons that gripped the skull at the neck. Only a small amount of edemic fluid appeared at the touch of the doctor's knife, most of which Diane Beckwith hosed away with a small jet of water.

Kristen Barron then handed the doctor a small, self-powered bone saw, a device cobbled together from odds and ends earlier by the Fiddlers. The doctor applied the saw to Plainfield's exposed skull and began.

Instantly, the air filled with the odor of incinerated bone. Kristen Barron became nauseated and had to leave, but Diane Beckwith was able to hold out, if barely. But even Hutchings was made sick by the odor of cooked bone.

Minutes later, the doctor removed a wedge of skull from Plainfield's head and deposited it in a small pan nearby. Diane Beckwith cleaned the exposed area of Plainfield's lower brain with a gentle fount of water, removing extraneous fluids and chips of bone.

"This is interesting," the doctor muttered after a moment's inspection.

"What's interesting?" Hutchings asked.

"That piece of skull I just removed came away with some difficulty. At death, cerebrospinal fluid pools in the lower skull. But here, there's very little of it. The trace apparently is grown through the cerebrospinal reservoir between the brain and the skull, adhering directly to the bone of the skull. It's unaffected by any edemic breakdown of brain-tissue fluids. It's as if it belonged there."

"Did you damage the trace any when you pulled the skull back?" Hutchings asked.

"Partly, yes. Here. Take a look."

Hutchings leaned over. The exposed window to the dead man's brain revealed the usual striations of the cerebellum. However, threading the horizontal fissures of the cerebellum were spidery filigrees of staggering complexity. The copper-blue and silver-gold arabesques clung to the crevices of the old man's brain and were clearly, Hutchings had to admit, a brilliant technological achievement, regardless of who had invented them.

"Miniature circuitry," Hutchings said. "And if these pathways are visible to the naked eye, then there could be all sorts of biotech machines in there. The natural electricity in the brain would be more than enough to power them, particularly if the molecules weren't all that large."

"Yes, but there's more metal present here than is healthy for the human brain," Bladestone said. "Something allows its chemistry to coexist without the brain absorbing any metallic poisons that might leach off."

"Unless the trace is made of metal alloys that are biochemically neutral," Hutchings said.

"Yes, but how did they get *in* there?" Diane Beckwith asked. "I don't see how they could do that."

"Klane said they were grown," Hutchings remarked.

The doctor's brow furrowed in thought. "The only

way that can happen is if they accumulate in vascular deposits that settle in the dura mater membrane that surrounds the brain. Once the deposits have a toe-hold, they could send biotech components out from there. They could move quite easily from the dura mater to the transverse sinus area at the back of the brain."

The doctor looked up at Hutchings. "If you dreamed this up, you're a genius."

"Let's save the parades for later," Hutchings said. "We'd better get Pablo in here before exposure to the air compromises the trace."

"Right," the doctor responded.

Ramirez had been waiting in the outer room with his Gleaner, having declined a ringside seat for the autopsy. He was not the bravest of men when it came to dissection, human or otherwise.

Ramirez walked in, this time wearing a hooded E-suit. He held his Gleaner ready.

"Here it is," Hutchings said, indicating Plainfield's exposed brain.

"Jesus," Ramirez said, peering in. "It *does* look like a tattoo."

"Can you Glean it? That's all that matters."

"Absolutely."

Ramirez engaged the device, its flat plate glowing slightly inches from the exposed portion of Plainfield's brain. Ghostly wisps of dissolution vapor rose from the target area as the trace disintegrated and was pulled atom by atom into the small containment tank strapped to the Fiddler's back. Every bit of trace exposed to the Gleaner's transformative field disappeared, ignoring, as it was programmed to do, the crenelations of the cerebellum, leaving even the fleshy bits of the brain untouched.

However, with the trace stripped away, the exposed section of Plainfield's brain revealed a severely traumatized surface area. It resembled something like badly spoiled meat.

"Man," Pablo said. He switched his Gleaner off. "It looks like once the traces are in, they're not to be messed with."

"If that's true," Diane Beckwich countered, "then how can they be decommissioned without damaging the brain?"

"I would say that the decommissioning must involve some process other than reducing them in size," Hutchings said.

"But ours *are* reduced in size *and* decommissioned," the doctor said. "At least according to Councilor Whitehall."

"I'm betting our amnesia is due to the decommissioning process itself," Hutchings said. "Or some other aspect of the trace physiology. This is going to be very tricky."

"And very dangerous," Bladestone said. "Particularly if what you have in mind doesn't work."

"We'll worry about that later," Hutchings said. "Right now, I want to see what these things are made of. Pablo?"

"Right," the Fiddler said.

26

Trembling and cold to her very bones, Kate starts to climb the gently sloping ridge behind her family's ranch house. Each breath she takes seems to suspend the molecules of her body, slowing down their nuclear forces. Even the sheepskin coat she wears, including the Acme thermal boots on her feet and the hot-wired gloves on her hands, are unable to ward off the chill.

The guard fences give off a gentle hum that touches her heart. It's an odd, spectral music—if it *is* music—and she yearns terribly to go home, back to where the skies are still blue and the weather always invigorating.

But now she is home.

Or she is *dreaming* of home?

Either way, the music of the fences makes her forget. Instead, she turns to the ridge behind her family's compound, beyond which are the panicked horses with the incredible saddles.

Yes, she decides, this is a dream. The one dream she has always had.

But something has changed in it. The horses are quiet now. The thunder of their hooves has ceased and in their place has settled a deathless calm.

The song of the fences compels her forward. All she can hear of the animals on the other side of the ridge is an occasional sputtering snort or whinnying that belies the danger Kate feels is still present.

This is what draws her on. She has to *see* the beasts, to confront their *meaning*.

Kate slogs her way up the ridge. At the top of the ridge is a gigantic cottonwood tree, bereft of leaves. Kate pauses near the tree, to catch her breath.

She is stunned by what she sees on the opposite side of the ridge.

Stretching out across the plain are thousands of horses. Their colors and hues remind her of a patchwork quilt. *A patchwork quilt?* She had once made a patchwork quilt . . . but for the life of her she can't remember when or where.

Kate scrutinizes the dazzling riderless saddles strapped to the backs of the magnificent animals. The studs are polished silver, mother-of-pearl. The embroidery is made of golden wire. Diamonds, emeralds, rubies! The saddles must weigh hundreds of pounds. Add a human rider and that would be far too much for an animal, even a dray horse, to carry.

Yet something is wrong here, Kate realizes. The horses seem to have become mired in the mud. They have sunk down to their knees. Halted by the force of a motion menace so common to dreams, they are unable to free themselves.

Kate knows what to do. She'll grab the bridle of

the nearest animal, and pull him out, hoping the others will follow.

But she discovers that *she* can barely move. Because of the wet snow, the soil has taken on the gluey consistency of gruel. She has sunk several inches into it.

With great difficulty Kate turns around, her boots making obscene sucking sounds. Her plan is to shout back across the barren pasture to her house. It is only a hundred yards away.

To her surprise, however, her family's house is not there any longer. In its place is a strange, Gothic-like structure of arched and pointed crystal, a nightmare cathedral of silver with elongated towers trimmed in gold and ivory. And the house of their immediate neighbors just three hundred yards to the east looks much the same. Beyond it are other unfamiliar structures, the glassy suburb of a phantom city growing like clusters of scrimshaw and crystal across the Wyoming plains.

"*Daddy!*" Kate shouts. "*Daddy!*" But her voice is an empty echo swallowed by the wind.

Kate grabs the communicator at her belt and punches in her family's code. "*Kingston!*" she cries, calling her brother. "*Kingston! Daddy! Are you there? Help!*"

The communicator yields only static. She switches to the emergency band and tries to raise the Department of Public Safety. "*This is Katie DeWitt! Can anybody hear me? I'm stuck in the mud and I can't move my feet!*"

Again, silence. The world seems bereft of human beings. However, she has stopped sinking.

She'll walk back to the ranch house *without* her

boots then. Boots are boots. All she has to do is slide her feet up and out and. . .

But she can't. Her feet seem stuck—and her toes . . . *twinkle.* It seems as if every nerve ending in her feet scintillates with a frizzy life of its own.

This is because her feet are sending out tendrils. Her toes are becoming roots. Or as Bebe would say—*does.*

Kate looks down to where the horses are also mired in the muck. Those beautiful horses . . . *Bebe Wasson's patchwork quilt . . . her does . . .*

The beautiful animals are quiet. Rhomboids, ellipsoids, delta shapes of radiant sunlight glance off the angled surfaces of the jeweled saddles. The sight has a strangely calming effect on her.

Suddenly, the saddles are changing shape. The stirrups reach downward, sink into the earth, the bridles become silver-encrusted vines winding about the horses' necks, winding down to the forelegs, searching for mud within which to take root.

Kate drops her communicator: The mud makes a mouth which swallows it whole.

Her fingers relax to the pull of gravity, reaching down to the rich, nourishing soil. She is no longer afraid. She feels the peaceful breath of sleep surround her and she fades. . . .

Kate jerked awake. It took a massive effort of will to escape the dream, but she forced herself out of her sleep paralysis, the paralysis that was about to send out roots from her toes. She forced herself to return to the real world.

However, rather than finding herself in her temporary quarters near the infirmary or even in with the little Girls, Kate opened her eyes to the floor of the Suncup facility. She had apparently been sitting at the main console of the Suncup when she had been taken by quick-sleep. She vaguely remembered that Alan Holly, at Ian's request, had given her a digitally cleaned-up recording of the strange music which came from Councilor Whitehall's message. Ian wanted as much input on it as he could get from anyone on the sunstation willing to listen to it. So Kate ran the recording through her own board in the 'cup facility.

That was the last she could remember.

However, the same episode of narcolepsy had also hit her assistant, Sheila Bakondi. Sheila lay on the facility floor completely rigid—like a tree ready for planting.

Kate sat up. Her mouth tasted like copper. It was as if she'd been chewing pennies for eight hours. She wanted to spit but didn't even have the saliva for it.

Kate checked the monitor console. Its indicator lights told her that all was well with the Suncup itself. The 'cup had taken a gulp of furious plasma into a separate fusion chamber and had processed it into the new alloy Pablo Ramirez had requested for the environment suits. *For the expedition...*

"This isn't right," Kate said. She and her assistant had blacked out at virtually the same instant. And that didn't seem possible.

She tried to recall her last moment of consciousness. Pablo had successfully determined the chemistry of the trace alloy which he had Gleaned from Edward Plainfield's brain. Ian, meanwhile, had sequestered himself in his own lab where he had set the two Bobs—Peters and Cady—to a special task which he wanted kept secret for the time being. Ian seemed unusually distracted. Not even Pablo knew what Ian was doing with his Fiddlers.

Then Alan Holly sent down his brief recording of the peculiar background sounds he had gleaned from Councilor Whitehall's harangue. Shortly after that, she and her assistant had collapsed and two hours had gone by. The alloy Ian requested had already cooled. There were gallons of it now, more than enough for several E-suits.

And Kate's toes *still* felt as if they wanted to send out roots, just like Bebe's big silver cactuses.

"Sheila, wake up," Kate said, kneeling at her assistant's side.

The redheaded engineer did not respond. Kate felt Sheila's forehead, which was alarmingly warm.

Sheila's lips, she then noticed, appeared to sparkle, as if just before she went under she had put on a new kind of lipstick, one that glittered with particles of silver. Which was, in itself, odd. Sheila did not use lipstick. In fact, no woman on Ra used lipstick. That, and all the other luxuries of the fashion world were not among their provisions on the sunstation. Theirs was a prison facility, not a beauty shop.

It was the silver dust, however, that caught Kate's attention. It was not only on Sheila's lips, it seemed everywhere about them: on the floor, the chairs, the console itself. And some of it had even gotten into her mouth. That was where the metallic taste had come from.

Then she thought: *Wouldn't the air filters have caught the dust and removed it from the ship's breathable atmosphere?*

Perhaps not. The partial power outage engendered by Dylan Oaks and Matt White had temporarily shut down the filtration system. They still had air, but it wasn't being cleaned as efficiently.

But *where* would the silver dust have come from?

Kate could only think of one other possibility. The little Girls had come into the Suncup facility to play while she and Engineer Bakondi lay unconscious. The Girls must have set up their crayons and paper and glue and scissors and Barbies and ponies and perhaps a Tonka or two, and had a wonderful time amusing themselves with their toys.

Except that such a scenario made no sense either. Lisa Anderson, had she been among them, would have tried to awaken Kate and Sheila. If she couldn't have, she would have been smart enough to have summoned a Grown-up.

But who would have *allowed* the little Girls into the Suncup in the first place? She would never have, nor would Sheila. Ian's new orders. No Children on the Suncup floor. *Ever.*

Then Kate had an odd thought and it came tied to a memory of her own childhood: the glitter. It was common enough when she was a little girl in kindergarten, but it was a commodity the little Girls on Ra did *not* have. Most of their toys were products of the inventive genius of the Fiddlers. Paper, scissors, glue, crayons, and clay, yes. Glitter, no.

The awful taste of copper *glitter* filled Kate's mouth. "Com, open, Ian," she said, feeling woozy.

Ian's voice, however, was not forthcoming.

"Com, open, Elliot," she then said.

"Right here, Kate. Fire away."

She suddenly felt the need of more sleep. Years of it.

"Ian isn't answering his com. I just called him."

"*He's in his lab. He said he's pulling a rabbit out of his hat.*"

"What?"

"*That was my reaction. Is there anything I can help you with?*"

"Elliot, it's happening."

"*What's happening?*"

"Whatever it was that got Clarissa and Bebe. It got both Sheila and me. Sheila's still unconscious. I can't get her to wake up."

Kate ran her tongue across her teeth. They felt like nodules of chromium and her saliva tasted like liquid mercury.

It was as if she was one of her dream-horses, teething impatiently on a bit made of metal. And the taste was ghastly.

"*I'll get Hugh. We'll be right there.*"

"It's too late for that," she said.

She then fell away from the control board and collapsed next to her second-in-command, the two of them having now officially become bindlestiffs.

27

A *man who was scared.* That's what Elliot Shoe-maker considered himself, if he was being totally forthright. The shake-up in the meadow had started it, and now events appeared to be snowballing.

At receiving Kate's call, the normally confident vice-administrator raced from the Brains, leaving the station in the control of an exhausted Larry Voorhees whose own stability was in doubt. Shoemaker desperately wanted Hutchings back in charge and their lives back to normal—whatever *that* meant.

What troubled Shoemaker more than anything was Hutchings's sudden inaccessibility. Ian was *never* unavailable, to anyone, for any reason, regardless of where he happened to be or what he happened to be doing. If they lost Hutchings through some misfortune or through the agency of the new illness, that would legally—at least by their own unspoken charter—place Shoemaker as head. And Shoemaker knew that he could never fill Hutchings's boots. In fact, if that ever happened they were as good as lost.

Shoemaker went directly to Hutchings's quarters. To his surprise, he found the two Bobs putting the finishing touches to the base of a platform that took up most of the space in the lab. The platform itself supported what appeared to be a gauzy, black cylinder approximately fifteen feet wide and about eight feet in height.

"Where's Ian?" Shoemaker asked beetle-browed Bob Cady. "We've got a problem."

"He's still in there," Cady said, pointing to the black cylinder which Shoemaker recognized now as a Renner force-field. The Fiddlers had evidently built a very large stasis chamber, similar to the ones down in the infirmary which now contained Clarissa Pickerall and Bebe Wasson—only this one contained Ian.

"What's he doing in there?" Shoemaker asked.

"He won't tell us," said Bob Peters, an electric drill snarling in his hand. "We'll tell him you stopped by, though."

But then, the black force-field of the cylinder suddenly vanished, dropping like a veil on a magician's platform.

"Elliot," Hutchings said, stepping down.

On the platform stood an extraordinary array of technical equipment, most of which Elliot recognized as tools of Hutchings's field of expertise—biotechnology. Also on the platform was a fold-up cot, a neatly piled blanket and two pillows. The small Sally and the portable john explained Hutchings's sudden inaccessibility. Just *what* Ian had been doing on the shielded platform, Shoemaker hadn't the slightest idea.

Hutchings looked tired and he also hadn't shaved.

It was either that or Hutchings had decided to start growing a beard—as if he had nothing else to do.

"We just got a call from Kate," Shoemaker said. "She's in the Suncup monitoring room with Engineer Bakondi. They're down."

"Down?"

"Stricken. Kate said that it's the same thing that struck Bebe and Clarissa. At least that's what she thinks."

Hutchings muttered a curse to himself. "Did you summon Hugh?"

"Right after I tried contacting you. He's there now."

Shoemaker had never seen Hutchings so preoccupied. It rather alarmed him. "Ian?" he asked.

Hutchings held up a finger. "Just a second." He directed the two Bobs over to his side. "You guys. Come here."

Hutchings retrieved two small cylinders from a table on the platform. He gave each of the cylinders—they had peculiar nozzles attached to their tops—to the two Bobs.

"The first goes to level six," he said. "The second goes to the infirmary. The Getaways should probably come next. Then the common rooms, the Fiddlers' Den. You know what to do with the others."

Only then did Shoemaker notice that about a dozen of the small canisters, each about five inches long and an inch or so wide, were standing on a counter in the small laboratory that had been enclosed between the two large Renner-shield plates.

"How do they work?" Peters asked.

Hutchings held one of the canisters and rotated a

small black plastic wheel attached to the nozzle. A hissing sound emerged from the canister and a cloud of mist launched itself into the air around them.

"Whoa!" Shoemaker said, stepping back reflexively, batting away the ghostly fog. The mist quickly filled the laboratory and Bob Cady sneezed explosively.

"Sorry," Hutchings said. "Pablo made them with hair triggers."

Shoemaker couldn't detect any particular odor in the mist and it faded away within seconds.

"Give this small wheel a twist—" Hutchings indicated the black plastic wheel at the top of the canister in his hand—"Then place them where I told you. It's absolutely important that you do this the way I instructed. You got that?"

"What about the Vapor?" Cady asked. "What are we going to do if the Vapor comes out and gets us?"

"You guys won't be going anywhere we haven't gone before. Eddie crawled throughout the ventilation system and the Vapor didn't come out and get him," Hutchings said. "When you set these in place, come back for the rest."

Hutchings indicated the remaining canisters on the table behind them.

The two Bobs seemed doubtful, unsure of their ability to do what Ian had asked of them.

"Go on," Hutchings said. "You'll be fine. If you run into anybody, don't tell them what you're doing. Just be casual about it. You'll be all right."

The two Bobs left the room, off on their mysterious mission.

Shoemaker faced Hutchings. "You want to tell me what's going on?"

"I'm not all that sure myself," Hutchings said. "But I'm beginning to get an idea."

"What are those things for?" Shoemaker asked, pointing to the remaining canisters.

"Insurance."

"What kind of insurance?"

"Life insurance."

"So when was the last time you shaved?"

"A couple of days ago, I think," Hutchings said, as he attached several of the canisters to his utility belt.

"A couple of *days*?"

"I'll tell you about it later," Hutchings said. "Let's go see about Kate. This worries me."

While Shoemaker had been hunting down Hutchings, the doctor and his assistants had gone to the Suncup facility to see about Kate and Engineer Bakondi. As it developed, two other Suncup engineers had arrived at the same time. They were thus present to help Bladestone load the two stricken women onto waiting hover gurneys. The doctor, in turn, contacted Shoemaker en route to the infirmary where everyone then met.

The infirmary now looked like a war zone. Cots had been set up for Kate and Engineer Bakondi in a newly sectioned ward, with tools and other equipment scattered around for the Fiddlers who were hard at work constructing two more slow-sleep chambers.

The doctor kept everyone out of the ward, leaving Diane Beckwith and Kristen Barron with the sick women, trying to make them more comfortable. Blade-stone then sealed the door and turned to the two relief Suncups who had helped with the rescue.

The first engineer was a Cornell University computer graduate, Paul Schoenberger, and the other was a metallurgist named Ken Howells. Mentally, they were in their late twenties—both only remembered the fledgling academic careers which they had back on Earth—yet they were biologically in their forties.

"Did you notice anything out of the ordinary when you found them?" Bladestone asked.

Schoenberger, a wisp of a man who wore anachronistic wire-rimmed glasses and had the demeanor of a Proustian recluse, said, "Not a thing. They were both on the floor when we found them."

"Was there anyone else in the facility?" Hutchings asked. "Or did you pass anyone in the halls?"

Ken Howells, a man who resembled an Arkansas farmer more than a scientist, responded. "Just the two stiffs in their flops outside the main lift. But they've been there for days."

"What about the Suncup itself?" Hutchings then asked. "Was there any damage to the computer or any of its program settings?"

"That was the first thing we checked," Howells said. "Everything's normal. The plasma ball's still in suspension and the new alloy is processed and ready for the Fiddlers. It's in the alpha chamber cooling."

The doctor looked through the partition of the door that led to the special ward. He spoke distractedly.

"There were no immediate signs of physical injury

to either of the women. We won't know until we conduct a full examination on them."

"You don't have to. It's the same affliction," Hutchings said. "The symptoms are identical. I just didn't think it would happen to them this soon."

"What are we going to do about Kate?" Shoemaker asked. "Are we going to send her up in this condition? Remember that Whitehall said they'd destroy anybody we sent up who was ill."

Hutchings shook his head. "We can't send anybody up until Larry has realigned the monopole tracking signal. Unless he did that while I was . . . occupied. Did he?"

"Not that I know of," Shoemaker said.

Hutchings removed one of the canisters from his belt and placed it on the room's large table. Shoemaker heard a small hissing coming from the nozzle. No one else seemed to notice.

"I think," Hutchings announced, "that we should assume this thing's very contagious, whatever it is."

"That what's contagious?" Paul Schoenberger asked. "What are you talking about?"

"You mean they've got a disease?" Ken Howells then asked.

The two Suncup engineers hadn't been aware that a mysterious ailment had been striking at their comrades. Even the death of Plainfield had been kept secret from the rest of the sunstation.

"We don't know what it is just yet," Hutchings told them. "But we've still got a little time left."

"Time left for what?" Schoenberger asked.

"Time," the doctor said, "before each one of us

succumbs to quick-sleep and Ra becomes a boat full of bindlestiffs."

"*What?*" Schoenberger said, swallowing heavily.

"That's one of the things we're working on," Hutchings said. "But right now we need you two men to operate the Suncup. Call your usual staff, those you can trust. Then lock yourselves in. You'll be safe in there."

"Safe from what?" Howells asked.

"I'm working on that, too."

Engineer Howells finally had the presence of mind to remark on Hutchings's unkempt appearance. "You look terrible. What in the world have you been doing?"

Hutchings rubbed his bristly jaw. "Working on a way to keep those motherfuckers from killing us."

"What motherfuckers?" Howells asked, completely bewildered.

Hutchings said, "You'd better get going. And remember, keep this thing quiet."

"So what *have* you found out?" the doctor asked when Howells and Schoenberger left.

"A few things," Hutchings said. "Let me show you."

On the infirmary computer Hutchings brought up a file which he had transferred down from his own lab computer. Above the holopedestal appeared the 3-D image of a fully expanded trace, the one that Councilor Whitehall had included in his message. The full trace looked like a tadpole standing on its tail—a tadpole of woven, convoluted metallic threads.

"The most complex part of the trace is centered just under the midbrain," Hutchings said. "I began manipulating the hologram and I noticed that if you systematically remove the outer layers of the trace—" Ian pressed a button, invoking the next stage in the sequence "—you can see that the trace doesn't make actual contact with the thalamus."

Shoemaker then asked, "Didn't Descartes call the thalamus the 'seat of the soul'?"

Hutchings shook his head. "The pituitary. But the thalamus is where all of the mind's cognitive processes take place."

Hutchings pointed to the hologram with a pen. "What I did next was analyze samples of neural fluid from Mr. Plainfield's hippocampus. I found an abnormally low amount of beta-serotonin. I then took a sample from Plainfield's thalamus and there I found no beta-serotonin at all."

The doctor sneezed mightily. Wiping his nose with a handkerchief, he said, "That doesn't sound right. Beta-serotonin is essential for mentation. There are dozens of neurological disorders that would also occur if the serotonin levels are suppressed, such as Alzheimer's disease."

Hutchings agreed. "I think that the traces have a major effect on endorphin production in the brain. If that's the case, then it's entirely possible that intelligence could be enhanced. Exponentially so, depending on the amount of serotonin produced."

He sat back. "This is what I want you to look into, Hugh. I want to know *how* the traces interfere with the thalamus. If a trace can exist in the lower brain without any sort of biochemical reaction, serotonin delivery would be much more efficient."

"A superconductivity of the brain?" Shoemaker asked.

Hutchings nodded. "Yes. I do know that the traces are so brilliantly engineered that their growth, or their reduction for that matter, is very rapid."

"You sound like you know what the traces really do," Shoemaker said.

"I have an idea," Hutchings said. "But I want to see what Hugh comes up with. I want to be absolutely sure that these things are what I think they are."

"That means digging into Plainfield's head again," the doctor said.

"One last time, anyway."

Hugh Bladestone stared through the window into the room with the new chambers. "We're going to need more equipment. And more time. A lot more time."

A commotion in the outer area of the infirmary caught their attention just then. Feet shuffled; a door opened.

They turned to see a gathering at the entrance to the infirmary. Paul Schoenberger was helping Newsome Klane carry in a barely conscious Rhonda Barrie. Engineer Howells trailed behind them. They had apparently met Klane emerging from the main lift and had rushed to help.

"What happened?" the doctor asked, rushing over.

"I thought I'd call your attention to Ms. Barrie's condition," Klane said in his usual laconic manner. "I found her in the common room."

They immediately took the still barely conscious Barrie into the wing where Kate and Engineer Bakondi now lay.

"I didn't think it . . . would happen," Barrie said weakly, catching Hutchings's eye.

"You didn't think what would happen?" the doctor asked.

The woman's eyelids fluttered like two dying butterflies. They finally closed.

Hutchings turned to Shoemaker. "Elliot, I think we'd better get every one of the new people down here. Fast."

"Right," Shoemaker said, prepared to leave, *glad* to leave on any excuse.

"I'm afraid you'll have a hard time getting Mr. Oaks to come down here with you," Klane said.

"Why is that?" Shoemaker asked the tall man.

"He's gone exploring."

"He's gone *exploring*?" Hutchings asked.

"That is what he told me. He had a coil of rope and a belt of those tools your Fiddlers carry with them. He said he wanted to see more of the sunstation."

"*Where* has he gone exploring?" Shoemaker asked, stepping forward. "Did he tell you?"

"I'm afraid not."

Hutchings said to Shoemaker, "Get Lorraine and her people on this. We've got to find him."

Klane then sniffed a couple of times, making a face. He looked at Hutchings. "I take it you haven't fixed the ventilation system yet. There is something in the air that is fairly unpleasant, at least to my nose."

"We're working on it," Hutchings said. He then turned to Shoemaker and said, "Let's go find Mr. Oaks before he kills us all."

"Right," Shoemaker said.

28

Hutchings lingered only long enough in the infirmary to see that Kate was made as comfortable as possible. That she had succumbed to the strange sickness did not really come as much of a surprise, though it pained him that there was nothing more he could do about her condition. His greater suspicion was that, eventually, the malaise would catch up with the rest of them, and that concerned him more.

This business of Dylan Oaks at large in the facility was another matter, however. Oaks had decided not to wear his parry, despite his initial fondness for the bracelet, and was therefore untraceable by the location-chip fused into its circuitry. Moreover, Oaks had not responded to a com summons by Hutchings—no surprise there—or from one by Klane, which *did* surprise him. A floor-by-floor search of the free zones therefore became necessary.

They first searched the ventilator and maintenance shaft networks that ran both horizontally and vertically through the sunstation. Hutchings was particularly bothered by the fact that Oaks, according to Klane, had climbing rope with him. The rope, the only rope they had, once belonged to Eddie Brickman and since Eddie's death, had been kept in storage in the Fiddlers' Den. Oaks also had a Fiddlers' equipment belt and all the goodies that went with it: a small, but powerful acetylene torch and several other metal-cutting, -bolting, -screwing or -unscrewing tools. And because of Oaks's physical size, the little man could probably crawl anywhere the duct system led in the free zones.

But they could not find him. Lorraine Sperry's deputies—there were five of them—also contributed to the search. All to no avail. Even Lorraine's Tonka corps was unable to locate Oaks. Their efforts had been hampered somewhat by Hutchings's reluctance to call a stationwide alert and get the functional members of Ra in on the task. He thought that such an announcement might lead to panic. However, random inquiries indicated that Oaks had not been seen recently by anyone.

Elliot, Lorraine, and Newsome Klane gathered in the Brains later when Hutchings called a cessation to the search. Only the Tonkas were kept on the job. The Grown-ups had to regroup and consider what they were going to do next.

Larry Voorhees, who should have been relieved of duty several shifts ago, had remained at his console and Big Board to aid in the effort. Mere exhaustion wasn't a good enough excuse for him to abandon his post when his talents were needed.

"One thing's for sure," the lanky Oklahoman said. "He didn't ride the Shunt. There's nothing here on my board that shows that the gazebo's been activated. But, hell, even if he'd gotten off the station without us knowing about it, he'd be in space now, just a string of a few billion atoms riding the monopole corridor, heading for Mercury."

"Well," Hutchings said slowly. "There's only one other place he could be."

"Where?" Lorraine asked.

"He's probably outside, climbing around on the hull."

Lorraine and Elliot spoke at the same time. *"What?"*

Even Klane was taken aback. "You must be joking," the tall man remarked.

"Not this time."

"How could he get outside the ship?" Klane asked.

"The same way Lyle, Eddie and I got out two years ago," Hutchings said.

Larry Voorhees leaned over his console and began typing commands. "We should have thought of that first thing."

There were four access ports to the outer hull located in the upper part of the sunstation. There were probably four others located in the bottom half of the vessel for servicing access when it was in dock. That, however, was only conjecture, since none of them knew what the bottom part of the sunstation looked like. The bottom half was the Forbidden Zone.

Voorhees whistled. "Wouldn't you know it."

"Know what?" Shoemaker asked, leaning over.

"When those little Boys diddled with the computer in the Suncup, it looks like they cut out camera four," Voorhees said. "Take a look."

On the Big Board in front of them Voorhees had brought up video screens of the four bulkhead exits. All four cameras appeared functional, all four exits appeared undisturbed. Voorhees, however, did something to his console and the delta camera blanked out.

"What happened?" Shoemaker asked.

Voorhees said, "Delta was taking its video feed from a loop from the beta camera. Delta had been switched off and Oaks must have rerouted the video image from beta back into delta. Looks like we've been hoodwinked."

"Com, open, Passmore," Lorraine said. "Respond."

"Right here, Lorraine," answered Lisa Passmore, the deputy who commanded the Tonka corps.

"Get to the delta exit as fast as you can and report on what you find. Examine the security camera, Eddie Brickman's shrine, the door. Anything. *Everything.*"

"Will do."

Shoemaker added: "It probably wouldn't take much for Oaks to get through the lock and into the outer bulkhead maintenance corridor. At least with the tools he's got."

"That's how Eddie did it," Hutchings said.

"And that's assuming that Oaks isn't really a three-year-old, but a fully capable adult," Lorraine said.

Hutchings looked up at Newsome Klane. "What do you know about this? Did he say anything to you about what he had in mind?"

"Not a word."

Hutchings turned to Voorhees. "What's the air like out there? Is it still breathable?"

Voorhees nodded. "It is. The ambient temperature is holding at eighty degrees Fahrenheit. It's a little warm to go wandering around in, but the atmospheric pressure on the hull is Earth-normal. It's tolerable, better with an E-suit, though."

"We should have pumped the air out when Eddie died," Lorraine stated. "We should have brought the Renner-shield layers flush to the hull and sealed all the free zone exit locks."

"We thought that Eddie might still be alive out there. Remember?" Voorhees said. "That maybe he'd held on and would show up some day with that big, dumbass grin of his on his face."

"It was only human for us to hope he'd make it back," Shoemaker said. "Too bad he didn't. Eddie was a lot of laughs."

"As long as Oaks is away from a computer terminal, I think we're safe," Hutchings told them.

"Unless," Shoemaker added, "he finds a way into the Forbidden Zones from the outside and manages to gain access to the Man from down there somewhere."

"Then we'd have trouble for sure," Voorhees said.

"Oaks would have to be one hell of a mountain climber," Hutchings said. "Remember, I've been out there, and the hull isn't designed for climbing in standard gravities. The way the sunstation is shaped, I don't think Oaks will be able to climb beneath the upper cap, let alone be able to reach the lower maintenance exits."

"Even if he gains access to the ship's engines," Lorraine said, "Oaks will still have to work his way through the repelling force of the Forbidden Zones.

In fact, it might even be worse down there than it is up here."

Hutchings then said, "Well, we don't have time to go chasing after Oaks right now. I think we should stick to our original plan. Put a Tonka at the delta exit, just in case Oaks comes back anytime soon. If he does, we'll nail him."

Klane's brow furrowed. "I must have missed something here. You have a plan?"

"Something else has come up."

"What has come up?"

"Circumstances require that I lead a small expedition into the Forbidden Zones," Hutchings told the man.

"You are being funny again. Am I right?"

Hutchings considered Klane carefully. "Don't think so. We have to get to the Man in order to make a series of repairs. And as soon as possible."

Klane seemed shocked by the very concept. "Do you have to go there physically?"

Hutchings nodded. "Larry can't realign the monopole signal coordinates from here. The guide signal can only be calibrated properly at the main board of the main computer down below. The people who built this place hadn't planned on someone like Dylan Oaks wiping out half of our vital software programs. We have to go down there and make the changes ourselves."

"As it is," Shoemaker told the tall man, "we're damn lucky to still be alive."

Hutchings agreed. "Without the monopole signal in its proper configuration, nobody's coming or going from the sunstation. There won't even be further shipments of alloys from the Suncup. We'll be stuck here forever like a wobbling top with no communication with the outside even possible."

"You're insane to even attempt such a thing," Klane said.

"Not insane," Hutchings confessed. "Desperate, maybe, but not insane."

Shoemaker added, "We also have to find the backup software for the Sally. Otherwise, it's tofu forever. And I *hate* tofu."

Klane took a deep breath. "The clearest solution to all of our problems lies in the amplification of the traces. I think it is evident that the people who put us here do not want us to reactivate them. Exploring the sunstation out of mere curiosity would be a grave misallocation of your efforts."

"It's more than curiosity, Klane," Hutchings said. "If we don't stabilize the station's axis alignment, the Man is going to break down."

"How will the Man break down?"

This was Larry Voorhees's bailiwick. "It's processing at maximum capacity right now, just to keep the station at our present alignment. Remember, the Man also juggles the Renner-shield layers, and that takes up an extraordinary amount of memory and power. Someone's got to go down there, find the backup files and reinstall them before the Man senses burnout and begins shutting down various functions. If one of those functions is the Renner shield, we're cooked. Literally."

Klane's eyes flashed with arctic fury. "Hasn't it become clear to you that we should be working on the traces? Once we get them back to their original dimensions, we can do . . . all of this." Klane gestured at the Big Board. "We'll be smarter. We'll get our memories back *and* our technical competency. We can solve everything from here, once we do that."

Hutchings folded his arms. "Klane, if we don't realign the monopole and get the Man to step down his processing speed, we're going to Pop. This is something we have to do."

Klane's frustration was manifest. "You would be making an enormous mistake."

"Maybe," Hutchings said. "But we're still going to do it."

Klane's long-fingered hand pushed back through his silver-blond hair. However, he caught sight of someone standing in the doorway to the Brains in the outer hall.

"*God's blood!*" Klane erupted.

Klane fell back against Shoemaker, but Elliot caught him and propped him back up. "Easy, there."

In the doorway stood a being entirely in silver. It was Pablo Ramirez. "So what do you think?" he asked.

Ramirez stood in a standard EVA environment suit, which included helmet and breathing apparatus on his back. The E-suit had been sprayed from head to toe in a bright silver alloy that, Hutchings knew, was mostly lithium and titanium, the prominent metals found in the Strathclyde traces.

"This is the first suit," Pablo said. His voice came from a small, external speaker mounted in his collar. "The others will be ready in twenty minutes. It takes that long for the adhesive to bond to the suit itself."

Ramirez crinkled as he walked.

"This is an abomination," Klane swallowed, standing back.

Ramirez approached him and looked up. "We're going to have to make a suit for you, so we'll need a few measurements."

"You are making a suit for *me*?"

"If you're going with us," Hutchings said.

"I am going with you?"

"Why not? I got the idea from you in the first place," Hutchings said.

"You cannot be serious. How did I give you the idea for these monstrous suits?" Klane demanded.

"When you rescued Plainfield from the Forbidden Zone," Hutchings said.

"I don't—'"

Ramirez jumped in. "The trace in your head is somewhat larger than the traces in ours and we think it helped you survive the Zone. You only got a slight headache whereas it scared the hell out of the rest of us. So we're going to see if we can get in with these suits covering our whole bodies, not just our lower brains."

"I am *not* going with you," Klane insisted. "I will not be a party to this . . . this *idiocy*."

"We may need your help," Hutchings said. "If there are some areas we can't penetrate in these suits, we may need you to realign the monopole signal for us. Larry can guide you and talk you through it."

Klane stood like a stone man. He addressed Hutchings. "How can I impress upon you the absolute *necessity* that *you* be the one to find a way to revive the traces? They are *intelligence* enhancers. There is no telling *what* we can accomplish when we reactivate them. *You* are the only person who can make that happen! This space-suit expedition is absolute nonsense!"

"Hugh Bladestone is pursuing the medical angle. I've pooled all the information I've come up with in the last . . . well, in the last twenty-four hours, let's say, and I've put it in a file which Hugh now has. One way or another, we're going to turn the tables on those bastards up there."

"You're at the wrong end of the table," Klane insisted.

"Not from where I'm standing," Hutchings countered.

Klane struggled with Hutchings's intransigence. But after a few moments of pondering the plan, as idiotic and suicidal as it may have been, he finally acceded.

"Oaks went too far," Klane breathed. "He should have been watched more closely. Common sense should have prevented this ridiculous situation."

"Common sense says we'd be in a prison in a more humane location," Hutchings said. "But this is the hand we were dealt so we're going to play it."

Hutchings faced Ramirez. "Are you ready for Mr. Klane's fitting?"

Ramirez nodded, though the silver orb sitting on his shoulders hardly moved. "You bet. Any time."

"I still don't like it," Klane said.

Hutchings slapped Klane on the back. "I don't like it either. But if we don't do it, we fry. And I'm not going to let that happen. Let's go."

29

The Forbidden Zones had vexed the Raians since the day of their incarceration. Every effort to penetrate them had been repulsed by a power none of them could explain. They couldn't even explain it in theory. Force-fields, they knew about. *Fear*-fields was something altogether new to them.

Then, of course, there was the Vapor. The mere threat of his appearance as judge, jury, and executioner, was itself a deterrence. Eddie Brickman, who may have been attempting to enter the Forbidden Zones when he and the others were climbing around out on the hull, had been the only Raian who did not fear the Vapor. Or much of anything, for that matter. For everyone else, however, the Vapor was a very real threat, never far from their minds at any one time.

This was especially true when Hutchings and the other four members of the expeditionary crew stood in the corridor where Edward Plainfield had wandered two days earlier. They knew they were about to break the rules big time, especially Klane.

"This will not work," Klane insisted over his E-suit's radio.

"We have to try," Hutchings said.

The five explorers stood there, each wearing an environment suit which had been coated in a polymer-bonded alloy. They could have been the Vapor's rumpled cousins, Klane particularly because of his height.

Joining Hutchings, Klane, and Pablo Ramirez were two Fiddlers. These were women who happened to be twin sisters, Arlene and Pauline Deyerberg. Their presence on Ra was as much of a puzzle as was the inclusion of the two Smith brothers, Don and Tom. The odds that *two* sets of siblings would be sent to Ra seemed so unlikely that no one knew what to make of it. The Getaways had puzzled over this for three years.

The Deyerbergs, however, were outfitted with spray guns, similar to the kind house painters might use. These were connected to large pressurized canisters clamped to their thighs. The canisters, and what they contained, were a last-minute addition, recommended by Hutchings.

"I still think you should have let us make real guns," Ramirez said, pointing to the spray guns the women held. "I mean something that shoots bullets."

"No guns," Hutchings said as he made a few adjustments to the heads-up display inside his visor and checked the interior atmosphere of his suit. "We can do this without guns."

"We shouldn't be doing this at all," Klane argued.

"Why is that?" Arlene Deyerberg demanded. Hutchings considered the Deyerbergs two of the most fearless individuals he had ever known, right behind Lyle MacKenzie and Eddie Brickman. They weren't afraid of anything—not the Vapor, not Klane.

"Because," Klane responded in a patronizing tone, "there is nothing we can do down here. That's why."

Hutchings tightened his alloyed gloves around his golden shackles. "You aren't an American, are you."

"My people are Quebeçois by way of Mars. Why?"

"Americans have a saying," Hutchings told him. "If something's broken, you fix it. That's what we're going to do."

"And what if you can't 'fix it'?" Klane asked.

"Then you beat the fuck out of the guy who broke it and make *him* fix it."

"Americans," Klane breathed.

"That's us,' Hutchings said, slapping Klane on the arm. "Let's go."

They approached the corridor S6. The hallway had been cleared of all ship's personnel, including two 'stiffs sleeping in their flops. Only a Tonka stood guard, a yellow crane.

Before them was the door which Plainfield had apparently been trying to reach before he collapsed. This was also the same door behind which the Vapor had disappeared three years earlier.

"Klane and I will go first," Hutchings said. "Actually, Klane will go first and I will go second. You three follow."

"This is not advisable," Klane insisted. "You should be upstairs in your laboratory working on the traces. They are the answer to our problems, not this foolishness."

"They might be the answer to your problems,"

Hutchings said. "But this is the answer to ours. Let's do it."

Klane turned and surveyed the hallway before him. After a moment's hesitation, he crossed over into the area of the strange repelling force.

Klane then took several steps past the spot where they had rescued Plainfield.

"What do you feel?" Hutchings asked.

"I *feel* that this is a bad idea. I *feel* that you and Dr. Bladestone should be devoting your efforts on the traces. I have this terrible intuition that if we don't—"

Hutchings broke him off. "It's the Zone, Klane."

"What?"

"The fear you think you're feeling? It's the Zone. That's how it works."

"I hardly think so," Klane insisted. "I *know* we shouldn't be doing this. I feel it at the bottom of my soul."

"Yep," Ramirez said. "That's the Zone talking."

The other four walked to where Klane presently stood.

"Feel it?" Ramirez asked Hutchings. Hutchings nodded.

"Feels sort of scary," Pauline Deyerberg said to her sister. "Not a lot, though," Arlene responded. "The suits are working. We can do this."

"We've got a way to go," Hutchings advised. "Expect it to get a lot worse."

Ramirez observed, "I'd say the fear is diminished about ninety percent. I'm just feeling a bit edgy. That's about it."

Hutchings walked past Klane and reached the door

at the end of the corridor. He noticed only the tiniest tremulations of fear within him. His heart beat faster and sweat had begun to moisten his palms. But that was the Zone working its mysterious magic.

"If it doesn't get any worse than this," Arlene Deyerberg said behind Hutchings, "we'll be all right."

Hutchings pressed the door's release button. The door was not a standard air lock, but merely a corridor seal. And lucky for them, it wasn't locked or fused shut.

The door, however, was slow to open, making a grinding sound from years of unuse.

"This is it," Hutchings said, and he stepped through.

A trail of small emergency lights lined the floor and Hutchings could see that they were in a utility corridor. Pipes of all sizes, ducts, and optical fiber tubing, ran along the walls, trailing off into the darkness at either end of the corridor.

"The first thing we have to do is find the source of the Zone's repeller field and disarm it," Hutchings said.

"Do you have any idea what that might be?" Klane asked.

"Frankly, no," Hutchings admitted. "This is all new to me."

The corridor led to a connecting passageway. Tiny motes of dust floated in the air stirred by their passage, caught by the crystal beams of their helmet lights.

"One thing we've got to do is fix the air filters," Pauline Deyerberg then said. "Get this shit out of the air."

Hutchings kneeled down and drew a gloved finger across the floor where the powder-fine dust had settled.

Ramirez pointed to the ducts running along the ceiling. "Maybe they shut down Environmentals throughout the Zones to lower the need for maintenance. You know, give the Man one less duty to carry out."

They pressed through the inner corridor with no noticeable increase in their feelings of fear. No tunnel terror awaited them; no baleful entity lurked around the corner, ready to pronounce judgment and obliterate them for their trespass.

The group came to what appeared to be a small common room. Inside, tables were overturned, furniture tossed around, debris of all kinds scattered along the floor.

"This is what the sunstation looked like three years ago," Ramirez observed. "What a mess."

The two Deyerbergs had remained in the outer hallway. They each had detectors in their hands that could pick up all manner of electronic signals. The two women swept their scanners about them. Klane, meanwhile, hovered in the background, waiting Hutchings's next idiotic command.

"Got something here," Pauline Deyerberg announced. A red indicator light on her scanner had begun flashing when she held it up to a ventilation grid in the ceiling.

Hutchings came over. "What is it?"

"A weak, localized transmission," she said. "It's got a broadcast radius of about three yards. And it seems to be coming from . . . right here." She pointed directly above them.

"Klane?" Hutchings asked. Klane's head was just inches away from the source of the signal.

"Yes, I feel it," Klane said.

"Here, use this," Arlene Deyerberg said to Hutchings, handing him a compact cutting laser. "You're taller than I am."

Hutchings sliced three sides of a square opening underneath the location of the repelling force. The material of the ceiling gave way, swinging down from the exposed vent as if on a hinge.

When it did, an object the size of a bowling ball plopped to their feet. Everyone jumped back.

The object was a mottled cream color and had a curious outer shell. Small, tenacious fibers, hairlike tendrils, clung to its surface.

Pauline Deyerberg held her scanner above it. "It's generating at sixty hertz. It's a repellant."

"Just enough energy for the hallway right underneath it," Pauline Deyerberg said, glancing up. "But it's not strong enough to penetrate to the Roughhouse which is on the next level above us."

"There could be hundreds of these things down here," Ramirez stated.

Arlene took out her spray gun and fired a jet of silver that quickly enveloped the sphere. It was the same bright silver alloy of their E-suits. Arlene then rolled the orb over with her gun's nozzle and sprayed the underside until the thing was entirely coated.

Hutchings found himself breathing a little easier. The proximity to the strange device had unleashed

all sorts of goblins into his mind . . . *the time he fought
a neighbor's Rottweiler dog when he was a teenager . . .
or that awful automobile crash when he was in college
that killed his roommate . . . or the fear he felt when he
saw Boörstam's comet for the first time. . . .*

Quite a lot was coming back to him now. He
looked at Ramirez and the two Fiddlers. They apparently weren't feeling it yet. Earlier, when they were
climbing into their E-suits, Hutchings had surrepti-
tiously opened one of the small canisters he'd attached
to his belt. The canisters contained what he hoped was
the solution to the problem of their amnesia. The chemical was fast-acting, but Hutchings didn't know how
fast—they each had different metabolic systems.

However, *he* had a head start. Not much of one,
but enough.

. . . *The comet. He and Kate had also seen it. They
watched it from a hotel window. They were in Kenya. . . .*

Kenya? He had the distinct feeling that this memory was only a few years old . . . *Nanyuki, Kenya, on
their way to the Yards.*

Yards? What Yards?

The airborne nanobot navy was working, escorted
to his brain by the fearful pumping of his heart. It
was only a question of time now.

"Is it dead?" Arlene Deyerberg asked.

Her sister's scanner registered a solid green light.
"As good as."

The group proceeded down the corridor with
Klane walking behind them, his hands guiding him
along the walls for balance.

Hutchings paused and crouched down. "This is
interesting," he said.

A line of boot prints stood out in the dust, like fossil tracks. They were slender, a bit too narrow for those of a human being.

Ramirez guessed the same thing. "The Vapor?" he asked.

Hutchings said, "That door back there was the last place I saw him three years ago. It looks like he came this way."

The corridor led them toward the center of the sun-station where all the main systems resided—the Renner-shield generators, the Man, and especially the flight operations compartment.

"I think we should turn back now," Arlene Deyer-berg said.

"Me, too. Let's go," said her sister.

"Hold on," Hutchings said. "It's the Zone. One of those things must be nearby." And he was thinking: *the Durkee Elevator Yards outside of Nanyuki, Kenya . . . the gravity plates the System Assembly employed to heave people and material into space . . . the only Yards world-wide that were still operable. . . .*

A cursory scan of the narrow corridor indicated a weak signal, but they found nothing hiding in the walls or in the ceiling or under their feet. They pressed on. As they did, the feelings intensified.

They rounded a corner and found themselves before a door that bore the words: FLIGHT DECK—FLIGHT PERSONNEL ONLY. Right in front of the door, however, was another repeller sphere standing guard.

Pauline Deyerberg kicked the orb out of the way with her boot and her sister sprayed the hell out of it, practically gluing it to the nearby wall.

"Don't waste the spray," Hutchings cautioned.

Arlene backed away, shutting off her gun. "I *hate* those things."

However, the uneasiness disappeared upon the drowning of the sphere.

Ramirez pointed at the door to the ship's flight compartment. "Don't you think Matt should be down here for this? He might remember something."

"Not yet," Hutchings said. "We'd only be asking for trouble." And he remembered . . . *meeting Matthew White at the Durkee Yards. White was a pilot of one of the lift vessels taking them up to the* John Baldry *in low Earth orbit. . . .*

The John E. Baldry?

The door to the flight compartment would not open all the way when Hutchings pressed the seal release. Its mechanisms were filled with the same silver dust they had seen everywhere. Hutchings had to force it physically back into its casing.

They stepped into the flight center. Twice as big as the Brains, the compartment was lost in darkness. However, the navigator's semicircular console, and the main board, which took up the entire wall before it, were still active.

"I don't like this," Klane muttered. "I'm getting a headache now."

"Another sphere," Ramirez responded. "Look."

A repeller sphere lay beneath the middle chair at the console. The console itself was horseshoe-shaped with seats each for a navigator, com-officer, and perhaps a copilot.

They immediately rolled the repeller sphere out into the hallway where the Deyerbergs sprayed it to death. They left it glistening next to its dead cousin.

Hutchings said, "Pablo, see if you can find some light for this room. What we need to do is—"

Klane began dancing.

But it wasn't dancing. The tall man had suddenly jumped back and started scrambling past the Deyerbergs toward the exit, a performance entirely inspired by a surge of unbounded panic.

"Hey!" Arlene Deyerberg said, flung to one side by the tall man's hasty retreat. "What's the idea?"

Klane tumbled into the outer hallway, nearly falling over the two drenched repeller spheres.

Hutchings turned to see what had frightened Klane—and almost jumped clear out of his E-suit.

Immediately behind the navigator's console was an elevated compartment protected by a pane of glass. Behind the glass pane was the pilot's chair. A small series of steps to the left of the compartment led up to that room.

Lying upon those steps was the form of something that once had been functional but had long since ceased being so. When it stood, it must have been nearly seven feet tall. It was vaguely humanoid and was made of a now-tarnished silver-plating.

"Jesus Christ!" Ramirez shouted, lurching backwards.

"I think," Hutchings breathed, "that we've just found the Vapor."

30

In the dream-that-isn't-a-dream, Kate opens her eyes. A forest of crystalline trees like prehistoric cycads, surrounds her. The sky is an incarnadine pink. A yellow cloud moves across the sun. It has taken the shape of a comet.

This can't be real, she thinks. *These are not trees found anywhere on the Earth.*

The forest gives off an eerie, if seductively pleasant trilling when the wind passes through. It is Alan Holly's music: something altogether transcendent, a sacred hymn of the Spirit, something to please a High Councilor or a Ward Elder. The shifting, syncopated harmonies of the forest speak of the empty reaches between stars and tedious journeys through space. It is all glory to them, especially in the one planetary system they have so recently chosen, the one that seems so promising.

That star is a silver coin, freshly minted, sparkling in the sky above the deserted plains of Wyoming. That star is the sun.

The sun. Something about the sun keeps nagging at Kate's mind. She considers the trees.

Thousands upon thousands of the polyplike trees sing in the wind from Canada—so this *is* the Earth!—across the flat Wyoming landscape now inhabited by structures of crystal and metal whose bark scatters rays of sunlight into shards of diamond and ice: this forest is all that remains of her riderless horses.

But is this a dream? she wonders. She can actually feel the ooze of the black earth around her legs and the cold, dry wind that shears across her skin. It's entirely *too* vivid. She can see all around her. She has 360 degrees of lateral vision. She can see without turning her head or her torso or moving her body in any way. In fact, she is lodged so firmly in the mud that any kind of movement is impossible. She therefore must have eyes around her skull—if she *has* a skull. There might not be anything recognizably human about her anymore.

She tries to speak but no words come. Her mouth is a closed grill beneath a tiara of silver spider eyes.

She tries again with a little more effort and words of a kind do appear: brittle, wind-chime sounds drift out.

"*Can anyone hear me?*" she cries. "*Is anyone out there?*"

The music ripples through the bizarre forest of metal polyps clattering like the blue ceramic wind-chimes her grandmother once made in her backyard kiln in Sheridan, Wyoming. Her Grandmother. That was *such* a long time ago!

Kate listens to the wind. The entire polyp forest seems to be sending out communications of all sorts, each at different timbres, each a distinct bundle of tonal colors. Some are faint and obscure; others revel in a simple *joie de vivre*, the pleasure of life on the endless plain. None of the communicative shimmerings, though, make any *human* sense to her.

"*Please*," she ripples again. "*Can somebody hear me?*"

The pain fills with the delicate choir of fractulated sounds, of wind-worn metal, smooth porcelain, the clanking of rhodium-stained glass. However, among the waves of gently, glittering sounds, Kate makes out a voice. Someone is singing nearby. The wind-chime sounds fade for a moment and Kate hears a melody sung by a little girl, a Child of perhaps three or four.

"*I love Pooter, yes I do . . . Boiled, broiled . . . or in a stew. . . .*" It is a human voice. A baby Girl's voice.

"*Bebe?*" Kate sends into a prismed air. "*Honey, can you hear me? Bebe?*"

"*Mmmm—*"

Bebe Wasson's baby-song rises on the wind and drifts away—mindlessly, happily. Kate yearns for her. She wants to hold her forever in a deep swell of unbounded motherly affection.

Bebe is singing a lullaby for Pooter, the kitty-person she had when she had been truly little, more than thirty yeas ago.

"*Bebe! Please wake up, sweetheart! It's time to get up!*"

"*Mmmm.*"

"*I'm making pancakes, Bebe. Do you want yummy pancakes for breakfast? You can have lots and lots of syrup.*"

"*Birdy-nose . . . birdy-nose . . . knock, knock, knock . . .*"

Kate scans the forest. Bebe is one of the trees nearby. Kate recalls from a dream of another world that Bebe had fallen ill and wouldn't wake up and she had to be sealed away until they knew what had happened to her. The nearest polyp is only a few yards away, but that one doesn't appear to be her. That structure has a "male" character to it. He sings his own song, happy to be feeding, there in the face of the sun.

No one has any arms to signal with, no one has a mouth to shout out cries of warning. They are no longer human. Silver butterflies flitter by, their metal wings like razors slice the air. On the prairie below tremble metal-embossed flowers. To the east at an incalculable distance races a whirlwind of silver particulates cresting a hill of platinum trees.

The prairie is now home to Ian's argentite birches, Lorraine's metal butterflies, Lisa Anderson's iridium posies, and Elliot's silver dust devil. The menace of the choking, sparkling silver ash spreads across the globe.

No, not ash, Kate thinks. *Glitter. The glitter on the floor of the Girl's dorm . . . the glitter that suddenly appeared in the hallways . . .*

Glitter that was not inert. Glitter that was *alive.*

Kate calls out, *"Can anybody hear me? Anybody! Please! We've got to wake up! We've got to wake up! All of us!"*

Her voice flings silver rings through the air. They ricochet through the forest, casting out reflective bangles of light.

Someone does respond, however. There is a familiar resonance to his voice. Kate can feel what's left of this man's actual consciousness. It hasn't quite gone away, but there's not much left of it.

"Who is it? Is it Kate?"

"I'm here! I'm here!" Kate emanates with the strength of her entire being. Desperately, she scans the forest of metallic polyps. *"Where are you?"*

"No need . . . to be frightened . . . Kate."

"Who is it? Who are you?"

"Feeding."

"Feeding?"

"Yesss—"

Feeding. A noun. Not a verb. A state of being, an essence whose purpose in life is merely to *feed*.

"Lyle, is that you?" Kate calls out.

But how can it be Lyle? They buried Lyle MacKenzie a long time ago. They buried him in the meadow.

The meadow?

Yes, she thinks. There *is* a meadow. And it's somewhere on the surface of the sun.

"What's happening to us?" she asks.

"Feeding," MacKenzie says. But he is quite nearly gone. He's held out all these years in his pitiful grave, a glimmer of awareness, a tiny star of consciousness slowly fading into the dream of the billion-year-old Feeding.

"I don't understand, Lyle."

The palimpsest of Lyle MacKenzie, a mere speck of his true Self, is all that remains of their brave expeditionary leader. It has held out until now in the grave, fighting all this time not to give in to the *feeding*, kept alive as long as possible by the vampirish appetite of the trace within. Now his thought-voice trails off into oblivion.

"They should feed on the light . . . the light . . ." he says.

She feels Lyle's weariness, the final succumbing to quick-sleep. Hugh Bladestone is beginning to feel it. It's what their bindlestiffs suffer from: It is the first stage of what can only be a form of sentience retraction.

Sentience-retraction? What in the world is that?

She remembers now: it's the Feeding. It was Ian's major discovery when he first analyzed the traces: larvae that turn into polyps, polyps that flower and move on to other planets, other worlds. They feed on humans to fuel their developmental cycle, on their way to flowering.

These are the Strathclyde traces: the microminiaturized yokes that have traveled a billion years to the verdant planets of Sol. Taking first Strathclyde Station on Pluto, having drifted across space on the wings of a comet. The glitter . . . bits of living metal wanting to become forests like those in Kate's dreamscape: billions of polyps twisting in the wind.

Yet not all of them have succumbed to the traces. Lorraine has survived. Elliot and Larry are still immune. So is Ian.

But Hugh is close. He is tired of *life.* Tired of fighting his conscience for what he thinks he may have done to his wife. He is *so* close to collapsing into quick-sleep that she can *touch* his mind. She sees him as he stands before a holopedestal, staring at a silver flower hovering in the air. A trace. A Strathclyde trace . . .

"Hugh,'" every atom of her being cries. *"Stop the traces! Stop the traces! They just killed Lyle!"*

Hugh Bladestone turned from the holopedestal which happened to hold the suspended image of the trace lodged in his very own brain. A sudden intuition had compelled him to go through the data files Ian had left before he had set off on his fool's errand into the Forbidden Zones. The doctor could almost *feel* the blood in his brain roar around the molecules of his Strathclyde trace. Ian had done something to them all before he left, put something in the very air. He—

—turned to Kristen. "Did you hear that?" he asked.

"Hear what?"

"I thought I heard a voice."

"I didn't hear anything."

"It sounded like Kate. I was just thinking that the traces just might allow for a telepathic link between us, only—"

Diane Beckwith appeared in the doorway to their small lab.

"I heard it," she said. "She said the traces killed Captain MacKenzie. I'm sure of it."

The three medical personnel looked to one another.

"Stop them. Stop the traces," resonated in the deep, deep survival-oriented regions of their minds.

Someone had spoken to them from the roots of their ancestral brain stems, to the seat of their souls which were now being surrounded, engulfed, smothered by the metal threads of an unwanted invader.

"I think I understand now," the doctor finally said in a whisper of astonishment. "I think I've got it."

31

Only Hutchings had the nerve at first to approach the wreckage of the Vapor. Everyone else stood back away from the shape of terror which had fallen in the corner. It was their greatest nightmare come true, except that the Vapor was unmistakably—and quite inexplicably—dead.

The robot lay wedged in the narrow set of stairs that led to the pilot's main control bay just above and behind the navigation console. The Vapor had apparently been trying to reach the pilot's berth when it expired. How long the Vapor had been this way, Hutchings had no way of knowing. But given the undisturbed footprints in the dust in the outer hallway, the Vapor had probably perished soon after he had taken Hutchings on his tour of the sunstation three years ago.

Pablo Ramirez crept up behind Hutchings. "You think he's been *here* all this time? I mean, lying here like this?"

"I'd say so," Hutchings admitted. He looked to the Deyerberg women. "Pauline. Bring your scanner. See if this thing's dead or not."

"No way," Pauline Deyerberg said. "I'm not going near that thing."

Hutchings walked over to where the Deyerbergs stood and snatched the scanner from Pauline's hand. Hutchings then made a careful scan of the robot, making absolutely sure that he was reading the scanner correctly.

"It's dead, all right." Hutchings handed the scanner back to the woman. "Let's get some illumination in this place. I want to see what this is about."

Arlene Deyerberg found an activation switch for the room, bringing alive the lights as well as the environmental systems, which included the ventilation. Air whooshed from vents, pushing out faint clouds of a luminescent dust—*silver* dust, Hutchings noted, like Bebe Wasson's playroom glitter.

They examined their bogeyman. As Hutchings had long ago described it, the machine was a gracile entity of shining iridium-titanium alloy. It had only the most abstract face with a meshed grill for a mouth. The fingers of its hands were at least seven inches long.

Hutchings noticed that Klane was taking the discovery the hardest. At the entrance to the flight command center, the tall man was bent over, his hands on his knees as if on the verge of being physically sick.

"Are you going to make it?" Hutchings asked.

"I . . . can't tell," Klane said with some difficulty. "I did not expect this."

Ramirez turned from inspecting the Vapor. "You know, this doesn't look like any robot I remember.

It looks like it might be partly biological. You think that's possible?"

"Ten years have passed on the Outside," Hutchings said. "There's no telling what direction robotics could have taken."

Here, Klane spoke. His voice was dry and reedy. "They have them."

"Who does?" Ramirez asked.

"The System Assembly. A new kind of all-environment worker," Klane said. "Their bones are plastic or modified silicon. Their muscles and tendons are metal fibers. They're designed to sustain themselves in environments that are prohibitive to humans. That is—" He nodded at the Vapor "—that is easily one of them."

"If Venus or Mercury can't kill it," Ramirez said, "how did it die in here?"

Klane shrugged. "It must have run out of internal power. Robots do that now and again."

Ramirez bent over the ruin. "I'd sure like to know how this fellow ticks."

"We'll figure that out later," Hutchings said. "When we've got more time."

Arlene Deyerberg, the braver of the twins, said, "So, this means we've got the place to ourselves!"

"Not yet, we don't," Hutchings stated. "Those repeller objects are undoubtedly everywhere. There's no telling what else is down here."

Hutchings didn't elaborate on his last remark. Instead, he turned to see Klane in the doorway. The man did not look well. "Klane?"

Klane's silver visor made his face unreadable, but his body language suggested a man in discomfort.

"It is possible that I am going to be sick," Klane said. "I don't think you need me. At least here. I would like to step out into the hallway until I recover."

"Your head was the closest to that first repeller sphere we found in the ceiling," Ramirez observed. "You think maybe that did it?"

"That is possible," Klane speculated.

"Well, don't take your helmet off," Ramirez cautioned. "If there are any other repellers nearby, they'll probably kill you outright, at least without any kind of protection."

"Perhaps it won't come to that," Klane said.

Like a dazed mantis, Klane walked unsteadily back out into the corridor, bracing himself, arms outstretched.

Once Klane left, Hutchings stepped past the remains of the Vapor and bounded up the short flight of steps into the pilot's compartment. The nook had a form-fitting chair and a scimitar of a monitoring board curving before it. The compartment's resemblance to the cockpit Matt White had created in his dorm room was uncanny. It was nearly identical.

Ramirez had also noticed this. "Man, this looks *exactly* like the setup in Matt's room. Even the screens on the console here are the same. How'd he do it?"

"Mnemonic resonance," Hutchings stated. "We all have it. They couldn't quite make us forget what we were."

Ramirez said nothing. The normally talkative Fiddler seemed unusually quiet and introspective. Hutchings did not want to reveal to him just yet that minuscule agents of change were already surging through his veins, *their* veins.

The com chimed in Hutchings's right ear and a voice immediately followed it without waiting for an acknowledgment. *"Ian or Pablo."* It was Bladestone.

"We're both right here, Hugh," he said. "What have you got."

"Message from Kate," the doctor said.

"Has she come out of her coma?" Hutchings asked.

"No. She's still inside her stasis chamber."

"But she sent you a message?"

"She told us to stop the traces."

"Are you sure?"

Diane Beckwith's voice appeared. *"Absolutely. I got the distinct image of a forest of some kind. There were skinny trees made of metal everywhere and they were in the process of feeding. It wasn't a dream and I didn't imagine it. Kate was there."*

"Kate was frightened, too," Hugh added.

"If she's asleep, maybe she's sending her nightmares over the trace-links in our heads," Ramirez speculated out loud.

"That's possible," Hutchings said.

"Ian, I need your opinion on this," the doctor said. *"Do you want me to continue with the adjustments to the acceleration hormone you've designed or do you want me to wait until you come out?"*

"No," Hutchings said. "Follow my instructions exactly. When you get the nanowaldos configured to the outer sheath of the molecular dreadnoughts, start mass-producing them. Don't worry about the bonding character of the trace polymer. The dreadnoughts will take care of them. We've got to make a few billion of those things. All I did was make an advance guard. If we're to get the full effect of the antidote, we'll need those things in the billions."

"The dreadnoughts unravel the bonding polymers, Ian. Is that the idea or am I missing something here?"

"You're not missing a thing. You got it exactly."

"Why didn't you tell me this earlier?"

"We were both busy."

"How many days did it take to figure this out?"

"Just two. Then two more to affect a solution for a few of us, the stuff in the canisters."

"What about Kate's message?"

"We'll take her at her word. She's a pretty smart cookie."

"Then we are in touch with each other through the traces?" Diane Beckwith asked over the com.

"Undoubtedly," Hutchings said. "If you get any more messages from her, let me know."

"There is one other thing."

"What's that?"

"The air in here's starting to smell funny."

"That's just Cady and Peters at work," Hutchings said. "I've got them fiddling with the air filtration systems in the free zones. Don't let it bother you. You'll be fine."

"Are you sure?"

"I am."

"All right, then. Out."

Meanwhile, Arlene Deyerberg had eased into one of the three seats at the navigation console just beneath the beveled windows of the pilot's booth. Being a Fiddler at heart, she began puzzling over the monitoring console, tracing the various function buttons, trying to make what sense of them she could.

To her sister, she said, "Paule, this looks like a standard orientation indicator. Come here. Take a look."

"Don't touch anything!" Hutchings commanded from behind the beveled window of the pilot's perch.

Arlene turned. "Paule's had master navigation classes. She ran in a sail-race around the moon when she was twenty."

"I did?" Pauline said.

"Don't you remember?"

"No, I don't."

"Well, *I* remember it. I remember watching it from Wilson Hall on my layover at Riordan Station in Earth orbit. I had that fractured toe when I kicked Brookshire in the ass when he came onto me in front of Bozo's Bus Stop."

"I don't remember any of that," her sister said.

"It just came to me," Arlene said. "But forget about that. Look at this board. You can work it, can't you?"

Pauline began scrutinizing the command features of the navigation console. She pointed a gloved finger. "Come to think of it, this does look familiar," she said in a soft voice.

Hutchings came down from the pilot's compartment, carefully stepping past the Vapor. "Don't touch anything. At least just yet."

Pauline Deyerberg ignored Hutchings and turned, instead, to Ramirez. "Hey, Pablo. I think this board here controls the lock on our monopole bearing coordinates. It's all done from this console. Look."

"Where?" Ramirez asked, coming around.

"The monopole alignment signal," Pauline said. "It's tied into the stability sequencing ratios of the Renner-shield layers as they're generated from here. Right here!"

Ramirez sat down in the middle chair at the console. "Show me."

The twins traded places and Pauline pointed to a screen on the console and a row of illuminated buttons just underneath it.

"These look like standard gyroscopic attitude locks," she said. "In this case, they're tied into the corridor generated by the Renner shield, here. And this row could be the lower alignment settings for the Anchor underneath us. Yes. I'm sure of it. And *this* is the station's positioning array."

"Except the numbers don't match," Arlene observed.

Ramirez nodded. "The left calibration figure is probably the default setting for the monopole corridor's proper coordinates. The right figure must be the current setting—"

"—the one Oaks knocked us into," Arlene Deyerberg said. "All we have to do is reprogram the settings and calibrate a match. It doesn't look like there's a lock placed on computer access from this particular console."

The two sets of numbers on the two gauges were off by only a single digit which, Hutchings knew, translated to a thousandth of a degree of axial deviation. But it was enough to throw the monopole corridor sufficiently out of whack to prevent communication with any vessel in the monopole corridor above them.

However, just beneath the right-hand indicator, the one that was off by a thousandth of a degree, was a smaller screen with a series of numbers that were now slowly decreasing in sequence.

"What do those numbers indicate?" Hutchings asked. "They've just started."

Ramirez leaned over, peering at the flashing indicator. "The tether," he said. "It's got to be."

The numbers moved from 2518 to 2517 to 2516, but did so at a very slow pace.

Pauline Deyerberg then said, "It looks like the Anchor is adjusting itself upward along the cable, perhaps for tighter steering control of the whole station."

"Com, open, Voorhees," Hutchings said.

"Hey!" Voorhees fairly shouted. *"What did you guys put in the air? My blood feels like it's pumping a million miles an hour!"*

"That's supposed to happen," Hutchings said, quickly cutting him off. "And you're going to get your memory back, too. But listen, are you fooling with the Anchor from your console?"

"I was just about to ask you guys that," Voorhees said. *"I've just had an alarm go off and it scared the shit out of me. I didn't know we had an alarm like that on this board!"*

"Sounds like he's had twelve cups of coffee," Arlene Deyerberg whispered to her sister. Of course, she herself was nervously tapping her foot. Hutchings made sure that his nanoboosters had a slight methamphetamine kick to them.

Hutchings spoke into his com. "Larry, can you tell

if the Man is making the adjustments to the Anchor on his own?"

"*I can tell you without looking. He doesn't have the time or the processing power to do anything with the Anchor.*"

Hutchings could almost hear the gears working away in the brains of his team, brains slowly returning to their normal capabilities, as they thought through all the implications of the situation before them and their possible options for response.

Voorhees got there first. He said, "*But you know, the Anchor's positioning would have to be part of the monopole signal's realignment. Hey! You think it could be done from the Anchor instead of at the Man's main board? We could readjust our position all from the Anchor while the Man concentrated on keeping the Renner shield active!*"

"We couldn't do it," Hutchings said. "But someone else could."

"*Someone like who?*"

"Dylan Oaks," Hutchings said. "My guess is that he's doing it from there right now."

32

Hutchings's memory started to return. What was once a trickle had now become a steady flow. Soon it would flood. But what he saw now was enough for him to go by. His imagination filled with images of a nanonavy of molecular "Fiddlers" at war in his brain. The artificial dextroamphetime sulfate molecules, common for use in fighting Alzheimer's disease, were designed to dismantle their foes. A wrench clutched in one fist, a crowbar in another, a drill in another and a screwdriver in yet another, Hutchings's blood army opened neural pathways, cleared connections and dismantled the Wall, brick by noetic brick.

And he didn't like what he now started to see through the chinks in the Wall.

"How did Oaks get down to the Anchor?" Arlene Deyerberg asked.

"He climbed down the tether," Hutchings told her.

"How'd he do that?" Arlene asked.

"With some of the equipment Eddie had made," Hutchings said. "And some that he brought down himself."

"You might have warned us," Ramirez stated. "At least we could have stopped him."

"I wanted to see what he was going to do," Hutchings said distractedly. "That, and a couple of other things."

Pauline Deyerberg then said, "We should have put him in jail the moment he got here."

"But who knew he'd want to escape so soon?" her sister said.

"Oaks is not trying to escape," Hutchings told them.

"He's not?" Pauline asked. "What's he doing, then?"

Hutchings did not immediately respond. The console before them indicated that the sunstation was indeed rising, if rather slowly, passing up the monopole corridor within the enclosure of the Renner shield without affecting the efforts of the Man to maintain their position. It was a tricky bit of flying, but Oaks seemed to know what he was doing.

"Com, open, Elliot," Hutchings said.

"Right here," came Shoemaker's voice. *"Are you in?"*

"We are. Listen, we've found the ship's flight control center. The repelling force in the Forbidden Zones is caused by spherical devices about the size of volleyballs. They're small enough to be just about anywhere. We found one in a ventilation duct, but they seem to be mostly out in the open."

"Does the spray solution work?"

"It seems to," Hutchings said. "Are you ready at your end?"

"As ready as I'll ever be."

"There's one other matter. You may run into Klane on your way down. He appears to be ill."

"What should I do about Matt?"

"Don't tell him anything yet. He's really pissed off at me right now and he might not cooperate. Just tell him what I told you, then play it from there. Out."

The Fiddlers looked at Hutchings, waiting for elucidation. Instead, Hutchings handed out orders. "You two—" this, to the Deyerbergs "—find as many of those spheres as you can and neutralize them. Go back the way we came and branch out from there. But don't remove your helmets. That's very important."

"Right," said Arlene.

"Signal us when you're ready to go down to the next level. We'll have reinforcements for you by then."

The twins left the way they came, each with her spray gun held out, eager to cast the repellers into the other world.

"Com, open, Lorraine," Hutchings then said.

"Right here. What's your progress?"

"We've reached the flight center and Elliot's on his way down. Klane has taken ill and is on his way back up. Dylan Oaks is in the Anchor."

"I copy that."

"It looks like your part of the plan will be necessary after all. Be prepared."

"I copy that, too."

Ramirez turned to Hutchings. "You've got a plan? I thought you told Klane you didn't have a plan."

"I think I've always had a plan," Hutchings said, studying the flight monitoring board. "It just depended on what the System Assembly was going to do."

"You know what's going on?"

"I do now. I didn't know a few days ago."

"How much of this do you want to tell me?"

"Enough to say that the System Assembly has employed Mr. Oaks to deliver the sunstation back to them, if all else fails."

"If all else fails? What 'all else'?"

"I'd rather not say just yet."

"You mean they want *us* first?" Ramirez asked.

"At the very least."

Hutchings indicated the monitoring console. "Elliot's on his way down. I want the two of you to unlock as many of the ship's internal systems as you can from here and get them back on operating status. But don't do anything with the air filtration systems. Don't listen to anybody's complaints about the air."

"I wanted to ask you about that—"

But Hutchings continued, "Then see if you can establish an override to the Brains. That'll free Larry up. We're probably going to control things from down here from now on."

"What about the Anchor?"

"The Anchor apparently has control only over our vertical ascent. I don't think we'll move laterally. Oaks knows what he's doing."

"What about Klane? Is he one of them, too?"

"It's hard to say what Klane is," Hutchings admitted.

"I don't like anybody being down in the Anchor, Ian. Someone's got to go down there and stop him."

"He'll be stopped."

"When?"

Hutchings turned and faced a sealed door opposite the one by which they entered. It led deeper into the Forbidden Zones.

"When I find out what's on the other side of this door."

In Hugh Bladestone's overworked mind, a soft, epiphanic light burned like an illuminated dagger in the sky. It didn't help matters any that his blood pressure was up and that he was running a low-grade fever. However, he knew that this time there was a reason for the fever: His body was purging itself of an affliction he'd had these last three years. Only now had he recognized it for what it was.

Foxy Ian, he thought. Hutchings had slipped them some sort of remedy, borne on the very air they breathed. Bladestone understood now as his memory began patching itself together. Ian had thought that a simple, naturally occurring hormone might inhibit the maturation of the traces. It was part of the limbic system's defense against intruders. And depending on the individual chemistry of the victims, this clash was the most likely cause of their quick-sleep which affected some more so than others.

Bladestone felt his heart race with excitement *and* the millions of amphetamine-amplified microsoldiers in his blood. They helped clear neural passages and bridge synaptical chasms once blocked by the bonding polymers of the traces. One legion of nanobots was fighting another: one army came from the breeding bins of Ian's lab . . . the other came in off a comet from some far corner of the galaxy.

"Hugh?" Kristen called from the doorway to the lab.

Ian's baffling food poisoning a while back now made sense. He had been working on himself all this time, devising nanosoldiers for their amnesia. And Hutchings kept on experimenting with himself, trying one solution after another, until he got the solution configured correctly. The man probably felt he *owed* it to humanity, given what it was he was supposed to have done to it.

Which, Hugh realized then and there, *was merely a fiction, given to them by the System Assembly, itself composed of traces wanting to mature.*

It was only recently, however, that Ian had perfected the kind of soldier they needed. Hugh now understood. The solution lay in a modification to Ian's literary Critic, the one that helped Steve Welch's natural brain chemistry pry loose those literature sems that had invaded the man's dreams and had made him so miserable. Those same Critics were now prying loose the anchoring templates of the Strathclyde traces, molecule by molecule, in all their minds—the true cause of their amnesia.

The doctor turned. "What is it?"

"It's Arliss Adamson," she said. "You'd better have a look at her."

In the room where the Fiddlers had frantically built the slow-sleep chambers, and were hurriedly constructing two more, the doctor found Arliss Adamson leaning against the black chamber that held Clarissa Pickerall in suspended time. Adamson's hair had gone almost totally white. On the floor was a sprinkling of silver dust.

Adamson looked up, the light of consciousness fading in her eyes. "They're going to get us all," she said. "We've got to turn the traces against them . . . make us smarter. We need to know what prevents them from expanding. We need to *grow*."

"We're working on that," Bladestone told her. He chose the words of his half-truth carefully: "Ian has identified a hormone that blocks the growth of the traces. It apparently triggers a defensive reaction by the brain which prevents electrical conductivity in the trace."

He could have added: *Without it, the soul freezes . . . people become pillars of crystalline metal, their will to live vanishes, they become as cold as interstellar ice. . . .*

"Those bastards," Adamson said. "You *have* to find out what the traces really are. We need them to grow. We need them to *think*. That's what they're afraid of. There's a lock on the templates. We have to find it and release it so the traces will grow back."

"We're doing everything we can," Bladestone said.

Adamson then looked around the room. "Where is Major Hutchings? He's the one who knows the most about them. He's the one who can get them growing again. He's the expert."

Yes, Hugh thought. *Major Hutchings.*

And *he* had been a Sergeant Major. Those were temporary titles of military ranking bestowed upon them for the duration of . . . what?

The Crisis. It was coming back to him now.

Adamson grit her teeth. "I want the cure," she said. "I want my trace expanded *now*. I want to *feed* on the bodies of my enemies."

Behind them a chime in a row of instruments went off and Adamson turned. "What's that?" she asked.

"What you asked for," Bladestone said. "The cure."

He pulled a small capsule from the synthesizer. It had twenty-five cc's of a pink chemical in it, a much more potent version of the antidote than Ian's jury-rigged commandos now circulating in the air.

"*That's* the cure?" Adamson asked, unbelieving.

"Yes."

"But, Hugh," Kristen asked, "don't you think we should run some tests on it first? We don't know just how it's—"

"There's no time for tests," Adamson said. "I'll volunteer. Try it on me."

Bladestone shook his head. "Clarissa, Bebe, and Kate need it first. We should have more of it made for the rest of us very soon. If there wasn't so much widespread damage to the Sally's processing software, we could make larger quantities of it almost immediately. As it is now—"

Adamson looked as if she were about to collapse. "What's the nature of the solution?" she demanded. "I was a scientist once. I've *got* to know."

"All of Ian's notes, his diagrams, and his formula are here on this tile." The doctor held up a standard data tile, which he, in turn, placed in a small medical tile pouch.

This he gave to Kristen. "Get this tile to the Sally in common room six. It's the only one that can handle the amounts we're going to need for the rest of the crew."

Kristen took the pouch. She left the infirmary in a rush.

Arliss Adamson looked fiercely at the doctor. "Please. I'd like to help any way I can. I *want* to help."

"We've done about all we can do from here," he told her. "It's now up to Major Hutchings."

"Where *is* Major Hutchings, anyway?" Adamson asked. "Shouldn't he be here? This is where all the equipment is—"

"He's doing his part," Bladestone said. He left it at that. He did not tell her there was a greater reason for her to worry: The sun had already begun to shine through the clouds above Chicago and it cast a whole new light on what had befallen Ostermann Station on Mercury three years ago, symbolized in his dream of the Ostermann hotel.

Now the battle could pick up where it had left off three short years ago.

33

Hutchings walked the hallways of Hell, a land of terror which no man, no woman, had seen in three years.

Sweat trickled down Hutchings's spine and his bladder filled as his deconstructionist Critics waged war in his brain and escourted the debris of the vanquished to his bloodstream. His formerly captive mind was now free of the crushing guilt he had carried all these years of the crime he never committed.

He knew now that he had killed no one—at least no human being.

Memories now came flooding back: *his grandmother's lemon meringue pie . . . his Uncle Buck's affection for camomile tea . . . the sahavas in India at the tomb of Meher Baba when he finally graduated college.* More memories: *Elizabeth Jean Bremser, the first woman he almost married because she lied about being pregnant . . . they argued in the snow before K-Dorm and broke it off. Memories of Carmen Bresnahan and Judith Watkins the night he and his roommate rappelled out of Sechrist Hall, nine floors up in a raging snowstorm just to impress the two girls.*

As Hutchings made his way down the narrow corridor, he began to notice that his apprehension was abating with nearly every step he took. Had he reached a region where there were no more repeller spheres? He thought not: The effectiveness of the repellers was diminishing in proportion to the trace being disassembled in his brain. In fact, the repellers worked *only* when the traces—or their anchoring templates—were present.

And he remembers—

—*waiting for the next antigravity shuttle to arrive at the Durkee Yards in Nanyuki, Kenya. He is coleader with Capt. Lyle MacKenzie. They and a crew of 110 brave souls are about to investigate a comet that has inexplicably decelerated on its way into the solar system.*

The prints Hutchings's boots made in the silver dust on the floor looked like trilobites of some distant world. *Comet dust. A dust of death brought in by an interstellar voyager. . . .*

"Com, open, Pablo, Elliot, Arnie and Paule."

"Right here," Ramirez responded. The others chimed in right behind him.

"Listen carefully," he said. "Do not remove your helmets. Do not breathe the dust at your feet. It's our worst enemy. Pablo, how many Gleaners have your people got?"

"Four. Why?"

"The dust has been spread throughout the Forbidden Zones and we'll need every atom of it sucked up and destroyed."

"Roger on that."

"Elliot?" Hutchings then asked. "Do you have Matt with you?"

"Yes."

"Did you give him some of the gas?"

"Yep. He didn't like it. He took a swing at me."

"Is he okay now?"

"I think so."

The young pilot from Texas came over the com. He sounded uncharacteristically mature. *"I want to know what this is all about, Ian. I'm tired of you guys picking on me!"* an adult Matt White said.

"We're not picking on you and you're about to find out."

Ramirez's voice appeared over the com. *"Hold it. You're bringing Matt down here?"*

"That's right."

"You're not going to let Matt fly this thing, are you?"

"That's the idea."

"I was hoping it wasn't," Ramirez said, but he, too, was coming around. He, too, was having his memory restored bit by bit, atom by atom, coming to perceive his own role in this as well.

Hutchings then said, "We'll give him time to familiarize himself with the controls. But we won't let him do anything until he says he's ready."

Silver dust cracked beneath Hutchings's boots as he edged down the corridor. "Arnie and Paule, are you there?"

"I'm here," said Arlene.

"Likewise," responded Paule.

"Have either of you seen Mr. Klane?"

"I haven't seen him," Arlene stated.

Hutchings noted the confidence in the woman's voice: Arlene Deyerberg was also beginning to remember the forty-year-old engineer she had once been. *Arlene Deyerberg Littel,* he corrected himself, remembering now that she had been married back on the Earth.

"He's not around here," Pauline said with the same assuredness. *Pauline Deyerberg Thompson.* An expert in remote-viewing and extrasensory perception.

Larry Voorhees's voice chimed in Hutchings's right ear. *"Open, Ian."*

"Go ahead."

The Oklahoman was clearly excited. *"Good news here. About thirty seconds ago we came up with a lock on the monopole calibration coordinates. The Big Board's showing all green on the original monopole setting."*

"What did you do?" Hutchings asked.

"I don't know if I did anything. What I have been doing is redistributing other processing chores in the Man's main drive in order to free up his RAM. The coordinates came in clean."

"What do you think happened?"

"I think the Man got some help."

"Some help?"

"From outside," Voorhees said. "Topside, actually. When the Man came back on-line it seems that he somehow had snagged a broad-frequency signal above us in the upper Renner corridor. The beacon's gone now, but its source was in the corridor long enough for the Man to calibrate the monopole signal back to its original default setting."

"You think it was *Bold Charon?"* Hutchings asked.

"Yes, I do."

"Then they knew we had been knocked off our axis signal."

"Looks like it."

"What about the gazebo? What's its status?"

"The Shunt is showing green straight across on my board. No problem there."

"And the Suncup?"

"Copacetic, all green."

"Okay. Our next step is to transfer control from your board to the Man's board down here. Pablo's there now and you should be hearing from him as soon as he becomes more acquainted with this console. It looks very similar to yours, except that it's bigger. It'll take at least three people to operate it efficiently."

"Got it."

"When Pablo switches you over, shut your board down completely and lock it. Then get down to the flight center as fast as you can. We'll need you, Elliot and Pablo sitting at that console so Matt won't be distracted."

"Distracted from what?"

"We're going to try to lift off the sun."

"You can't be serious."

"Is the com system operable stationwide?"

Voorhee's voice seemed to lower an octave as he realized the utter seriousness of their situation. *"It is now."*

"Stay on line. Com, open, Klane," he said. "Klane, this is Hutchings. I want to know where you are. Acknowledge."

No response came from Klane; but then, Hutchings didn't expect one.

"Larry, have one of Lorraine's people locate Mr. Klane."

"You bet."

Hutchings crept down the hall and found himself standing before a door that was partially open, rare for a corridor seal. He forced it open and eased inside.

He stepped into a silver forest.

"Oh, wow," he breathed.

The room appeared to be a laboratory or a work station similar to the Fiddlers' Den. However, this room was filled with silver structures that resembled trees. They were slender, gangly affairs with drooping limbs—if they were limbs—with vines or appendages wrapped around them sinuously.

Hutchings's helmet light glanced off their metallic bark, sending lances of light everywhere. He counted twelve of the silver structures growing from floor to ceiling: Without the greenery of real tree limbs, they could have resembled his white birch forest in the meadow upstairs.

The workroom itself, like much of that part of the Forbidden Zone, was a wreck. Many of the monitoring consoles, however, were still activated, glowing with yellow and red lights, indicating that they were still on-line. Someone, he guessed, had had the foresight to leave them on in case the worst had happened, which, evidently, it had.

Hutchings eased among the rococo pillars of twisted metal.

At the far wall he found a computer station where a message appeared on a single screen that was dull and phosphorated by time. A message blinked on the screen: PRESS ENTER TO ENGAGE.

He pressed Enter.

The face of a man appeared on the dusty, ten-inch-square monitor screen and Hutchings stepped back.

"Isn't *this* interesting," he breathed.

His last forgotten memory suddenly reappeared and everything fell into place: The face on the screen was *his*.

He was dressed in a military uniform, but the uniform was torn and blackened in places. Hutchings turned up the audio.

"*—absolutely important. I've sent down schematics for the deconstructors. Your synthesizers can easily produce them and the micro-soldiers will go to work almost immediately.*"

Static garbled the sound. Then: "*—the 'bots also have a timed thioridazine-chlorpromazine accelerator component. That's the key. It, too, can be synthesized easily and can be deployed in serum or aerosol spray. I recommend the spray. As a gas it gets in the bloodstream quicker. Its only side effect appears to be the suppression of sexual desire. I don't know why just yet. But that's not important . . . this thing we're dealing with—*"

The message was garbled for several long seconds, then: "*. . . are extremely adaptive and incredibly old . . . a billion years, maybe older . . . Pablo Ramirez thinks they're Von Neumann machines, partly biotic, partly artificial . . . but they only replicate when they flower, and only if they've successfully anchored themselves in the brain. And that, we can stop.*"

The image on the screen nearly faded away entirely, but it quickly returned. "*. . . we can't raise anybody back on the Earth. You might be the last of us in the entire solar system. . . . If these things find that out, they'll come for you, too.*"

More static, then: *"—You'll know that you've got it if you feel the need for very intense naps . . . loss of memory comes later. . . . They're voracious . . . and they're intelligent, but we can now control their growth cycle. We can stop them from feeding. We can stop them from flowering!"*

Hutchings's heart fluttered in his chest like a cardinal in a cage.

"The John E. Baldry *is on its way . . . have hope!"*

The message disintegrated in a snowstorm of entropic static.

Hutchings stood alone in the forest of silver figures, the conquered remains of the original science crew of Ra. *A billion dead.* A human being could easily contain a billion of those *things.* The grains of dust they'd inhaled years ago were themselves tiny Trojan horses, packed full of the microminiaturized traces . . . ready to feed . . . ready to flower.

Hutchings heard a grating noise behind him. He whirled around to greet it.

One of the silver "trees" suddenly came at him.

Kate drifts in her dream state, fighting the somatic paralysis that's slowly taking over her body. It's a sleep caused by the dust which the crew of the *John E. Baldry* had unwittingly inhaled when they set out to fight the scourge from the stars.

But Kate won't let it get her. The forest of grotesque metallic polyps that covers the Wyoming plain sing their hosannas of glorious consumption. They were the first life-form to emerge in the Milky Way, progeny of its earliest suns. Ancient, predatory, and ruthless, they lived by their visceral urge to feed and flower. It was their calling.

Kate listens as her mind drifts, held captive by the delicate, invading polyp that now clutches her brain stem. She has heard the names they have for themselves. They are the Stellar Emergent . . . Eaters of Life . . . Those Who Tread the Righteous Path . . .

All that matters is that they flower and move on from the system of Sol, the domain—the *former* domain—of *homo sapiens interplanetarus*.

But someone has stopped them and they can't flower.

Kate knows this now. Some miracle of human intervention in the real world has prevented the traces from flowering. And if they can't flower, they can't mature. And if they can't mature, they eventually degrade and die. Someone has figured this out and Kate knows who: Ian! Appointed Major to lead the civilian contingent of the *John E. Baldry* into space, he had found the solution to their problems.

This is all Kate needs. This is all the reason to keep on living, to keep on fighting.

The traces have come for her *family* and she isn't about to let that happen.

34

Standing in the center of the infirmary hub, Hugh Bladestone trembled with barely controllable rage. Long-concealed memories were now beginning to crowd for space in his mind: memories of his wife, Cassie; memories of his life before the crisis.

The Wall that had been holding back the waters of his life had sprung a fairly substantial leak, thanks to Ian's unflagging efforts to combat their extraordinary enemy.

Hugh knew now that he had murdered no one. He had, in fact, saved thousands of people, particularly children, worldwide. He was one of the leading experts in reconstructive diencephalic microsurgery. Together with Ian, a renowned biochemist, they headed a formidable team in the war against a malady that had struck several outer-system stations.

If he *had* committed any kind of a crime, it was in failing to foresee what the traces were capable of doing and failing to warn his family in time.

On their return from Cormoral Station in orbit above Titan, the second human settlement in the solar system taken by the pernicious microaliens, they had, as a team, decided not to contact anyone. They did not want to cause a panic. So when they returned to the Earth, it was only to take on a larger military contingent, led by Capt. Lyle MacKenzie, for a direct assault on the comet that brought the invaders in. That comet, a vast artificial ship, was now on its way around the sun and they were going to meet it. In this effort they also enlisted master second-story-man Eddie Brickman, the only person known to break into the Pox Palace in the Tellenes Redoubt on the moon.

Yet somehow the dust had reached the Earth ahead of them and entire nations were succumbing to its somatic spell. And he was helpless to come to the aid of his family in Chicago. They were left to be taken over . . . left to become the Ice Men.

Or so his buried guilt told him in his dreams. . . .

One of the Fiddlers who had been working in the stasis-chamber room appeared at the door to the doctor's lab. "Hey, Doc? We've got a problem here."

Diane Beckwith appeared behind the Fiddler. "It's happening to Rhonda!"

Bladestone rushed into the slow-sleep ward. The stasis chambers which contained Clarissa Pickerall, Bebe Wasson, and Kate had recently been fitted with Ian's new atmospheric pumps that contained his solution. But the other two chambers, the ones that would be used for Sheila Bakondi and Rhonda Barrie, were still incomplete. The two stricken women lay on cots several feet away, trembling in their private universes.

Rhonda Barrie, they discovered, might not be needing her chamber after all.

The Fiddler construction crew—there were six of them now—stood back and stared at the *thing* which lay on Rhonda Barrie's cot, the thing which used to be a human being.

The woman was morphing right before their eyes. Her hair, once blonde, had now gone gray, writhing like iron worms. Her skin color, drained of blood, had turned a deathly bluish white. They watched in horror as Barrie's arms began to elongate, with her fleshy *human* skin rending audibly, revealing bright metal beneath. *Something inside the woman now wanted out.*

"Clear the deck! *Now!*" the doctor commanded.

The Fiddlers scrambled from the ward and Bladestone hurriedly sealed the only door that led to the wing.

"Doc, what's happening to that woman in there?" one of the Fiddlers asked.

"In a minute," Bladestone said. "Com, open, Voorhees."

"*I'm real busy, Doc—*"

"I need you to seal the ventilation in ward three in the infirmary, as fast as you can."

"*I got orders from Ian to keep the ventilation system open everywhere in the ship. He's got this stuff that's—*"

"I know," the doctor said. "But I need you to seal off ward three now. I don't want what's in there to get out and it might try through the vents."

"*So what's in there?*"

"You don't want to know. Just do it for me. Out."

And the doctor thought: *Their individual seeds re-*

semble buckminsterfullerenes: large molecules like Trojan horses filled with microsolders inside. Their larval stage is when they're the most dangerous. They take over any advanced life form with the capacity for consciousness. Some of them can even shoot—

Thoughts and memories avalanched in Hugh's brain as he breathed Ian's invigorating airborne armada: *His son! Memories of his son came back to him. he had nicknamed him Heater because when he was a little baby he would sit in Hugh's lap in the dead of the Chicago winter, toasty in his diapers and pajamas, like a little portable heater. . . .*

The doctor stood at the sealed door to ward three, staring through the window at the monstrosity on Rhonda Barrie's cot.

"I made an error," he said. "We should've given the solution immediately to Barrie and Bakondi because they're still in real time. Clarissa, Bebe, and Kate could have waited."

They heard the ventilation system in ward three shut down as locks and seals to the air ducts clamped tight, sectioning off the room.

Rhonda Barrie was no longer recognizable. She had become an elongated caricature of a human being. Her skin was some sort of pliable metal, her torso twice the length of a human's. She had also developed what appeared to be extra arms—arms which might have been adaptive extensions of her rib cage except that they exhibited no hands of any kind. They moved in and out like a set of bellows. It was a thing of terror.

Bladestone turned to Diane Beckwith. "We've got

to get Ian's solution to every person on the sunstation, preferably by injection. That's the fastest."

"What about Kate and Bebe?" Diane asked.

"If something as powerful as the sun can't crack a Renner shield, then I don't think that thing in there can. They'll be safe."

"But what *is* it?" Diane asked.

"I'd say it's a short-lived foot soldier of some kind," he told them, remembering: *how the pernicious invaders had taken over the bodies of the Elders who met them before the transition to Mercury Farside where the John E. Baldry was to attempt the rescue of the Ostermann colony there. All of the doctor's skills at microsurgery could not save the transformed men who had invaded the Baldry. He remembered blaming himself. It was his first professional failure. The silver dust was too insidious, too fast. . . .*

Bladestone got everyone out into the main corridor. He palmed the lock to the infirmary, sealing the place.

"Com, open, stationwide," he then said. "This is Hugh Bladestone. I want everyone to go to their duty stations immediately. I want all Children to return to their rooms and lock themselves in. I want the bindlestiffs back in their dorms and I want the halls cleared. This is an order, priority one!"

Memories rained through his consciousness like leaves stripped from a maple tree in an autumn ice storm . . . *the maple tree out in front of their home in Chicago . . . Roxanna fell out of it one day and broke her arm . . . Roxanna, his daughter!*

Then the doctor felt a surge of sudden panic. Arliss

Adamson was gone and Kristen hadn't called back from common room six.

He bolted down the hallway toward the main lift, the first time he had run anywhere in the sunstation since his incarceration.

"Damn!" he said, coming upon her.

Kristen Barron lay sprawled on the floor before the doors of the main lift. She had never made it to common room six with the data tile that would have allowed them to manufacture massive amounts of Ian's antidote. Someone—or some*thing*—had doused her with a sparkling glitterlike substance, which she had been unable to avoid breathing, and now she lay unconscious.

The pouch she carried was gone.

Lorraine Sperry had heard the doctor's stationwide announcement. But rather than return to her usual duty station at the Tonka banks down below, she stayed where she was, in the meadow. Having been gassed with a small dose of Ian's blood army, she was slowly coming to understand what they were up against and was determined to follow Ian's instructions.

The gazebo lay just thirty yards from her position in the forest where she hid. In her hand she clutched her concussor, their only real weapon. A Mills concussor could cause a hell of a lot of damage if fired at close range. It could easily kill.

The question was: Could *she* kill a person? Even when she volunteered for the expedition to the comet she didn't know if she would respond properly as a dutiful soldier. She didn't know if she could kill.

Larry Voorhees had restored much of the meadow's usual daytime program and the wind in the trees seemed almost normal. It wasn't, however, enough to distract her from the sounds she heard coming from a maintenance tunnel across the meadow opposite her position in the woods.

Someone was climbing up into the meadow—*sneaking* into the meadow—having decided not to take the faster, more efficient main lift. Ian had earlier told her that someone was probably going to attempt to leave the sunstation via the Shunt. However, he had not told her that such an individual might not be human.

What emerged from the forest was an elongated, multiarmed monstrosity with one set of normal arms and rows of others around its midsection.

In its hands it clutched something of apparent value. A pouch. Stolen from the infirmary. As Ian said one might be.

"Com, open, Elliot, private," Lorraine whispered.

"We're a little busy here, sweetheart," Elliot's voice said from deep inside her left ear where only she could hear.

"I've got one hell of an intruder in the meadow!"

"Who is it?"

"It looks like the Vapor, except that this one's got a whole bunch of upper arms. But it's not a robot. I think it's alive!"

"Be careful—"

The creature headed directly for the gazebo. As it did, it appeared to be shedding some of its skin as it walked, a flaky outer material—scabs—that looked to her like butterflies . . . *the silver butterflies that fluttered through her nightmares.*

Lorraine stepped from the trees. "Hold it right there, friend."

The thing turned on the gazebo steps. It had the rudiments of a face, a mouth like a grill, eyes ringed its head like a crown. But it did not speak. Instead, its rib-cage arms opened out and before Lorraine could react, one appendage exploded with a pneumatic burst of air and the appendage, now an eight-inch silver dart, shot forth with extraordinary speed.

It plunged into Lorraine's side and the pain she felt came as a sunburst. She stumbled back, falling to the grass.

The creature extruded an opposite "rib" and took aim once more. But Lorraine had her concussor up and she pulled the trigger, hard.

Balls of bursting light, hundreds of them, exploded around the creature, each burst rending it—as well as the gazebo and the Shunt mechanism underneath—into thousands of pieces. She emptied the gun of thunder and lightning and rage, never wavering in her aim. Bits of wood, machinery, and creature rained about her, with some of it ricocheting off the dome of sky above. No one survived a Mills "kiss", as her bobby friends back in London used to say of the world-famous concussors.

When the gun ran out of power, there was no more creature and there was no more gazebo, just a black spot on the meadow, a smoldering crater of death for the metal masters who tried to defeat them a second time—and a second time *failed.*

"Gotcha," she breathed, falling back to the peaceful fold of Ian's hard-won meadow.

35

Hutchings backed away from the metalloid creature Klane had become. That transformation had happened somewhere in the outer hallway and the creature was now using a pair of gracile arms to tear away the distinctive E-suit Klane had worn.

"Com, open, Pablo!" Hutchings shouted as the entity inched its way toward him, flinging aside the useless human apparel.

No response. But then, the creature had just come from the direction of the flight center where Hutchings had left Pablo—alone.

"Your friend has fallen," the talking devil said in a voice that sounded like crumpling silver foil.

Hutchings kept his distance. The creature's elongated body forced it to crouch as it threaded its way toward him through the metal forest.

"Com, open, Elliot!" he shouted.

"Ian!"

"We've got trouble down here!" Hutchings shouted before his friend could say anything further.

"You're telling me we got trouble! Somebody's shot Pablo and there's this silver shit all over the place!"

"That was Klane. Didn't you see him?"

"No. We just got here."

"Call Hugh!" Hutchings quickly said. "Tell him about Pablo, then close off this level as fast as you can!"

"What about you?" But Hutchings didn't respond.

Hutchings glimpsed the entity as it stepped past one of the silver columns. Hutchings now noticed that, unlike the Vapor, this one seemed to have parallel rows of smaller appendages fixed to its upper chest. These had been moving in and out like bellows aerating a furnace, but Hutchings didn't think they had anything to do with something so mundane as creaturely respiration.

One of the strange "ribs" then levered out at him. A sudden, unexpected burst of compressed body gasses, sent a projectile of some kind flying right at him.

Instinctively, Hutchings brought up his left wrist. Hours of practice in the Roughhouse had made it an automatic gesture. The dart shattered like an icicle off the gold shackle hidden beneath Hutchings's E-suit. A powdery silver glitter exploded around him . . . *seeds for more creatures.*

Hutchings lurched to the side, keeping the pillars between him and what Klane had become, thinking: *They should have scanned Klane's body as well as his skull. Had they done so they would have seen that most of Klane's inner body had been consumed, waiting for the right moment to burst through and attack. That awful oatmeal Klane kept eating must have been a temporary form of sustenance—until the time for real "food" was at hand.*

Hutchings switched his suit's communications over to audio as he edged toward the door. "So do you want to talk about this or do you want to destroy us all first?"

"We do not answer you," the creature said as it picked its way through the silver columns, kicking aside overturned furniture.

Hutchings switched off his helmet light, plunging the disheveled workroom into darkness. Only the computer monitors along the far wall behind Klane shed any illumination.

Hutchings neared the door as the creature came out from behind a column. A sense of desperation—or sheer appetite—seemed to inform its movements.

"Your flowering days are over, friend," Hutchings said.

"You have found the solution—" Klane said. *"It is what we came for—"*

Hutchings merely nodded. He remembered it all clearly now: *The* John E. Baldry *in orbit around Mercury. Its desperate human crew trying to find a cure for the dust—the little machines that became bigger machines. Hugh Bladestone successfully removing a living trace from an officer stricken at Ostermann Station. Hutchings, in turn, discovering how the trace—an extraordinarily complex organism made of metal-bonding nanobot polymers—evolved, grew, and replicated.*

But then tragedy had struck the expedition. The virus had gotten loose in the *John E. Baldry* and the crew began to succumb. At that time Hutchings had only a temporary cure, the Critic, one that reduced the trace to its anchoring templates only. *But they needed to get word down to Sunstation Ra. They were the last stronghold of human beings in the solar system whom the traces had yet to infect.*

That was the message Hutchings had seen on the console behind him. But it had been sent too late.

Klane rushed him.

But Hutchings was ready. He had worked his way over to where a fire extinguisher hung clamped to the wall. This he grabbed and whipped around, spraying a fan of slick white foam across the floor. Klane scrabbled awkwardly upon reaching it and he lost his balance. He crashed headlong into one of the grotesque columns, knocking the whole thing loose. Together, Klane and the dead trace—the silver column—fell hard to the floor.

Hutchings reached the door and ran like hell back the way he had come removing his E-suit as he went: He wasn't going to need the alloy's protection from the repellers, now that the traces in his brain were being deconstructed by his Critic.

Bursting into the main navigation room, he found a horrified Elliot Shoemaker, helmetless in his E-suit, gaping at Pablo Ramirez who was standing behind the navigation seats. Ramirez held in his hand a twelve-inch dart. His other hand clutched his right hip which was oozing blood. His helmet was off as well.

Ramirez was, however, alive and standing. That's all that really mattered to Hutchings.

"He shot me in the ass!" Ramirez said. "I tried to hide under the console when I saw him coming." Ramirez held up the silver dart which he had yanked from his hip by sheer willpower. "Is this thing poisonous?"

"Probably, but Hugh's got a more powerful formula cooking in the infirmary. You'll live."

That almost made Ramirez laugh, but instead he said, "I was in the middle of switching control of the ship from the Brains to this panel when that thing, whatever it was, showed up."

"You might have told me Klane was headed my way," Hutchings said.

"I was *busy*," Ramirez said.

"That thing was Klane?" someone asked behind Hutchings.

This voice came from the person now sitting in the pilot's chair in the booth above them—Matthew White.

"Klane, or the trace that took over his body," Hutchings said.

White wore an expression that was a mix of anger, confusion, and not a little bit of fear. Hutchings spoke to him carefully.

"Listen to me, Matt. I put something into the air that's going to bring back your memory—and with it your piloting skills."

Matt White nodded. Hutchings could see that his airborne armada was already working in the pilot.

"But don't jump the gun," Hutchings insisted. "Just familiarize yourself with the controls for now. When Pablo gets the flight-deck computer on-line, I want you to locate those programs at your station there that are designed for automated flight. But *don't* do anything until you hear from me. Got it?"

Matt White was tense to the point of paralysis. "You're going to let me fly the sunstation?"

"With any luck," Hutchings said. "But only when we're ready and only when I say. You got that?"

The pilot who was no longer a little Boy nodded.

"Right," Hutchings said, racing from the room.

Now that the electrical systems throughout the free zones were up and running, Hutchings left corridor S6 and took the spook hole up two levels to the infirmary. He jumped out into the corridor, startling everyone there when the wall seemed to part magically and spit him out.

He also must have surprised them because he was just wearing a pair of khaki hiking shorts and his gold shackles. Everything else he had discarded.

The infirmary staff and several Fiddlers were huddled around Kristen Barron who lay upon the floor of the corridor. Kristen appeared to be coming out of a state of unconsciousness.

"Ian," Hugh exclaimed, rising to his feet. "One of them's in the infirmary. We had to close it off." An insistent pounding could now be heard on the opposite side of the sealed infirmary door.

"Is it Pickerall?" Hutchings asked.

"No," Bladestone said. "It's Rhonda Barrie."

"What about Arliss Adamson? Where is she?"

Hugh's eyes darkened. "We don't know. She ran into Kristen, here, and knocked her out. She could be anywhere."

"I don't think she's just anywhere," Hutchings said. "I think she's going to try to leave. She'll either attempt to get to the Anchor where Oaks is, or she'll try for the gazebo and ride the Shunt. My guess is that she'll go for the gazebo since that can only be activated from *Bold Charon* and Larry says there's already someone up in the monopole corridor waiting."

"There is?" the doctor said.

Hutchings nodded. "That's how Larry realigned the monopole signal to its previous default setting. He had help."

"Uh, Ian?" asked one of the Fiddlers. "You want to tell us what this is all about?"

Hutchings nodded. "The short version is that we've been carrying around some sort of microscopic machinelike organism that has the ability to take over any creature with an advanced encephalic system. We fought them to a standstill the first time around. But since they don't waste food, they put us in storage. Now they've come back for us."

Kristen rubbed a large lump on the back of her head where she had been clobbered by Arliss Adamson. "But now they've got the cure," she said weakly. "It was on the tile in the pouch, wasn't it?"

The doctor shook his head. "Actually, no. I gave her a blank data tile. Ian saw this coming. If she goes anywhere, she'll go empty-handed."

"They're not going to be too happy about that," another Fiddler said. "I mean those people up there."

"We're not dealing with people up there," Hutchings said. "We never have been. Right now we've got more pressing concerns. Hugh, Pablo's been wounded in the flight center. Elliot and Matt are with him. We also have to make sure everyone gets a full dosage of the advanced formula you developed. I don't know how long my solution will fight off the traces. They're pernicious and *very* adaptive and that dust is everywhere in the Forbidden Zones. Right now, that's our main enemy."

"What dust?" one of the Fiddler's asked.

"The silver stuff that Klane spread around," Hutchings said. "They're *babies*, very small self-replicating trace linkages that go directly to the bloodstream and go right to the brain."

Hutchings pointed to the infirmary. "*That* thing in there is at its late-juvenile stage. In that stage, they can shoot darts that can inject the particles into the blood. Pablo got shot with one of those darts and he's got to get an increased dosage of the antidote now. Com, open, Larry."

"Right here," Voorhees returned.

"What's the status on the gazebo?" Hutchings asked.

"Funny you should ask. I'm showing a line of pretty red lights on my console which I guess means that it's not there anymore."

Hutchings felt a tightness in his gut. "Lorraine must have taken it out."

"Lorraine?" Voorhees asked.

"I told Lorraine to blow up the gazebo if any of the new people so much as came near it. When did it go off-line?"

"About ten minutes ago."

"Have you heard from her since then?"

"No."

"Com, open, Lorraine," Hutchings said.

When no response came, he looked aside to Hugh. "The meadow. Fast as you can. Lorraine's in trouble. Pablo can wait."

"You two come with me!" the doctor told two of

the Fiddlers. "You stay here," he said to Diane and Kristen. Bladestone and the Fiddlers ran for the main lift.

"Larry," Hutchings continued into his com. "What's the status with the Anchor?"

"I'm still showing green on my board," Voorhees said. *"But we're definitely gaining in altitude. Relative to our former position, we're rising at about two hundred feet per second. We'll be entering the lower reaches of the chromosphere in less than an hour. But it's ten times as hot up there as it is down here in the photosphere. And steering through the magnetic convections isn't going to be easy, no matter who's flying the ship."*

"How are the Renner layers holding up?" Hutchings asked.

"Within their design parameters. But that ain't gonna last if Oaks keeps this slow speed. He'll kill us all."

"Why is he going so slow?" one of the Fiddlers asked.

Hutchings considered this. "Either he wants to turn the heat up under us and make us sweat, so to speak, or he's just being careful. Steering the sunstation from the Anchor is probably very tricky. Remember, he also has to maintain the monopole bearing *and* steer at the same time; but the Anchor, I think is probably designed for such precision flying."

"Odds are that he'll still kill us," Voorhees contended.

"How long can we stay in the chromosphere?" Hutchings asked.

"At twenty million degrees Fahrenheit? If we're right in the middle of it, I'd say we'd last about forty minutes before we overexert our main reactor. The Suncup's got

*about twenty tons of solar plasma in suspension and we
can tap into that for auxiliary power if we have to."*

"How much time would that buy us?"

*"Thirty minutes, maybe more. Remember, Ra was origi-
nally shot down to the equator at twenty times our current
speed. It didn't stay in the chromosphere long enough to
overload the Renner systems. Once we get into the chromosphere, we're gonna have to haul ass or it's goodbye
Charlie."*

"All right then," Hutchings said. "What's important for us right now is keeping the monopole signal
locked onto at its original heading. Without it we
have no way of communicating with anybody at the
top of the monopole corridor."

"You think they're going to want to talk to us?" Voorhees asked.

"Definitely."

*"You think they're crazy enough to risk a ship in the
chromosphere just to get us?"*

"I'm convinced of it," Hutchings said. "As long as
Oaks doesn't reel us out too rapidly, we've still got
time. Let me know if you get a hailing signal from
Bold Charon, Larry. Got that?"

"What if it isn't Bold Charon? *What if they send down
a battleship?"*

"It just might *be* a battleship. But right now, watch
for the signal. Then call me."

"What are you going to do?" Voorhees asked.

Everyone in the hallway had overheard and they,
too, were wanting to know.

"I'm going to see about Mr. Klane."

36

The past came back to Hutchings in a kaleidoscope of memories. Back came the first graduate seminar he taught at Boston University, BiChem 655, on past-life memory retrieval via photon-capturing memory chips lodged in the human brain. Back came an image of walking the obsidian sands of King Joe Cay in the Caribbean where he and Kate had vacationed before they left the Earth in pursuit of a comet. *Kate had all along been much more than just a bedmate.*

Hutchings paused before the spook hole. "Com, open, Elliot," he said.

"Right here," Shoemaker said.

"Has Klane come back your way?"

"No. We've sealed every sealable door on this level and we've locked ourselves in."

"Is Larry there?"

"Just arrived."

"What about the maintenance tunnels? Are they still open?"

Shoemaker paused at his end as he considered the

Big Board in the main flight center. *"You're right. We've got a breach. There's a vertical maintenance tunnel running along the inner bulkhead next to the Suncup."*

"Where is the next seal to that tunnel?"

"Above or below the Suncup facility?"

"Above."

"There's one flanking the Roughhouse. The dorms are just above that."

"We can't let him reach the dorms. Block the vent above the Roughhouse and get someone to clear the dorms just in case."

"But not the Roughhouse?"

"There's no one in the Roughhouse at the moment. If we can get Klane to come out there, I think I can stop him."

"The Roughhouse isn't empty," Matt White abruptly announced.

"What?"

"Bobby's got a Dumb Ball game going. I was supposed to play, but you locked me in my room."

"We've got a stationwide emergency!" Hutchings said. "How can they be playing Dumb Ball at a time like this?"

"They probably haven't been exposed to your airborne Critic yet," White said. *"But we can channel some of the new air that way."*

"It's too late for that!" Hutchings said. "Tell them to clear the Roughhouse! I'm on my way! Out!"

Hutchings jumped into the spook hole. Blood rushed to Hutchings's feet as the lift shot up. The hidden door then snapped open and Hutchings was thrown out into the hallway. He bolted down the hall as fast as his shackle-laden legs could carry him wondering what sort of contingencies had the trace's "commando team" anticipated? What were they prepared to meet down here?

Heading for the Roughhouse, Hutchings encountered a stampede of frightened Children. There was a lot of screaming and shouting and pushing and shoving.

Hutchings swam past them, reaching the observation lobby of the Roughhouse. There, through the large plexiglass wall, he saw several Boys floating helplessly in zero gravity, attempting to get to the nearest exit where the other Children had fled.

At the far end of the court, floating away from a popped vent screen was the elongated monstrosity that Newsome Klane had become—a creature of smooth silver metal with odd appendages and a slender, multi-jointed body. All attempts at mimicking the human form had been abandoned. This was a Warrior designed for all manner of combat and species survival.

Bobby Nakamura, caught in the air, was screaming and flailing about: *"It's the Spanker! It's the Spanker! Help!"*

Bobby happened to be floating nearest the door set in the observation wall. Hutchings reached in and grabbed the little Boy by the jersey and yanked him to safety.

Bobby came crashing out into the Earth-normal gravity of the observation deck and landed with a *thud!*

Hutchings hauled him up. "Get into the control booth and do *exactly* as I say!"

The Boy's eyes were wide with terror.

"Just do it!"

Inside the zero-G environment of the Roughhouse, three remaining little Boys were screaming in helpless suspension: the Spanker was coming for *them*.

Hutchings took a running leap into the open zero-G arena, his momentum carrying him directly toward the swarm of helpless Children.

Hutchings grabbed the first Boy he reached and flung him back toward the observation-room door. This, in turn, sent him spiraling awkwardly in the opposite direction, forcing him to use his zero-G rebounding skills to reach the other two Boys and push them to safety.

The creature, meanwhile, clawed and swam in the empty air. It did not appear to be an environment it was comfortable in. It had apparently been taken by surprise when it fell into the zero-gravity field of the Roughhouse.

Hutchings reached the last little Boy and propelled him back to the observation deck. Hutchings turned his attention to the alien soldier who was now only a few yards away.

The being of living metal floated toward him. Arms out, its prismed eyes considered him. Hutchings was no more than food now and the entity's first instinct was to *eat*.

The creature then began to make a kind of trilling sound, a sibilant, hypnotic music similar to the "music" encrypted beneath Councilor Whitehall's pronouncement. It was Alan Holly's melancholic *Let's give-up-and-go-home* music.

A spider singing to a fly: Come rest in my arms.

The entity, however, was having trouble with the null-gravity field. Hutchings recalled Arliss Adamson's reaction to the Roughhouse. They all feared it. They were ultimately land dwellers and hated being weightless, as they had been for so long as their "comet" traveled the empty reaches of space.

The creature had evolved to such a point now that it was no longer capable of human speech. Instead, it levered out its deadly riblike arms.

The projectile hissed and Hutchings jerked to one side as the dart whizzed past him. This, in turn, sent the creature flying in the reverse direction. It then crashed into the far wall, bounced up off the ceiling—and came right for Hutchings where he hovered helplessly in the air.

Hutchings popped off his right shackle and, holding it to his chest with both hands like a basketball, thrust it toward the approaching creature. This, in turn, pushed Hutchings out of reach.

The shackle itself struck the being in the lower part of his body, surprisingly, breaking it in half. *The zero gravity had apparently weakened the molecular cohesion of the trace linkages!*

Hutchings bounced off the glass wall of the observation room, ricocheted down to the floor, then shot up once again.

The creature, however, wasn't entirely incapacitated. His top half still functioned—a floating silver spider, its arms out, ready.

Hutchings snapped off his left shackle and took greater aim. He flung it as hard as he could.

The entity saw it coming and used his large right arm to deflect it. This was successful, but at the cost of the hand. It broke into several pieces and floated away.

Hutchings, careening backwards, slammed into a wall. He then rebounded to the floor where he tried to brake himself with his feet. But his momentum was too great; he shot upwards.

All the beast now had to do was wait for him to

float into his arms where flesh would give way to barbs of living metal and tiny Von Neumann machines would tunnel their way back to Hutchings's brain *do something asshole use the talent God gave you pretend it's the NCAA Zero-G Team Championship and Jeannie Owens Ann Luchart Julie Lightner are watching the whole world's watching do something porky as Eddie Brickman would say. . . .*

Hutchings kicked his right foot at the ceiling, which snapped away his right shackle. He started tumbling in the opposite direction. He then kicked off the left shackle and began tumbling the other way. All this to confuse the creature.

The alien's head, with its tiara of "eyes", kept following his progress and kept firing darts behind him to propel him toward Hutchings. This barrage sent it in all sorts of directions. And one of those directions would soon intersect with Hutchings's path.

Hutchings shouted up to Bobby Nakamura now in the control booth. *"Bobby! Three gees!"*

The little Boy in the booth threw a switch and the two opponents went crashing to the Roughhouse floor. Hutchings landed hard, but he managed to roll over on his stomach in the gravity that now pressed down upon them.

The creature came crashing down as well. Disoriented, yet desperate, it started inching toward Hutchings, fairly trembling in anticipation of victory.

Or trembling because of the terrible gravity.

"Bobby! Six gees!" Hutchings shouted. *"Turn it up!"*

Hutchings struggled in the sudden press of six gravities, barely able to breathe. He crawled for the open door of the observation deck.

Behind him he heard an ugly crunching sound, but he did not look back. It was the crumpling of weak metals and joints cracking, structural supports breaking with loud snaps. Hutchings didn't dare look back.

Hutchings pulled himself across the floor, leaving a trail of sweat. Bobby turned up the gravity another two Gs. The crunching and crackling behind Hutchings got worse. The creature let out a trill of outrage and anger. *Food was fighting back! How can this be?*

A giant hand pressed down upon Hutchings, forcing air from his lungs. But he did not stop. He could not stop. The observation deck was just a few feet away.

There, two little Boys, Rod Santos and David Baker, had remained to see the fight. They helped Hutchings to his feet when he reached the lounge and Earth-normal gravity.

The crunching and crackling behind him had now stopped. What remained was a flattened sheet of alloy, the compacted remains of molecule-sized machines now rendered useless. Without the bigger machine to carry around the smaller machines, the creature was effectively dead. All those solitary hours in the Roughhouse punishing himself in heavy gravities for something he did not do had finally paid off.

"What do you want me to do?" Bobby Nakamura spoke into his microphone from above. "You want me to turn it off?"

"No," Hutchings said, breathing heavily. "Never turn it off. Leave it on forever."

Hutchings wiped the sweat from his forehead and stood up. He felt remarkably buoyant: he was without his shackles.

He had forgotten what it was like to be free.

37

In the main flight center, Pablo, Elliot, Larry, and Matthew White had come into their adult memories and had figured out how to override the locks in the computer and gain control of the sunstation.

Pablo sat in his chair at the navigation console with his left leg sticking out to the side. Diane Beckwith had patched his wound and pumped him full of the doctor's amplified serum. As it was, the Fiddler was barely conscious, practically delusional.

In worse shape, however, was Lorraine Sperry. The doctor sent word down from the meadow that he had located her but that she was in critical condition. He was doing surgery at that moment in the meadow under a blustery New England sky.

Hutchings staggered into the flight center. "What's our status?" he asked.

"We're not dead yet," Shoemaker said.

"We're still climbing," White reported. "We've also increased our rate of ascent. It looks like they're taking us home."

"No, they're taking *me* home," Hutchings said.

"You, they will feed on. And when they get what they want from me—what they _think_ I have—they'll feed on me, too. How is the Renner holding up?"

Ramirez said, "We've got an increase in temperature inside the buffer zone just outside the hull, where you guys went climbing."

"What is it?" Hutchings asked.

"Two-hundred fifty-one degrees Fahrenheit."

"We're now in the lower chromosphere," Matt White said. "This is where the sun's convection cells heat everything up."

"How hot is it outside the Renner shield?" Hutchings asked.

"Approximately twenty-thousand degrees Fahrenheit," White told him. "It's only going to increase as we rise."

"Pablo, flush the atmosphere from the buffer zone," Hutchings said. "Then collapse the Renner shield all the way to the hull. We don't need that extra heat pushing up against us."

The sunstation rose up the monopole corridor like a bulge rising up a million-mile-long throat.

"Larry," Hutchings asked. "Is the Man still locked onto the correct monopole signal coordinates?"

The Oklahoman nodded. "Right on the beam. Whatever else Oaks is doing in the Anchor, he's keeping us on the beam."

"They sure had their bases covered," Shoemaker muttered.

Hutchings noticed that the body of the Vapor had been removed from the flight compartment. It had been placed, in the narrow corridor that led to the tech room filled with the silver invaders halted in their polyp stage.

"What can you tell us about the Anchor?" Hutchings asked their pilot. "Do you know what it is?"

The beveled glass window before White's chair now held a dozen or more projected screens and indicators. "I've got an exterior video feed," their pilot said. "It's located below the main steering engines, centered directly beneath the sunstation."

A simple gesture with his finger brought a screen on the Big Board to life, depicting the Anchor as seen from above.

"Ain't nothin' I've ever seen," Voorhees stated.

The Anchor was a teardrop-shaped vehicle, blood red. It was not a ship of earthly origin.

Matt White's eyes roamed the screens on the glass before him. "Okay, people," he said. "We've risen to the middle range of the chromosphere now. We're up to sixty-five-thousand degrees Fahrenheit outside the last of the Renner layers. It's going to get nasty from here on out."

"How much control of the sunstation do you actually have at this point?" Hutchings asked.

White responded, "Main engines are activated. Two are fully functional, one is at eighty percent. The last one's out. We can fly on two, if we have to. However, the engines can't be fully activated until we break away from the Anchor."

"Why's that?" Hutchings asked.

"Because they've got a systems-override in the Anchor, probably in case something like this ever happened. It controls us as long as it's attached to the station."

A light appeared on the Big Board. Voorhees announced: "Heads up. We've got a visitor Topside, above us in the corridor. He's sending down a handshake signal."

"A handshake signal? A handshake signal for what?" Ramirez said. "The Shunt platform's been blown to pieces."

"But the Suncup hasn't," Matt White said. "I'm showing that the handshake has just been accepted by the computer in the Suncup."

At that moment a yellow light appeared on the Big Board beside the first one.

"What's that?" Hutchings asked. "An echo?"

"No," Larry Voorhees said, their signal expert. "It's not an echo of the original handshake signal. There's a second ship in the monopole corridor. It's right behind *Bold Charon*."

"They're coming to meet us," Hutchings said.

"That's it then," Shoemaker said. "They've got us."

"Not yet, they don't," Hutchings said. "How far away are they?"

"I'm showing the alpha signal, which is probably *Bold Charon*, at fifty thousand miles," White said. "The beta signal is only five thousand miles behind that . . ."

"That puts them both well above the chromosphere," Hutchings said. "They're right in the corona, right in the worst of it."

". . . and delta is only three thousand miles behind beta," White added. "Coming in fast. They're hungry, all right."

"There's a *delta* signal?" Hutchings asked.

"There is now," Voorhees said.

Ramirez, meanwhile, created on a separate video screen a 2–D visual representation of the ships crowding the monopole corridor above them. Locked onto Ra's monopole signal coordinates, the three ships were coming to meet them. He said, "Oaks is taking us to them. One way or another they're going to get us. We've got no way to fight back."

"Yes, we do," a voice said behind them.

Hutchings turned and saw Kate and Diane standing in the doorway. Diane had brought her down from the infirmary.

Hutchings stepped over and put his arm around Kate's shoulders, taking over from Diane.

"You're dripping wet," Kate remarked in a weak voice.

"I got in some exercise," he told her. "How did you get out of the infirmary? What happened to Rhonda Barrie?"

"She collapsed," Diane Beckwith said. "The trace inside her grew too fast and she had a grand mal seizure. When we found her, she was dead. That's when we got Sheila, Bebe, and Kate out. We gave them Hugh's formula."

"What about Pickerall?" Hutchings asked.

"She's still inside her chamber," Diane told him. "She's still suspended in slow-time."

Hutchings looked at Kate. "You said we have a way to fight back."

Kate pointed to the Big Board. "There are ships locked onto our monopole signal-heading directly above us?"

"Pretty maids all in a row," White stated flatly.

Then she asked, "Is the Suncup still operational?"

"What do you mean?" White asked.

"Has it been harmed or compromised since I've been out?"

"No," Shoemaker said. "In fact, your backup crew is locked in there waiting to hear from us."

"Good," Kate said. "That's all we need then."

"What do you have in mind?" White asked.

But Hutchings had already guessed. "The Suncup is our weapons system."

Kate nodded. "It was something that Lyle told me during our last contact, our last dream, just before he finally let go."

"Lyle spoke to you?"

"Part of him did, I think. A small part that's been alive all this time living in a dream state. He's gone now, but he gave me an idea."

"What was that?" Shoemaker asked.

"He told me to show them the light." She turned to Voorhees. "Larry, send up a lock-confirmation signal to alpha. When they're ready to receive, we'll send them a tiny bit of what's in the Suncup. There should be at least twenty tons of compressed plasma in there right now—pure hydrogen fire. They probably intended to use the 'cup as a backup means of transport, if all else failed. I think that's why Dylan Oaks got into the Suncup computer. When he was there, he left some of the dust that eventually got Sheila and me."

Ramirez nodded. "You know, the Suncup's alloy transmission filters were restricted when we got here. With the right override codes, they could have enabled the 'cup to send up multielemental substances. Like human bodies."

And Kate added, "Remember when Marlissa tried to get off the station by using the Suncup? It's possible that her trace *knew* that it could be done. Like our traces talking to us in our dreams. That knowledge could have crossed over into Marliss's unconscious mind and driven her crazy, crazy enough to try getting off the sunstation in the Suncup."

"There are six ships now in the upper Renner corridor," Matt White announced. "And we can't go around them. We've got to do something and soon."

Kate turned to their pilot. "They'll be expecting some sort of signal from us, Matt. All we have to do is acknowledge it. They'll tell our computer to send up whatever's in the Suncup. Instead of Mr. Klane or Arliss Adamson, we'll send up a few hundred pounds of highly compressed nuclear fire, little packages of it, the size of grapefruits."

"Bombs," Hutchings said.

"Once they're reconstituted in their Shunt chamber, which will be instantaneously," Kate stated, "they'll blow any ship in half."

"Larry, acknowledge the handshake," White told Voorhees.

Voorhees made a slight adjustment to his console then nodded. Looking at Kate, he said, "Ready when you are."

"Wait until you hear from me," Kate said and raced off toward the Suncup facility.

Hutchings let her go. He'd seen that determined look on her face before. She had her own score to settle and she didn't need his help to do it.

Shoemaker mused aloud. "Well, they've lost ore scows in the monopole corridor before."

"They've never ventured this close to the sun for an alloy shipment," Ramirez added. "They probably expect to lose a ship or two, to get what they want."

"They're desperate," Hutchings agreed. "Larry, lock the transmission codes onto the alpha position only. Don't acknowledge any other handshake yet."

"Let's just hope we've got enough plasma to take out those ships," Ramirez said. "Lord knows we've sent them enough metal over the years to build a fleet of spaceships."

"Okay, boys," Kate's voice appeared over the com. She was now ensconced in the Suncup facility with her own crew. "I'm ready here."

"All green here," Voorhees responded. "We're locked onto alpha and they're ready to receive. No questions asked."

"Here comes the sun," Hutchings said. "Fire away."

Hardly a shudder went through the sunstation as Kate released the first bundle of plasma via the Suncup's own Shunt, just a handful in terms of the fiery mass they had in suspension. All eyes were fixed on the Big Board in the flight center.

One moment the alpha ship, Bold Charon, was on their screen, the next moment it wasn't.

"Yes!" shouted Voorhees.

No explosion, no fiery debris fanned out in the narrow Renner-enclosed corridor. The alpha ship's devastation would have been instantly absorbed by the Renner-shield layers.

"Okay," White said. "Let's see what they do."

The next several moments were tense ones, but Hutchings had a pretty good idea of what the aliens would do now. They wanted the magic formula that would allow them to flower and they would go to any lengths to obtain it.

Calmly and quietly, the beta ship took over the alpha position and it, in turn, sent down a handshake signal, demanding acknowledgment.

"Beta's moved in," Ramirez announced.

"Delta's right behind it," Shoemaker added.

"Acknowledge the new alpha's handshake signal. Kate—" Hutchings said into the com. "Send on their command."

"*Two's away*," Kate returned.

The beta ship, now the new alpha, simply disappeared from the screen, its handshake signal vanishing.

Hutchings's heart soared. All along his beliefs had been intuitively on target. He had never been an Annihilist . . . at least to the people of Earth. However, for those *not* of the Earth, he was the greatest adversary they had ever encountered. He had put a stop to the billion-year spree of Cor'y'ax'xi, the name he now knew of the ancient race.

One by one, the alien ships appeared in the monopole corridor and, one by one, they received what they hoped was a member of their commando team and the key to their flowering. The Cor'y'ax'xi knew the corona was dangerous, even with Renner-shield technology. They knew they would lose a vessel or two as they had in the past.

But they lost them all. Thirty-one vessels appeared

and thirty-one vanished. Thirty-one ships built with the alloys sent up to them from Ra, hoping to use them to facilitate their mission to pollinate the next star system.

The process of their destruction took approximately twenty-two minutes and by the time no further signal appeared in the monopole corridor above them Ra was well into the corona.

In that time Matt White had gotten his entire range of piloting skills back, including knowledge of those Raians who had the technical expertise for running the ship's systems. As dollops of compressed plasma were flying up to the alien ships, Matt White called out one name after another over the com, commanding the original crew of the *John E. Baldry* to their battle stations. They were about to do the most dangerous flying of their lives.

A series of yellow lights appeared on the console of the navigation board in the flight center. Several alarms also sounded off.

"Trouble, guys," White said. "I think it's Mr. Oaks." A rosary of sweat covered the brow of their pilot as he gripped the control waldos of his armrests. "I think he's decided to slow our advance. Shit! He's put the Anchor in reverse thrust."

"We can't stop now," Shoemaker said. "The Renner layers are barely holding. We've got to keep moving!"

More yellow lights began to appear as various shipboard systems began closing down in response to the Man's furious devotion to maintaining the Renner shield outside.

"Renner shielding has now entered overload,"

Ramirez announced. "We'd better do something *real* fast, compadres."

"Com, open, Cady, Peters," Hutchings said. "Respond immediately."

"I thought you said we'd be the only engineers going down here," Bob Cady said over the com. *"You didn't tell us there'd be a whole convention!"*

"They're there because they're going to help run the ship," Hutchings responded. "Have you found the tether control facility, yet?"

Bob Cady then said, *"I've got a board here that seems to be functioning all on its own. It's a coupling unit of some kind with an exterior communications lead. It looks like it was installed after the ship was built."*

Ramirez looked at Hutchings. "That's got to be the tether housing. And the communications lead probably goes directly from the Anchor to the Man."

Hutchings looked to their pilot. "Matt, how much control do you have now?"

"At the moment, I've got the main engines fully activated, holding in neutral. The main gyroscopic computer is up and running. We can fly—if we get the chance."

Hutchings spoke into the com. "Cady, you've got the tether housing right in front of you. Disengage everything there, particularly the exterior communications lead. There's probably a trigger there for the exterior bolts. Throw it."

"I don't know about this," Cady said hesitantly.

"Do it! Do it now!" Ramirez shouted, jumping up.

"I'll do it," came a different voice. *"Get out of the way!"*

It was the voice of Arlene Deyerberg-Littel. Master

Sergeant Littel had been one of the main engineering technicians of the *John E. Baldry*. She would know what the tether housing looked like and she'd also know how to disengage it.

So she did.

Suddenly, the sunstation pitched, but ever so slightly, a rolling motion akin to what they had experienced during the meeting of the Meadow Council. This surge, however, was due to the Anchor, the tether itself and the bolting assembly dropping away from Ra, plunging down into the monopole corridor, squeezing to a stream of molecules bound for the center of the sun.

Dylan Oaks was about to join Eddie Brickman in Hell.

Matt White sat upright as his pilot's chair automatically gripped him and started feeding information directly into his neural system, now that he had full control of the sunstation.

"We're rising! Hold on for maximum acceleration within the corridor!"

"What about the Renner shield?" Hutchings asked.

"Holding steady," Ramirez told them. "But just barely."

"How long can it hold?" Hutchings asked.

"We'll know soon enough."

"Full power to main engines," Matt White said. "Kate, I want every ounce of plasma that's left converted into power and I want that power sent over to the Renner-shield generators."

"*Done*," came Kate's voice.

"You think we're going to make it?" Pablo Ramirez wondered out loud as the seconds ticked by.

They found out eighteen minutes later when, still intact, they dropped the Renner shield thirty-million miles out from the sun, well beyond the orbit of Mercury and traveling faster than any human-built ship had ever traveled before. The loss of the compressed hydrogen plasma "bombs" had so lightened their load that escape from the sun's gravity well was made easier by a factor of twenty.

And when they returned to normal space, there wasn't a Cor'y'ax'xi ship anywhere nearby. In fact, as they found out later, there wasn't a Cor'y'ax'xi ship left anywhere in the system. They had all been used in their desperate attempt to find a solution to their inability to flower. In the service of that one racial imperative, like lemmings they sacrificed all their remaining Matures, their Soldiers like Klane and his commandos, and the Quisling Councilor Whitehall. Gone forever, all of them.

Space opened out to the freed men and women of Ra, and the sun was soon far, far behind them.

Epilogue

Under the bright sun of an early spring day, Ian McFarland Hutchings walked out across a real meadow—the south pasture on his family's farm outside Lowell, Massachusetts, back in what was left of the United States. The crisp air chilled his unaccustomed bones as the wind drifted with a myriad of odors, scents, and smells which his friends—his *team*—in their enormous capacity for invention, could never have devised for their artificial meadow on the sun.

Now, however, their penchant for creative solutions would be put to the test for at least the next decade.

By Elliot Shoemaker's estimates, only half a billion human beings throughout the solar system survived, and most of those were on the Moon, Mars, Ganymede or living in the two L5 colonies in orbit around the Earth. But they *had* survived the appetites of the Cor'y'ax'xi. That's all that mattered.

However, Hutchings had come to respect their adversary's cunning. Convincing the crew of the *John*

E. Baldry that they were criminals was a stroke of perverse genius. He guessed that there must have been several humans in-system who conspired with the Mature traces, if only to save their skins. Anything was better than consumption.

So the Cor'y'ax'xi sent them to Ra for storage. And only when it was too late for them did the Cor'y'ax'xi decide on a desperate mission to trick Hutchings into finding a key to trigger their flowering.

Hutchings's family's farm was an example of what had happened worldwide. Here and there in the fields loomed giant silver columns of the embryonic Cor'y'ax'xi, halted by their inability to fully consume their hosts and flower into maturity. The humans inside were quite dead, but then so were the Cor'y'ax'xi.

Those humans who had avoided the dust of Boörstam's comet had taken to the high deserts or the tundra or the open seas where the dust did not fare so well or evolve so fast. Hugh Bladestone's son, Jefferson, they discovered, had made it to Anchorage with his fledgling family. But Hugh's daughter and his wife were yet unaccounted for. They were, presumably, Ice Men now. And forever.

However, enough people had survived to start their civilization anew. The System Assembly itself remained intact, and much of the necessary technology to maintain an interplanetary culture survived as well. This included the quite miraculous survival of the Durkee Yards in Nanyuki, Kenya, where the antigravity space lifts, each a magic island, would be available to assist in humankind's rehabilitation.

Humanity had survived, but just barely.

A shout came over Hutchings's private com, breaking his reverie. *"Hey, cowboy! Look what I found!"*

Hutchings turned around. In doing so, his head spun vertiginously. Most of the Raians had bouts of agoraphobia, having been cooped up for so long inside the sunstation. He blinked and regained his equilibrium.

Riding high in the cab of a bright yellow road grader fifty yards away, Kate waved to him as she pulled the big-wheeled vehicle off the road that flanked the pasture. This vehicle, however, was no Tonka toy.

Kate spoke over her com. *"Pablo found this in a warehouse in town. We can use it to push off some of the cars blocking the Interstate."*

"I didn't know you could drive something like that," Hutchings said. *He* certainly couldn't.

"Cowgirls can do all sorts of things."

"You can say that again."

Now that the traces were gone from their bodies, their libidos had returned in full force. Kate soon was pregnant, as was Lorraine, Bebe Wasson, and Engineer Bakondi. Hutchings didn't want Kate doing manual labor and seeing her bounce around in the giant Tonka alarmed him somewhat. But Kate always knew what she was doing, and there wasn't anything he could have done about it anyway.

The irony was that the traces would have died out eventually. As Hutchings had originally suspected, a naturally occurring hormone in the thalamus blocked the traces, stopped them cold. The traces still could kill; the grotesque silver structures that now peppered the Earth were proof of that. But the Cor'y'-

ax'xi had never encountered a race like human beings before—a race of creatures with *souls*.

Hutchings had only found their solution in the last hours on the *John E. Baldry* as it orbited Mercury, before they fell victim to the insidious traces. But Hutchings, knowing that the Matures would never "waste food", sent a last desperate message down to Ra which was itself already in the midst of being taken over. That message, dutifully recorded and saved, was a bluff.

Hutchings had to get them to *think* that he had the means to help them flower. Even if he didn't. And though he was unable to get the de-anchoring solution back to the Earth, he knew that someday the traces would realize that they were stymied and that perhaps *he* held the key to their growth. So they came back.

Now all of the Matures were dead. Their reign was over, their galactic travels at an end.

Kate spun her grader around on the road on its man-sized bright black wheels as if she were riding a horse at a rodeo. She let out a squeal of delight as she did, and Hutchings, for the first time in a long time, also managed a laugh, a laugh in the bright distant sunlight.

THIS SIDE OF JUDGMENT

by

J. R. DUNN

"An impressively told story."—*Science Fiction Chronicle*

The woman was found nude in the snow, in plain sight, as if she was meant to be discovered. At the same time, a computer intrusion occured at the local bank. It was a sloppy job, as if the invader didn't care if he were detected. There's no link, at least as far as the Montana police can see. However, in Washington, Ross Bohlen, an agent for the Computer Subversion Strike Force (COSSF), finds a connection that leads all the way back to a Chiphead—a cybernetically enhanced person. But there's a problem: the Chipheads are all supposed to be dead—either murdered, or as hopelessly insane suicide victims. In a dark, new twist on the Frankenstein theme, three men—a madman drunk on power, a hunter weary of bloodshed, and a protector who can no longer protect—come together in a debut novel that is part sci-fi thriller, part high tech, and part page-turning madness.

(454863—$5.99)

"I read it in California and didn't even notice the earthquakes!"
—Geoffrey A. Landis, Hugo and Nebula award-winning author

*Prices slightly higher in Canada.